Nine Meals

Mike Kilroy

Fishtail Publishing

ISBN-13: 978-1500326357

DEDICATION

To Dahn for believing in me.

Part I
Chapter One
When Fletching Gets in Your Eye

Cheese Ravioli, Beefaroni or SpaghettiOs? That was the big decision to be made on this day. Well, on any day, really. He was Billy Shepard – his friends, of which he had none anymore, called him Shep – and he had his pick of those and many others. Cans, hundreds of them, filled with all sorts of things like soups and broths, meats and SPAM, were stacked high in the pantry on shelves that ran the length of the wall in the cellar.

That pantry was his world now. His salvation.

He stroked the coarse hair on his chin and contemplated his choice. It wasn't one that should be made lightly. After all, the decision would determine his culinary selections for days.

SpaghettiOs. Yes, SpaghettiOs it is. Can't go wrong with SpaghettiOs. It was his guilty pleasure. It had calories. That was the most important thing. Life takes a lot of calories after the Ejection and he needed all he could consume.

He grabbed a can, stuffed it into the pocket of his tattered gray tracksuit jacket – he so loved it and couldn't bring himself to get rid of it, even in the ragged condition it was in – and made his way up the narrow steps into his kitchen, which had seen better days. *Everything had seen better days.* The floor was warped and the linoleum cracked and peeled. The mustard yellow plaster walls were crumbling like dried-out and stale shortbread and the light that shined through the filmy window did little to make the room more attractive.

That was the point, though. The gangs didn't raid the dank places, the dirty places, and the decrepit places. They raided the places that looked better than the squalor where they eked out an existence.

It was all about appearances now.

He wanted his house to look as if it was the worst place on the planet to be. He was doing a pretty good job of that, he thought.

The fabric of his black track pants swished when it rubbed as he moved through the living room. He stopped as memories flooded in. He hated when that happened. He remembered the flowers that used to rest on the mantle of the fireplace. It was falling apart now. A sledgehammer saw to that.

He remembered the smell of Pine-Sol on the hardwood floors. Nothing smelled better than when the living room was freshly mopped. He remembered where the couch used to be. Soft. Comfortable. A great place to sleep. All that was left in the room was a trophy case and a bookshelf, taller than him and worn and beaten by time and life. The varnish that protected the oak was peeling and bubbled. Some of the shelves were warped from the weight of all the books and the constant pull on them by gravity.

All the classics were there. *Catch-22, The Great Gatsby, The Catcher in the Rye, Slaughterhouse-Five.* He wasn't much of a reader, but he had pored over the pages of those books many times. He marveled at how with each read, he received a different message, as if the words on the page had changed depending upon his mood.

He rather liked that.

There was even the *King James Bible*, tucked between *Dante's Inferno* and *Fahrenheit 451.*

He always snickered at the irony.

The case was full of trophies – gold ones and silver ones, bronze ones and cheap metal ones – of all different sizes and dimensions. He remembered how he won each and every one of them. It was the only thing he was truly good at and the only thing he felt he had mastered in the forty years of his life. Well, that and self-loathing.

Everyone was good at that.

He was about to make his way across the room to the bookshelf to grab a particular selection that had captured his fancy when he caught a glimpse of his reflection in a large mirror, now cracked, that hung above the fireplace.

Gray peppered his beard. Crow's feet peeked out from behind the thick, dark frames of his glasses. He was slimmer now than he had been the last time he saw himself in a reflection. He sucked in his gut to make himself look even thinner and patted his belly before he let it out with a long exhale.

How did I get so old? Probably before the world went dark and mad – well, even madder than it had been. Probably before the growling, rumbling pains of hunger became commonplace. Probably before the desperation, that real, scary, palpable desperation that sullied even the most noble and unyielding of men, took grip.

Life was just as hard then as it is now. It was just a different kind of hard.

And there's still SpaghettiOs, so, how bad could this life be?

He broke his gaze from the mirror and again began to make his way across the room to the bookshelf when something else grabbed his attention.

He peered out the window, across the brown grass and the knee-high weeds, and saw three figures making their way through the field. He couldn't see them in much detail as far away as they were. One looked like a man. The other was definitely a woman. And the third? He couldn't tell.

It wasn't a Sasquatch; he knew that much.

"Shit," he whispered. *Are they coming toward the house? Are they lost?*

"Shit. Shit," he repeated again. They were walking with a determined stride toward the front porch.

They had found him.

He didn't get many visitors these days. He preferred it that way. He wasn't a very gracious host after the Ejection. Then again, he wasn't a very gracious host before it, either. There were no dinner parties with wine and cheese followed by a fancy meal. Not in these times, certainly.

There was no occasion to entertain.

The trio moved closer and he could make them out a bit better. It was a man with threadbare clothes on his back and dark whiskers on his face. He had sunken eyes and dirty long hair, which stirred in the wind. His appearance didn't surprise Shep in the least. It was very much the norm in these brutal, desperate times.

He was a frail man.

That's what I'll call him. Frail Man.

The woman didn't look much better. She was rail thin, obviously malnourished, and her gait was more of a stumble than a stride. *If this were a disaster movie, she surely would be a zombie.*

Shep squinted and determined the third figure was indeed a young girl. She trailed behind them, walking slowly before speeding up at the urging of Frail Man. She didn't look like she wanted to be with them, trudging through a field on the way to a house filled with unknown dangers.

It was always risky to approach a house unannounced. But

travelers had become more brazen. Misery and sorrow does that. Those rumblings in your gut have a certain command that overtakes any sense of reason or self-preservation.

This was going to be trouble.

He jogged upstairs, his pants swishing again, his sneakers pounding the steps and making the boards creak. He reached the bedroom door and stopped. It always took him a minute to go inside. How long, he thought, had it been since he stepped inside that room? Months? Shep always had an exceptional sense of time. He dazzled his friends – when he had them – with the atomic-like accuracy of his internal clock. He would be at a picnic or on a camping trip and far away from the trappings of time, and they would ask, "What time is it, Shep?" and he would answer with astonishing accuracy.

He was like a carnival entertainer. They delighted in his odd skill.

That was gone now, though, like so many other things. Time didn't have the same meaning, the same hold as it did before. He concluded that was one of the good things.

He pushed the door open and stood in the arch. The room was very much like it was, like he remembered. The bed, still covered with a crisp white sheet, sat against the wall to the left. The alarm clock, long since dark, sat on the nightstand along with a lamp with a base shaped like a dolphin. The carpet was plush and green and the chocolate brown curtains were open and let in ample light.

He opened the closet door. Stuffed in the back, amid random things like a basketball, a Wiffle Ball bat and a football signed by some former Pittsburgh Steelers' player, he couldn't remember who, was an old recurve bow. It was a fine example of craftsmanship, made of sturdy yew and had served him well in many competitions. A back quiver with four arrows stuffed in it sat next to the bow among the clutter. *That should be enough.*

He slung the quiver over his shoulders, raced down the stairs and back into the living room. The trio was on the porch now and Frail Man had the crown of his head pressed against the glass of the front window, his hands cupped around his eyes for a better view.

Billy Shepard froze. Scenarios played out in his mind. None of them were good.

"Holy fuck, there's someone inside." Shep heard the muffled voice of Frail Man as he turned to speak to the woman. There was nothing for Shep to do now but to confront them.

His stride was long as he entered the kitchen and slipped out the side door. He crept around the house and quickly pulled an arrow out of the quiver. He turned the corner and his eyes locked on Frail Man. Startled, the man stood up straight and grabbed the arm of the girl.

"There's nothing here," Shep said in a voice as firm as he could make it. The bow was still at his side. "Might as well keep moving."

Frail Man tried to speak, but nothing came out. His grip on the girl became tighter and obviously pained her. Unlike the other two, she looked healthy and fit. Her deep blue eyes stared at Shep and her lips quivered. *Was she afraid of me or them?*

Finally, Frail Man was able to make words escape his lips. "My family, my daughter, we're just looking for something to eat. Maybe you can help out a poor, hungry soul?"

They retreated off the porch, Frail Man still holding the girl firmly as he dragged her down onto what used to be a lush green lawn that was now brown and wilted.

Shep couldn't break his stare from the girl. She clenched her jaw and squirmed a little. Her raven hair blew back in a gust of wind to reveal a fresh gash, the blood dried and matted on her scalp. Sweat rolled down her cheeks and nose and dripped off her lower lip and down the dimple on her chin.

He didn't know why he was going to do what he was about to do. The cautious play, the correct play, was to say there was no food or provisions to be found and to thank them kindly to keep moving.

That's what he should do.

That's not what he was going to do.

There was something about her, something familiar and beguiling, something that told him she needed help, desperate and immediate aid. She was no more than sixteen, maybe seventeen, and he feared she wasn't going to survive another day with them.

Shep grabbed the riser of his bow in his left hand and pulled the arrow back, pointing it at Frail Man. "I think you should be going now."

The man raised his right hand, the fingers of his left still gripping the girl's arm tightly, leaving it depressed and ruddy. The woman stood behind them now and peered at Shep through the gap between their shoulders.

"Wait a second! Wait a second!" Frail Man was panicked. "We just need some food or water." He turned his head to look at the girl and then back at Shep as he continued his plea. "Please! For my daughter."

Shep smiled as his cheek pressed against the bowstring. "She's not your daughter."

"Really?" Frail Man seemed offended. "And how do you figure that?"

She didn't want to be there, clearly. That's how he figured that.

Then again, what teenage girl wants to be with her parents? That's how it used to be, anyway. That wasn't how it was now. Now, families stuck together, or at least made the effort.

Shep yelled back. "She has a cleft chin. You and the woman don't." He could thank *House M.D.* for that observation. All those doctor shows he watched on television in that old life had paid off.

Frail Man pulled her in closer. She tried to fight but his grip was too strong. His right hand was still held up in an unthreatening way. There was nothing unthreatening about his gaze, or the woman's.

"Just give us some food and we'll leave you alone. No one has to get hurt."

Frail Man was wrong.

Wind? About ten miles an hour, gusting to about fifteen. His height? About six-foot-two. Distance? About 60 feet. He pulled back on the arrow a little farther and anchored the tip of his middle finger into the corner of his mouth. His index finger rested on his cheekbone and the fletching tickled at the side of his nose.

It was how he shot his very first arrow when he was a little boy and it was how he was going to shoot this one. The bowstring strained the wood just before he let the arrow go. He could hear the fletching hiss through the air as it sped toward the target.

The bolt pierced the right hand of Frail Man, right through the middle of the palm. He let out an "arg!" as he immediately released his hold of the girl and dropped to his knees; His left hand snatched his right wrist.

The girl toppled to the ground, too. The woman reacted quickly by pulling an old revolver from somewhere, Shep didn't quite see from where, and pointed it at him.

She wasn't happy. "You sonofabitch!"

Shep slowly reached over his shoulder and plucked another arrow, set it on the string and aimed it at the woman. He stated what had become painfully obvious, at least to Frail Man. "I warned you to keep going. Now go. But the girl stays."

The woman thrust the gun forward at Shep. It was an old gun, a dirty gun. It looked like it hadn't been fired in years, if ever.

"One more chance," Shep yelled. "Go! I'm not going to say it again."

The woman wasn't going to go anywhere. Neither was Frail Man, who stood and squinted at him now. Blood dripped onto the brown grass from his wound, the arrow pointed down at the soil.

This was their last stand. Their Alamo. It was going to begin or end here. No more scrounging for food. No more begging. No more praying each night for salvation when none was coming. No more falling asleep to the sound of a gurgling tummy.

The girl was probably to be their meal ticket. People still had compassion for young things, not so much for mangy, malnourished adults. They see a dirty face, those deep blue eyes and feel compelled to give what they can. It was a sound strategy. Every strategy had its flaw, however, and this was one of those flaws.

Shep was going to have to do it. This was about survival. He chuckled, inside, at the thought of this situation. It wasn't very long ago when he would have welcomed death. Now, he wanted to get as far away from it as he could. And that meant doing something he loathed.

Wind? The same. Height? She was about five-foot-six. Distance? About 55 feet now. She inched closer, still thrusting the gun forward at him in an attempt to fright.

Shep pulled the arrow back, held his breath and prayed for forgiveness. *We are all going to meet our maker someday.*

He hoped his maker would understand.

Shep whispered, "I'm sorry" as the arrow's fletching whistled against the wind. It was on target.

The arrow went clean through her right eye. It dropped her quickly into a heap on the dead grass, her legs tucked under her limp torso.

She was dead before she hit the ground. The bolt, made from only the best materials, passed cleanly through her temporal lobe, nicking her brain stem, just like he intended. It was the only humane way to do it.

Frail Man collapsed to his knees and frantically crawled over to her. He cupped her head in his shaking left hand and cried, "No! No! No!"

The girl stood, stared down at the dead woman, her eyes big and round and her mouth ajar, and then peered back at Shep. As she walked slowly toward him, he muttered, "I had to do it. It's all right now."

Shep cleared his throat and bellowed at Frail Man, who crouched and mourned, "I trust you will leave now. I'll bury her. She deserves that at least. If I see you again, you'll be right next to her."

Frail Man stood, emotionless now, turned and walked back the way he came. The arrow was still sticking out of his hand and blood dripped from the wound as he lumbered, though he didn't seem to care much about it now. Wind whipped through his long black hair that reached down to his shoulder blades and Shep and the girl watched him trudge away, some of his steps a stumble, until they could no longer see him.

Just then, something occurred to Shep. "I really hope I was right about them not being your parents. That wasn't your mom, was it?"

She shook her head. Her eyes were large, almost freakishly large. That's what shock must look like, he thought.

"That's a relief."

Shep was about to round the corner of the house when he looked back to see the girl still starring at the corpse. He clapped his hands and she jerked out of her stare, looking back at him.

"I'll take care of her later. Come on. Let's get you something to eat."

The girl followed, hesitantly at first, but she quickly made up the gap between them.

Part I
Chapter Two
What a Lame Armageddon

She shoveled the SpaghettiOs into her mouth as quickly as he had ever seen. He didn't think it was possible to eat so fast. He thought, maybe in that other life and in that other time, she may have been a competitive eater. He found it odd now that there were such things, eating for sport, eating for entertainment. People were quite good at it, too. He thought she must have been one of the best.

Now people only ate when they could and only to survive.

She couldn't have even tasted any of it. *No matter. It was sustenance. No more.*

"What's your name," he asked. *They should at least be on a first-name basis.* After all, he rescued her. After all, she witnessed him taking another life.

Between jamming a spoon full of pasta soaked in tomato puree into her mouth, and her infrequent gasps to take in air, she responded, "Antigone."

He smiled. *What a splendid name.*

"Billy Shepard. Nothing as special as that. You can call me Shep. Everyone does."

She nodded and scooped up another spoonful from her bowl.

"You can call me Tig," she mumbled while she chewed. "So, have you killed many people? Is it a hobby of yours?"

She's direct, this Antigone. He gave her credit for that much.

How many was many? More than a few and less than a lot? If that was the criteria, then, yes, I have killed many.

"I freed her."

She put the spoon down, swallowed her last bite and stared at him. It was an eerie kind of stare, one he used to get when he was a kid from his mother when he swore or when one of his errant backyard fastballs found a window instead of the strike zone. It was a disapproving look and it put him unexpectedly on edge.

Her words were terse and scolding. "Seriously? That's your justification?"

Shep leaned back on his chair and, after a long pause, asked, "How long were you with them?"

"I don't know," she shrugged. "A few days? A week?"

"Judging by how fast you inhaled those SpaghettiOs, I'd say you didn't have a bite to eat, did you?"

She nodded. "The woman snuck me a little, but, no, not much."

Shep leaned forward and placed his arms, folded, on the table. "She won't have to worry about starving to death. She won't have to go to sleep each night with her belly empty. I showed her a tremendous amount of mercy. It was the best way she could have gone.

"And him," he added with a derisive snicker. "He won't bother us again."

He had used the word "us." *She probably thought I was talking about her, that she and I were the us.*

Her head tilted. He could tell she was carefully choosing her next words as they would be very important.

He didn't want to hear them, at least not yet. He stood, scooped up his bowl and set it into hers, and then grabbed them both and carried them to the sink, which was empty and dry for a long time now. It was just a habit. Water hadn't flowed from those pipes in how long? That, too, escaped him, much in the way he escaped that line of conversation.

"Do you have any family?" He asked.

"Yes," she said. "But they're not all here. My parents were in Greece when the Ejection happened. My older brother … he's at Halcyon."

Ah, Halcyon. He had heard of that place. Just about everyone in this life had. The rumor that swept the land, defying the limitations of communication in this sans-technological world, was that there was a government bunker carved deep into Cheyenne Mountain in central Colorado. It was a place that was spared, where food grew and was ample, where livestock thrived, where people lived by the rules of civil obedience.

Shep didn't believe such nonsense. *Those places never existed in that other life, sure as hell didn't exist now*. But he concluded long ago that it was necessary for some to cling to such a hope, in the belief that somewhere there was a place far better than this. Hope was as rare as milk and as hard to find as a juicy apple. Hope, too, was dangerous, more perilous than the raiders and gangs and marauders who brutalized any who wandered into their territory.

"I have to go bury her now before she starts to rot," Shep said abruptly and walked out the kitchen door.

He had the hole nearly dug when Antigone wandered out into the field. He hoped she wouldn't notice the spots where he had dug three other graves – he couldn't remember how long ago that was – but she did.

Observant is this Antigone. He gave her credit for that much.

"Looks like you've done this before," she spoke boldly. "Where'd you put an arrow in them? Heart? Throat? Left eye? Who's in there anyway?"

Shep continued to dig. *Not who was in there, but what was in there? His humanity. His conscience. His soul.*

He picked up the woman and flung her over his shoulders with a grunt. He was shocked at how light she was as he dropped her into the shallow grave. He began shoveling dirt on her; that one eye stared at him. The other was full of fletching.

"So, you're just going to bury her in this graveyard of yours and then, what? That's it?" Antigone showed no fear, which struck him as odd. He was digging his fourth makeshift grave, after all.

"Pretty much," he said, wryly.

Once he had finished covering her with soil, he patted down the dirt with the back of the shovel. "And so it goes," he muttered, and then walked back toward the house. Antigone followed close behind.

Inside, Shep wiped his brow with the back of his hand. Judging by Antigone's grimace, she had seen the large scar that ran across his forearm.

"Old war injury?" She asked sarcastically and smirked.

He smiled and leaned against the sink again. "Something like that."

Antigone slumped in a chair at the table now and stared at him with disdain. "What now?"

"You can stay as long as you want." The invitation was genuine. She needed to stay, if but for a day or two or three. He needed her to stay as badly as she needed that meal she had wolfed down. He needed to know that not all of his humanity was ripped from him, that he was still capable of compassion and tenderness. He needed to feel benevolent again.

He had spent so much time surviving that he forgot how to live.

He turned and peered out the kitchen window, out over the rolling hills of his land. Memories flooded back of picnics and friends, of hot dogs and hamburgers and bratwursts – oh, how he loved bratwursts. He loved the smells, the feel of a cool breeze on his face, the sound of laughter. There wasn't much to laugh about now. He missed those things. They were never coming back and that made him wistful.

"You're wrong, you know." Her words broke him out of his gaze and tore him from his stare into the field and into the past.

"Wrong about what?" It was a fair question. There were so many things he had been wrong about.

Her eyes narrowed and her jaw clenched before she spoke. "He'll be back. You don't know what he is capable of."

Frail Man didn't look all that fierce with an arrow stuck in him. In fact, he looked timid. People are duplicitous, though. Always were. The Ejection hadn't changed that so much. People were always good at hiding themselves away behind false smiles, false hellos. People were always good at shaking your hand while at the same time wishing to slap you silly with it.

They were just a little better at it now.

He knew that. He figured she probably hadn't learned that lesson yet.

What did he do to her? Did he beat her? Did he rape her?

Maybe I should have put an arrow into his brain, too.

"I can handle him." He was defiant. He had handled worse.

"Sure. Whatever."

She stood from the table and walked through the half-moon arch into the living room. She was curious and he let her explore. He followed her into the room as her once white sneakers browned by the earth made the floor whimper with each step.

He noticed her shoes had the Nike swoosh on them. The logo was faded now, but still visible. He was excited a bit by that revelation because it was a reminder of something normal, something undefiled by the way things had become. *If there was girls out there like her, walking through a living room with squeaky Nikes, then maybe there were other normal things out there, too.*

It was a happy thought.

She walked to the trophy case and stood in front of it. He could see her eyes wander from one trophy to the next, her smile growing bigger.

"You win all these?" She asked excitedly. "Now I know how you put that arrow right in her eye like it was nothing."

He was proud of those trophies. After the Ejection happened, he didn't have the heart to hide them away. He liked looking at them. It reminded him of better times.

They were won in target competitions and field competitions; in 3D competitions and even in a Clout competition in London. He had put arrows in targets, both hung in open fields and tucked between trees in rough terrain. He had put arrows in 3D animals and in concentric circles drawn in the earth two football fields away.

And one in a woman's eye. *There was no trophy for that.*

Antigone pointed at one with a marble base. A golden figure of a man, pulling back on a bowstring sat atop it. The trophy itself was unremarkable; where it sat in the case was, however.

"Why is that one over there?"

He wanted to tell her, to open up the magic curtain and reveal to her all of his secrets, but hadn't an idea of why. Perhaps it was because there was something special about this girl. He had come to that conclusion the first time he saw her, grimacing in the clutches of Frail Man. A strange feeling had come over him the moment he peered into those azure eyes of hers.

Shep grinned. "Let me show you."

He walked to the bookshelf and grabbed the *King James Bible*, tucking it under his arm. He then made his way the short distance to the trophy case and stood next to her. She looked up at him, her eyes knitted close together and her nose scrunched.

He opened the glass doors of the case and put his hand around the marble base of that special trophy. It wasn't all that special, really. All the trophies were similar to that one in some form or another. Some were big. Some were small. Only so many ways to make a trophy for an archery competition, he concluded.

He picked it up and a whirring noise echoed through the mostly empty room. She was startled by this. She let out a small surprised gasp and turned to see from where it came. The bookshelf, which masked a three-foot thick steel blast door, slowly swung outward. Artificial light flooded the dim room from a long cement corridor, well-lit, leading downward in a gentle slope.

"Holy shit," she muttered. It was not unlike the reaction he received the last time he revealed the passageway to someone.

It was too late to change his mind now. He had let her see something few ever had.

That was a dangerous thing.

But he had done it, for a girl he had known for just a few hours, for a girl he knew next to nothing about other than she had a unique first name and skill at scooping up SpaghettiOs with a spoon.

"Come on," he said. "Let's get you someplace to sleep."

She ambled down the corridor behind him; her eyes flittered about and her mouth dropped open. He had to stop walking a few times to let her catch up. He watched as she drifted down the passageway, her lips curling to make a crooked smile.

You haven't seen anything yet.

They reached another blast door and he opened up a panel that hung on the wall next to it to reveal a keyboard. He punched in the numbers – 271234559 – each press of his finger producing a loud tone. Once he was done he turned the wheel on the door clockwise and pulled it open with a grunt.

Warm air rushed in to meet them as they walked in. Soft ambient light filled the room from fixtures mounted on the pewter walls. A cream chenille area rug lay in the middle of the room, covering most of the rich brown laminate floor. A 52-inch plasma television hung on the wall to their left, while a beige leather couch, complete with brown satiny throw pillows, sat against the wall on their right.

A consol table rested beside the seating area. Glass lamps with crisp white shades sat on each side of a smattering of trophies from more of his archery triumphs.

The ceilings, where vents poured in recycled air, were high, about twenty feet, making the room seem even more spacious.

"OH. MY. GOD," Antigone babbled. She wandered into the middle of the room, almost tripping over the oak coffee table positioned just in front of the sofa. "OH. MY. GOD!"

She hopped about the room. "Electricity? You have electricity. How do you have electricity?"

"Solar power."

She chortled. "That's a little ironic." She twirled and skipped into the kitchen that was just off the living area. It was complete with stainless-steel appliances and a marble counter top.

"You have a microwave. A fridge!" She opened the refrigerator door and light bathed her. It was largely empty save for a case of Iron City beer and few bottles of wine and water.

She closed the door and bounded back into the living room. He delighted in how her face lit up and the way tiny wrinkles formed around the corners of her mouth when she smiled.

He led her down a hallway. Four sets of bunk beds were built into the walls, each with soft mattresses and down pillows. They reached another sealed door and he swung it open. Inside the air was muggy. Sweat beaded quickly, dotting their foreheads with droplets of water like dew. The sound of trickling water was loud and reverberated in the chamber.

"What is this?" She walked over to a large bin that looped the room and peered into the water. "Are those fish?"

"It's an aquaponic bay. The fish crap and it feeds the plants and the plants filter the water. The water comes from the surface. When it rains, it drains down here. It's like a self-contained ecosystem. It doesn't produce much food, but enough to supplement the canned goods I have."

"This is amazing." He followed her as she glided back into the living area and over to a cream door about twenty feet from the television.

"What's in there?"

He was no longer delighted.

"That's not important," he said tersely.

Antigone sat on the leather couch now and peered about the room in wonder. A half-smile crossed her lips.

Then a grim cast came to her eyes as she looked at Shep, who was standing guard in front of the cream door.

She swallowed hard before she spoke. "Did you see it?"

There was no need to ask for clarification. "Did you see it?" was a common question after the Ejection. It had the universal feel of "Where were you when Kennedy was assassinated?" or "Where were you on 9/11?"

"Yes," Shep said somberly. "I saw it. That's something I will never forget. I didn't think the sky could burn like that."

"I saw it, too. I thought it was the most beautiful thing I had ever seen. All the colors rippling across the sky like waves. Then the burnt red. It looked like a sunset, but everywhere at once, you know. Who knew it was the end of the world, right?"

Shep always thought the end would come from an asteroid with a funny name, or a super bug unleashed upon the masses, or a nuclear war, or even Yellowstone blowing its top.

This end of days was caused by a belching sun.

As Armageddon's go, this one was pretty lame.

But it was one hell of a burp.

Antigone's words were sullen. "I just can't believe something as beautiful as that caused all of this."

Shep explained to her that sometimes the things couched in the most beauty were the most dangerous.

The sun was known to hiccup from time to time, sending solar flares and sometimes a Coronal Mass Ejection toward the Earth. Most were harmless, doing nothing more than providing a vivid light show of brilliant aurora for those nearest the poles.

This one was different. This one was the biggest CME ever witnessed by man and it hurtled toward the planet, vengeful like a jilted lover. It was the universe's way of smacking our bottoms, her way of reminding us that in the grand scheme of things, we barely rate.

If that fickle bitch was keeping score, we were surely still stuck on zero.

The event itself didn't kill. No. The "Ejection," as it came to be called, didn't take a single life.

It lifted no knives to plunge into civilization's heart. It fired no guns. It slit no throats.

The people did that.

All the Ejection did was fry the satellites in orbit and destroy the power grid, rendering technology useless. All the Ejection did was slap the human race back a century.

With no communication and no electricity, things began to unravel quickly, like someone pulling a loose thread from a knitted scarf. Stores were plundered for food and water, the shelves cleaned out within a day. People began to starve within a week. Society began to crumble within a month.

Those who didn't starve to death killed for food to survive.

It all happened rather quickly and shockingly.

The human race had de-evolved.

It darkened many men, just like it had sullied Shep. It whittled him down like the wind on the face of a mountain.

It changed him.

It made him shoot arrows into hands and eyes. It made him wall himself up. That made what he had done for Antigone all the more remarkable.

Shep told her all of this and she sat forward on the couch, her eyes like blue ice, wide and staring at him the entire time. He thought he saw some tears well up in them, but she had quickly blinked them away.

He was sure she had her own stories. Perhaps she would tell them in time. For now, he needed to check on someone.

He grabbed the remote control that operated the television and handed it to her.

"Watch TV. There's a movie cued up. I don't remember which one."

Any movie would do, he surmised. He figured it had been a long while since she had seen one, probably with her boyfriend in a dark theater somewhere. Maybe at one of those quaint drive-ins with the song about going to the lobby to have a snack.

He opened the cream door just wide enough to slip through, and then quietly shut it behind him. The light was dim, but he could still see her gaunt face as she gazed blankly ahead.

He stared at her for a moment. Her brown hair was thin and stringy, her lips dry and cracked and her hazel eyes sunken in as if dragged down into her skull by illness and time. A column of dried, red tomato sauce ran from the corner of her mouth down her chin. Shep wet his thumb with his tongue and wiped it clean.

She was only in her mid-thirties, but looked much older.

In his eyes, though, she always appeared as she did the first day they met. Her skin was always glowing, her lips always full and lush, and her eyes always warm and full of a spark of life, not dull and dead as they were now.

She lay in their bed, tucked under a white comforter with aqua blue dolphins on it. On the nightstand beside her sat a clock, blinking 12:34, and a Glock pistol rested close to a bowl of, he couldn't remember what, probably SpaghettiOs. It was hardly touched and there was a dried red film on the top, cracked like the earth when it was thirsty for water.

Suddenly, she stirred and looked at him.

"Billy?" she asked. She always called him Billy. She hated it when people called him Shep. She always said it sounded like he was one of the Three Stooges. He would always say, "No, baby, that's SHEMP," but she didn't understand the difference.

"I'm here, Anna. I'm always here."

He heard the door creek open. He meant to fix it; he just had never gotten around to it. *This is such a busy Armageddon.* Antigone peeked in, her mouth gaped. Shep shot her a look and she quickly shut the door.

"We have a visitor," he whispered. "I figured you wouldn't mind. She kinda reminds me of you. I'm helping her. You proud of me?"

She nodded and smiled. "I'm always proud of you, Billy. Don't be rude. I'll be all right. Let me sleep."

Part I
Chapter Three
Their Life Before the Ejection

He awoke to her tapping on his forehead. Anna Shepard did that when she was angry.

Then Billy Shepard heard why she was so angry.

Stomp! Stomp! Stomp!

Each morning at five o'clock, the neighbor's feet banged on the floor above them.

Stomp! Stomp! Stomp!

It must be five o'clock.

Stomp! Stomp! Stomp!

"You hear that?" she said, annoyed.

"Now I do," he replied groggily. *Who needs a wailing alarm clock when you have a finger poked into your forehead?*

"I wish he didn't have to go to work so damned early," she whispered.

He rolled over, tucked his hands under his pillow and sighed deeply.

"Why is he so loud?" she continued. "He must have elephant feet."

He laughed, imagining the upstairs neighbor with four giant toes. "Some people are loud walkers. You're a loud walker."

She playfully smacked him. "No, I'm not!"

He snickered and lightly slapped her face. "Loud walker."

Her voice became like that of a TV evangelist. "He walketh about, seeking whom he may devour … like my sleep."

She liked quoting lines from the Bible out of context. Perhaps it was her way of rebelling against her religious father, who sent her to Bible school very much against her will. Or perhaps she loved the power that the words possessed, the poetry ingrained in each syllable. She had a copy of the *King James Bible* on her nightstand and would read a few passages each night before she went to sleep. Deep down, he thought, she was inspired by the words.

He reluctantly rolled out of bed. *No sense trying to get a few more minutes of shut eye.*

It was about time for him to rise anyway. He wasn't a morning person, but it was his job to trudge into the police station, still groggy and half asleep, and collect the misdeeds of others as told by the underpaid and bored officers in typos and poor grammar.

He wondered what amusing shenanigans people of this small city had gotten themselves into last night. Perhaps someone had called the police because their Farmville money was stolen again.

Very rarely was there major news to report on the police beat. There had been very few murders in the five years he had been employed by the hometown newspaper, a small operation with a fair circulation. It wasn't the Post-Gazette, but he liked it that way.

There were the usual violations of the law: assaults, drug busts, even a prostitution sting. It was a rather mundane beat, but it fit him well.

He slipped on his khaki pants and tightened his belt. He had to move up another notch, even when he sucked in his stomach. He needed to go on a diet. *Yes, a diet. Tomorrow. I'll start on one tomorrow.*

Anna stirred again. "Get a Powerball ticket."

"Sure," he said, rolling his eyes.

Their apartment on the first floor was small. One bedroom, a cramped living room just big enough to squeeze in an old couch inherited from his parents and a chair covered in polyester that was as uncomfortable as it was ugly. They had an old tube TV, a monstrous thing, hooked into a cable plan that gave them just thirteen channels.

That's all they could afford on the income of a reporter and a project manager at Iron Mountain in Boyers, Pennsylvania.

Locals called it "The Mines" and she had worked there for the better part of a decade. It was a sprawling network of tunnels, old limestone corridors carved into the mountain early in the 20th century. It was abandoned and then repurposed as a subterranean storage facility for rare documents and recordings. It even had a mysterious name, "Room 48," that added to its mystique.

When Shep would ask Anna what went on down there, she would quip, "I could tell ya, but I'd have to kill ya." She also joked that she hoped she was at work when Armageddon came for she would be safe two-hundred feet underground in the bunker while he would be "fried like a marshmallow over the fire."

Happy thoughts.

The Shepards did just fine. They got by. They had enough money to pay the rent, the utilities, to eat and put clothes on their backs. They had enough money for one car payment, his student loans and to rent a few movies or take in a ballgame or two. They had three hundred dollars in their checking account and another two thousand in their savings, not to mention the hundred-dollar bill tucked away under the mattress for emergencies.

It wasn't a bad life. It was a simple life. A quiet life. It was their life, and that was all that mattered.

They were happy.

He closed the front door quietly behind him and made sure it was locked, and then walked past the row of mailboxes when he heard those clumping steps again rumbling down the stairs.

Stomp! Stomp! Stomp!

It was Paul Bray. He was a large man, more stocky than fat. His neck was broad and his hair was trimmed short. He had thick eyebrows and he had stubble poking out of his face even though he probably had just shaved moments before.

He was wearing his blues. The radio attached to his shoulder screeched with police chatter.

"Hey, Shep," he said, walking faster toward him. "Check this out!" He turned and lowered his collar. There was a fresh tattoo low on his neck. It looked like a fancy letter 'n.'

"What's the 'n' stand for?"

"What?" Bray was confused. "No."

"It stands for no?" Shep liked messing with Bray. He was an easy target.

"No, man. It's not an 'n.'"

"It looks like an 'n.'"

"Nah, man. It's the symbol for strength."

"It's an 'n.' A fancy 'n,' but it's still an 'n.'"

Bray waved his beefy hand at him is a dismissive way.

"Not my fault you are too much of a pansy to get one. You should get one, dude." He punched Shep on the arm. It hurt. It hurt badly, but he resisted the urge to rub it for fear of being called a pansy again. "That's if you're not too pussy-whipped."

Shep shook his head. He wondered how people like Bray did it, always jovial, always crude. He figured that sensor that most people have that keep them from saying the first thing that popped into their heads didn't work in some people.

Bray was one of those people.

He had known him for three years, since the day he and Anna moved into this apartment building. Bray thundered down the steps to greet them with that goofy smile of his, rolled up his sleeves and helped them move in. He cracked open a few beers for them and told stories of his early days on the force, of how someday he wanted to be a detective and solve those "seriously fucked-up cases."

To do that he worked double shifts. He rose at ungodly hours – didn't he and Anna know that. He volunteered for overtime.

The world was full of people who did what they needed to do to just get by. There were people who gamed the system. There were people who thought everything was owed to them, that society was there to prop them up and keep them warm and fed and comfortable.

Bray was not one of those people. And Shep admired that about him.

"Gotta go catch the bad guys," Bray said with a snort and another punch of Shep's arm. It throbbed worse than the last one. "Don't pass no wooden nickels."

•••

M&Ms, Kit Kat or 3 Musketeers? That was the choice before him as he gazed down at the rows of boxes in the candy aisle of the convenience store. It was such a perplexing decision that he paid no attention to the ringing of the bell when someone walked into the bustling store, or the cold air that rushed in and slapped him on the back of the neck.

He ignored the din of the conversations around him, people greeting people on the way to work, grabbing donuts with tongs out of the case, sipping the hot coffee they had just purchased to give them a pick-me-up for the long workday grind ahead.

It was his routine. He would get the police reports and take them back to the office, sift through them, type in the ones that were interesting or relevant, make a few phone calls and then get a snack at the convenient store down the street. He rarely made eye contact with anyone in the store even though he saw the same familiar faces each day. He didn't want to know any of them. Good people they were, he thought, probably with the same problems, the same joys, the same hobbies. They probably even liked the same television shows.

Sure, he would nod and smile at them as they passed. He may have even blurted out a "good morning" or "have a good one" from time to time. It was common courtesy, after all.

On this day, though, an unfamiliar face caught his eye. She couldn't have been more than thirteen. Her black hair was dirty and tangled. There was a film around the edges of her cracked lips and she looked weak and hungry. Her dark eyes darted all about the store, stopping on the cashier, who was distracted now by a steady stream of customers.

Shep grabbed a bag of M&Ms and quietly walked around the corner to where the mittens and cheap knitted hats hung. She looked around nervously, grabbed a couple of candy bars – he could tell she didn't have the same quandary that he had when choosing sweets – and tucked them into the pocket of her stained gray sweatshirt.

She tried to slip out the door, but a hand reached out and snagged the hood, yanking her back.

"Empty your pockets," he said sternly. He had been quietly stocking shelves in the corner. She hadn't seen him. Neither did Shep.

"Get off me!" she wailed and squirmed and tried to break free.

Before Shep could stop himself, there he was, pulling the girl out of the grasp of the employee.

"I'll pay for those," Shep said, then smiled at the girl. "My daughter forgot she put them in her pockets, isn't that right?"

Her big black eyes looked up at Shep and her mouth dropped open as she nodded. The employee shook his head and said, "Whatever," as he walked away.

"You want something a little more ..." he began to ask her, but before he could say "substantial," she was out the door and sprinting, weaving between cars on the busy main street. She moved almost too fast for her legs to keep up.

He stood in line and thought about her. He felt sorry for her, hungry all the time. *Where were her parents? Was she a runaway? Did she at least go to school? At least there she could get one good meal every day.* He didn't know why he was dwelling on it so much as the line slowly moved, third from the counter, now second from the counter. But he did. He was disturbed.

He was broken out of his trance by the cashier. "Buddy, the M&Ms, is that all?"

"What? Sorry," he said, reaching into his pocket to pull out a folded ten. "No, two more candy bars."

The cashier mashed the buttons on the register. Each press produced a beep.

"Oh," he said, panicked. "And a Powerball ticket."

•••

Nearly a week had passed before he saw her again. She walked into the store wearing the same clothes and her hair was just as unkempt.

Her eyes locked on him and she nervously tried to turn and leave. Shep, though, was able to stop her.

"Hey, not so fast." He grabbed her hood, much like the store's Employee of the Month did a week ago.

"Let me go or I'll scream."

He let go of the hood and held his hands up. "I just want to buy you a decent meal, something a little better than a PayDay."

She looked at him curiously, cautiously. He could tell she was trying to size him up. "Sure, okay," she relented. *She wasn't about to pass up a good meal.*

"Good. Let's get you something to eat."

They walked down the street to a little café. There was nothing particularly remarkable about the food, but the service was fast.

She sat across from him in the booth, the backrest of the red vinyl bench rising high above her head, and picked at the loose pieces of skin on her fingers. She wasn't much of a conversationalist. He ordered the pancakes with a side of syrup for himself and the same for her, but added two scrambled eggs and a large glass of orange juice.

The food came and she dug in. He marveled at how efficient she was at devouring her meal. He guessed it was because she didn't have much time to savor whatever scraps she could get her hands on.

"What's your name?" he asked. *He was buying her breakfast. They should at least be on a first-name basis.*

"None of your business," she snapped back.

Well, maybe not. "Do you go to school?"

"Yes. I'm not stupid." She finished the last bite of her eggs and took a large gulp from her glass of OJ. She slid out of the booth and began to leave, but stopped after a few steps to peer over her shoulder at him.

"Thanks," she muttered.

"We can do it again tomorrow if you like?"

She nodded and walked away.

They had breakfast again nearly every day for the next two weeks. She still wouldn't tell him her name. They had turned it into a game. He asked and she answered with some rude retort, or a made up name like Eileen Dover, and they would share a laugh. He was quite enjoying her company, even though they barely spoke. Every now and then she would drop her guard a little to reveal her dream about going to college to become a social worker, or a dancer, or a doctor – it changed frequently. It didn't matter to Shep because all of those dreams were worthy ones.

It was a rainy Wednesday when he waited for her. He fidgeted his hands in his pockets, spinning the spare change around in his fingers. He peered out the glass doors and watched for her. The day before she said she would be there and they would share a booth again at that café. But she was late.

Very late.

He saw just about all of those familiar faces, the ones he, for some reason, had grown to loath as they came and went, oblivious to the fact that a hungry girl had been among them for so long. They had no idea what he was going through. *What had happened to her? Was she okay?*

After an hour, he finally gave up. He grabbed a bag of M&Ms and slowly walked to the counter. His mind spun with scenarios of why she didn't show up. *Maybe, tomorrow. Yeah. She'll be here tomorrow.*

"Is this all?" The cashier asked.

"No," his face was grim. "And a Powerball ticket."

•••

He awoke to her tapping on his forehead.

She was blurry at first, and then Anna's face came into focus. She was holding his white iPhone in her hand.

"You better take this. It's Perry."

He could hear his editor's frazzled voice before he even put the phone to his ear.

"Shep! Shep!" It took a lot to get Perry this riled up. He had been the editor of the newspaper for, well, he didn't really know how long. Shep had worked there for five years and he had never called him at this hour.

"What's up, Perry?"

"I need you to get out here. There's been a shooting. Right down the street from the paper. The police are everywhere. The scanner chatter was about a gunfight. We need a story for tomorrow."

"On my way." Shep was wide awake now. Anna looked at him puzzled.

"What's going on?" she asked.

"There's been a shooting near the paper. Perry wants me down there." He quickly slipped on his jeans and a black long-sleeve V-neck shirt. He pushed his hands through his hair and began to make his way for the door when Anna pulled him close and kissed him hard on the lips.

"Be careful," she whispered.

•••

The strobes from the police cars splashed pulses of red and white light on the business fronts and pavement, which was still wet from the day's hard rain. People milled about outside the yellow tape, some half dressed with their arms crossed bracing against the chill, others smoking a cigarette and whispering rumors to each other.

Shep flashed his press pass and the officers let him through the first line of tape. He had been on the beat for quite some time now and he knew the police chief well. They had even played golf together once.

Thomas Crenshaw was a decorated man of the law for twenty years and chief for the past decade. He had seen a lot, and it was evident in his build and harried face. He was shaped like a pear and his face was round and flushed like an apple. He had mutton chops, which only made his face look even more misshapen. He always had a smile, though, and his eyes, even tired and sunken, always seemed to have a pleasant gleam about them.

But not tonight. Crenshaw was visibly shaken as Shep approached.

"What's wrong, Tom? What happened here?"

Crenshaw shook his head and stared down at the pavement. He swallowed hard, glowered and sighed.

"We had an incident, that's all I can say on the record."

"What can you say off the record?"

Shep caught a glimpse of Bray out of the corner of his eye, sitting on the bumper of a squad car. He was giving a statement to man in a suit. He said something, laughed, and slapped the suited man on the arm.

"Was officer Bray involved?" Shep's voice jumped an octave.

"Yes. Officer Bray was involved … off the record. He was responding to a robbery call at the convenient store. He witnessed three youths running from the store, and then a fourth came out. He said he saw the suspect reach into a pocket and pull out a gun. He shot the suspect."

"It wasn't a gun, was it?"

"No," Crenshaw said, biting his lower lip. "It was a PayDay bar."

Shep could see the body laying about a hundred yards away, covered by a sheet. Police stood near it. Shep's heart pounded. *No. It couldn't be.* Before Crenshaw could stop him, Shep sprinted toward the body. Officers who could have stopped him looked on stunned. Shep made it to the corpse and quickly pulled back on the sheet, then slumped to his knees onto the wet pavement.

Her dark eyes were still open wide and staring at him, much like they did when they ate breakfast together. She was wearing that same ratty sweatshirt – he had offered to buy her a new one but she said something like, "nobody dresses me but me." *Why didn't I insist on buying her a new sweatshirt?*

This one was covered in her blood from a wound in her chest.

He felt a tap on his shoulder, but he didn't turn to look. Instead he kept staring into those eyes that would never see the sun shine again.

He felt another tap on his shoulder. This time he looked up. It was Bray.

"Did you know her, Shep?" Bray's voice rang with concern. Shep nodded. He felt a tear stream down his right cheek.

"Shit, man. I thought it was a gun. Her accomplices had guns. The cashier said as much." It sounded to Shep like Bray was doing his own reasoning. "How was I supposed to know it was a PayDay bar? I mean, what's she doing in there at this hour anyway with those guys? I was just doing my job, man."

And Shep was doing his. He rubbed his hand over her eyes, shutting them. At the same time, his became open to what he already knew deep down, but didn't want to admit. *Life was cruel and unfair. If a sweet girl like this, full of dreams and promise, could be thrown away, was there hope for any of us?*

He prayed she was in a better place, at least.

Part I
Chapter Four
The Skye Before the Ejection

Her name was Skye Padme Walker and her parents were geeks. She was fourteen. Her father was an alcoholic and disappeared when she was only three. Her mother was a junkie who loved the needle more than she loved her.

Skye fell into the wrong crowd two years ago. Experimented with drugs herself before she quit, not wanting to turn into her mother. She didn't drink. She didn't smoke. Her day consisted of trying to find something filling to put into her belly so she didn't have to fall asleep to the sound of her stomach barking.

She was just tagging along that night. That's what the three boys who robbed the convenience store, no more than eighteen themselves, told the police when they were captured two blocks away while they attempted, in vain, to climb a chain-link fence. They told the police they actually tried to keep her away.

She didn't listen.

At about the time Bray was blowing a hole in Skye's chest, the Powerball numbers were announced. Shep didn't find out the ticket he bought after he waited for Skye had matched the drawn numbers exactly – 2 7 12 34 55 and the Powerball number of 9 – until after he had filed his story about the robbery and the tense confrontation with police that resulted in one death.

His fingers trembled as he typed. He had to go over the story three times to fix all the typos he had made.

•••

Anna threw her arms around him before he could even get through the door. He felt her heart thumping, even through several layers of their clothing.

"We won!" she screamed. He was stoic. All he wanted to do was sleep and forget. He pulled away from her embrace, and her excited smile turned to one of concern. "What's wrong? What happened?"

A girl died because Bray shot her, but he might as well have been the one pulling the trigger. He should have let her get caught. Then, at least, she would be in juvie or in a foster home somewhere instead of lying dead on Main Street. At the very least he should have taken her in. He could have convinced her. He could have taken her back to their apartment and fed her and gave her a warm place to sleep on their second-hand couch.

He didn't do any of those things.

He wanted to tell Anna all of that. Instead he muttered, "I need to sleep," and brushed past her on the way to the bedroom. He didn't even bother loosening his ever-tightening belt. He just fell backward onto the mattress, pushed his glasses up on his forehead and draped his arm over his eyes. He tried to shut out the outside world the best he could.

Anna's hand brushed his arm and he pulled it away. She looked down at him and combed her fingers through his hair like she always did when she tried to comfort him.

"No matter what, Billy, I will always be here with you."

"I'll be okay," he whispered. "Let me sleep."

•••

She stood in the corner of the dimly lit hotel bar. She appeared very much like Shep had remembered her. She looked innocent, but he knew better. That innocence had been snatched from her by fate, by circumstance, maybe even by the amateur chemist who made the meth her mother snorted, smoked and injected. So many people and so many things conspired against Skye Padme Walker – *perhaps even her geeky name* – and set the wheels of her doom in motion.

She looked right at him with those dark eyes. He tried to ignore her, tapping his Highball to get the bartender's attention. The whiskey sloshed into the glass and he scooped it up and knocked it back with a harsh swallow.

He grabbed a couple of almonds from the dish that sat in front of him on the bar and tossed them at her, prompting the bartender to utter something in anger, something like they were for eating, not throwing. Shep wasn't paying attention because Skye was still there.

Dark crimson blood began to spread out from the middle of her gray sweatshirt. It spread like the ink from a fountain pen dripped onto a piece of paper. Her eyes got big and round and she mouthed a few words. He couldn't make out what they were.

Shep quickly shut his eyes. Tight. He clenched his jaw and whispered through gritted teeth, "Please. Just go away."

"Go away?" Bray's voice boomed as he slapped Shep on the back. "I just got here."

Bray slid a stool closer to Shep. The sound of the legs dragging on the floor made a horrible screech.

"Hey, Officer Bray. It's been a long time." Shep's words were indifferent. Bray was the last person he wanted to see, except for maybe Billy Shepard in the reflection of the mirror behind the bar.

And Skye Padme Walker, who haunted him.

Bray grabbed a couple of almonds and popped them into his mouth. "It's Detective Bray now. Yeah. Got promoted. Livin' the life, you know. What the fuck are you doing here slummin' it, Shep? Can't you just buy your own bar now?"

Shep forced out a fake laugh. He didn't want to tell him his marriage was falling apart, that he himself was falling apart. He had a beautiful wife and a beautiful home on a hundred acres of rolling land with fertile soil. Isolated. Idyllic. Perfect. Yet he was in this filthy, dark and dank bar having a drink with him … and her.

He didn't want to tell him that under his home was a lavish shelter that he insisted on building. That Anna had indulged him for as long as she could until he pushed too far. The drinking. The quiet. The retreating down into the depths of the dungeon he had built for himself to get away from everyone and everything.

She ripped out a line from the Bible for just this occasion – earlier on this night, in fact – before he despondently packed a bag and left for this sterile, lifeless shithole of a hotel. He figured it suited him the best.

"No one can serve two masters," she had said, bitterly.

Anna Shepard had reached her breaking point. He had abandoned her long ago in mind, now she wanted him gone in body, too.

The only thing Shep wondered as he climbed into his Mustang convertible and drove away was, "What the hell took her so long?" It had been years since he was the man she fell in love with. He was incapable of being that person now. He had spiraled into a deep depression and was always forlorn. Nothing gave him pleasure, not even shooting arrows into targets on their sprawling land. Anna tried to help him. She was so patient and caring. But even she had her limit.

He didn't deserve her. He thought maybe he never did. His soul was as black as a moonless night and as dark as a casket – and he figured he might as well be in one, too.

Now he was sharing a drink with Bray. He was wrong. *Things could get worse.*

"How do you do it? Tell me." Shep's question caught Bray off guard. He backed away and cocked his head ever so slightly.

"What do you mean, friend?"

"We're not friends. When were we ever friends? We were neighbors. That's all. We had conversations in the hall before we went to work. You showed me your goddamned stupid tattoo. That's the extent of it. But, how do you do it?"

"You've had a little too much to drink. I think I should drive you home."

Shep laughed. Deep and hard. Laughed and laughed and slammed the bar with his hand. "Home? Home? I am home. We're separated. I have a ten-million dollar bomb shelter under my beautiful home and I'm staying in a fifty-dollar-a-night hotel that probably has hourly rates. You haven't answered my question, *friend*. How do you do it?"

Bray put his hand on Shep's shoulder and he slapped it away. "I don't know what you are asking. Let me help you to your room, then."

"No, dammit. I want an answer. How do you do it? How do you kill a girl and go on like nothing happened?"

"You're not making any sense."

"I see her all the time you know. She's right over there in that corner just looking at me through those cold black eyes of hers." Shep put his arm out to point to where Skye stood, her lips still moving to make words he couldn't quite hear. His arm swayed terribly; he was too inebriated to keep it steady. "Right there. There she is. She's trying to tell me something, but I can't hear her."

"Who do you see?" Bray turned to look to where Shep was trying to point.

"Eileen Dover." Shep giggled.

"Okay. Let's get you up to your room so you can sleep it off."

"Not until you tell me how you do it. How do you pull your gun and shoot a girl and act like nothing happened?"

Bray lowered his head, a loud sigh escaping his lips. He looked up at Shep, a cold look in his eyes. "Dude, it was an accident. I know you think you were somehow responsible, but it's nobody's fault. Shit happens. It always has and it always will. You gotta pull yourself together man and get over it. Jesus!"

Bray slid off the stool and grabbed Shep around the shoulders, trying to lift him up. Shep shook him off violently, made a fist with his right hand and swung it at Bray. It crashed against Bray's lip, flush. Even numbed – by how many shots, he couldn't remember – he still felt the sting pulsing through the knuckles of his hand. Bray's head snapped back, and then straightened. His lip was split and he wiped the blood from it with the back of his hand as he moved his jaw side to side and opened and closed his mouth. Shep could hear the bones click as he did. As quickly as Bray had finished sizing up the damage, Shep found himself face down on the sticky floor that smelled faintly of booze. Bray had flung him there once his jaw was back in alignment.

"You're one crazy motherfucker. You know that?" Bray screamed, towering over him. "I should throw your ass in jail, but that won't do any of us any fucking good. Let her go."

Oh, if it were that easy. He'd snap his fingers and she'd be gone and he would whistle and go about his life carefree and fanciful. It didn't work that way, at least for people like him. Maybe it worked that way for cold bastards like Bray.

He laughed. *Bray the Bastard. It had a nice ring to it.*

"Someday, something is going to be taken from you," Shep said, callously and with great disdain. "I hope I can be there to see it."

Bray lifted Shep off the floor, flung his arm under his pit and held him up. "Come on, you crazy fuck. Let's get you to your room."

Skye disappeared. He oddly missed her.

Part I
Chapter Five
The Things They Missed Now

"I miss ..." Antigone said that every night before they went to sleep. What she missed varied. Hot showers. Milkshakes. Twitter.

His answers were the usual fare, too.

Baseball. Bacon. Driving a car with the top down.

Normalcy is always the first thing you miss. He longed to watch the Pittsburgh Pirates, even though they lost more than they won. He longed to hear the crunch as he sunk his teeth into a crisp piece of bacon. He longed for speeding down a straightaway with the wind howling against his face.

"I miss going to work." It was an odd admission for Shep. There were days in that other life when he loathed getting up early, putting on a shirt and tie and going into the office. But he would have given anything to do that again.

"I miss M&Ms," she said, giggling as she lay on the bunk across the corridor from him, swaddled in a red fleece blanket.

He laughed at her answer, but not because he thought it foolish.

"M&Ms, huh?" He rolled out of the bunk and stuck his landing. *The Russian judge would even give me a 10.* His bare feet patted at the floor as he walked into the kitchen and opened a door that revealed a walk-in pantry, larger even than the one in his cellar. These shelves, though, were mostly barren save for a few cans of SPAM, chicken and beef broth and some jars of mashed pumpkin. He knelt, pulling a brown box off the bottom shelf and opened it. In it, packed to the top, were bags and bags of plain M&Ms. He grabbed two and smiled as he made his way back to her.

He tossed a bag onto her head and it slid down the bridge of her nose, coming to a rest on the red fleece blanket. By the time he had crawled back onto his bunk, her eyes were big and those wrinkles, the tiny adorable lines, were back around her the corners of her lips.

"At least I can cross one of those off your list," he said as he pulled his bag open. *Oh, that smell of chocolate, trapped in that bag for so long, now released.* He took a big sniff and held it, never wanting to let that aroma escape his nostrils.

She sat up and excitedly ripped the bag open, shaking out a handful into her left palm. Some green. Some yellow. Some brown. And some red. He remembered there was a myth about those red ones in that old life. Red dye No. 2 caused cancer. Red dye No. 2 caused birth defects. Red M&Ms were actually removed for a time in the 70s and 80s until the hokum of the claim was exposed.

Green. Yellow. Brown and red. They all tasted the same to him.

She popped the whole handful into her mouth. She didn't chew. She just let them melt – that whole melt in your mouth, not in your hands thing. That was a thing once, back when times were a different kind of complicated, back when simple pleasures were still simple and didn't require hoarding 99-cent bags of chocolate, squirreling them away in a survival shelter because they were worth more than nuggets of gold.

She finally swallowed and closed her eyes in pleasure. He wondered if there were many moments like that for her, or anyone, anymore. Probably not, he figured.

There were no delicacies. Food was no longer there to be savored and enjoyed. It was just a means to survive.

He took pleasure in her pleasure. She emptied the rest of the bag in her palm and popped them into her mouth. He could tell it gave her just as much satisfaction as the last mouthful.

"Here," he said and tossed his bag across the corridor to her. It landed just under her chin and slid down onto her lap. "Have the rest."

He hadn't seen a look like that from her since she had decided to stay. She was reserved around him. He could see and feel that. Untrusting of him. Leery. Guarded. She accepted his food and shelter, but he knew she was conflicted about it. Perhaps it was difficult to trust a man who had shot an arrow into a woman's brain and left her lying limp and dead on the ground without much of a care.

Those mannerisms, that attitude, had melted away now, much like those M&Ms had melted away a moment ago in her mouth. She had an odd smirk on her face and her head was cocked slightly as she poured what was left of his bag into her hand with two quick downward thrusts. Her eyes – those eyes again – never left his.

Perhaps those M&Ms were even more valuable than nuggets of gold.

"Let me ask you something." It was the first time she had asked him anything, other than if he had seen the sky turn red. She hadn't said much. He didn't, either.

"Go for it."

"Why don't you sleep in there?" She pointed to the main room, but he knew where she was really pointing.

"She needs rest," he answered. Her eyes narrowed and she bit her lower lip as he continued. "I could never really sleep well in there anyway. She understands."

"Who is she?"

"My wife. Her name is Anna." He found it difficult to say her name in front of Antigone. That troubled him. "She is the love of my life."

"What happened to her?"

Oh, so much, he thought.

"She's sick. Very sick. I can't leave her. I never could."

She wiped her eyes with her fingers, slightly stained with chocolate. She moved her lips to say something, but nothing came out. She was at a loss for words. *A first time for everything.*

"I need to give her some medicine." He stood and Antigone looked up at him. *Was that pity in her wet eyes? Yes, it most surely was.* He didn't want pity. He didn't deserve pity. There was nothing to pity.

Shit happens. It always did. It always will.

He opened the door and closed it quietly behind him. Anna lay in the bed very much like she always did. She stared blankly ahead at a fake front page of a newspaper that hung on the wall across from her. It celebrated their wedding, all those many years ago. He had forgotten just how long. Under normal circumstances, that would have meant the cold shoulder and even the silent treatment.

These weren't normal circumstances.

He walked across the room to another door that opened into one of the two bathrooms he had installed in the shelter. He peered at himself in the mirror that hung above the sink. He looked even older today. His dark hair was a mess, pushed up to a point on his head. He had been wearing the same black thermal shirt for days and his jeans were worn and dirty on the thighs. He reeked.

He ran his hand through his hair and sighed. He knew what he was going to find in the medicine cabinet when he opened it. Every night it was the same. It was irrational to think anything was going to change. Yet, he did it anyway.

He did it again.

Inside the cabinet were rows of prescription drug bottles, some with his name on the label, some with hers.

All were empty.

He slammed the cabinet door shut and left the bathroom in a huff. Anna was still staring blankly ahead. He'd let her rest. She needed her rest.

Antigone stood at the open door. She was snooping again and he didn't much care for it.

"Don't disturb her."

He forced Antigone to backpedal into the living room and closed the door behind them. He walked sullenly back to his bunk with Antigone trailing him with a slow, nervous walk. When he glanced back at her, she had a disturbed look on her face.

He imagined there was one on his, too.

There was nothing he could do for Anna. He was powerless. He wasn't much good at being powerless. It made his skin crawl. He was never one to let things be. He always had to tinker. He always had to fix things, even if they were unfixable, even if his efforts were futile.

Everything had changed around him. Just like that. Snap. Everything was different. Fundamentally, though, at his core, he was unchanged. The things that bothered him before, the small things, the insignificant things, bothered him still. The big things, too. It was his weakness. He knew that, but he couldn't change it anymore than he could make the world as it once was.

He was beginning to think Antigone knew that about him, too.

She sat with her legs folded under her on her bunk and rocked to and fro. He also did that when he was upset. It calmed him. Maybe it was because it was like the sensation they felt when they were infants, being rocked to sleep in their mother's arms.

"Now let me ask you something," he said. Her movement stopped. "It's easy to tell who is going hungry and who is not. You were not going hungry. Where were you?"

"My brother, he's kind of a big deal. My family is wealthy and pretty paranoid. We had a shelter. It wasn't like this one, but it was okay."

It made perfect sense. In that other life, people scoffed at the preppers, the people who hoarded food, hoarded SpaghettiOs and Cheese Ravioli and Beefaroni, broths and SPAM and jarred fruits and vegetables by the ton. They shook their heads and laughed at the people who spent thousands of dollars on shelters, on vehicles that ran on used motor oil, at the people who filled ten-gallon containers with rice.

They weren't laughing now.

The preppers were the people who were the best equipped to survive after the Ejection. But even their stores diminished over time.

Shep knew the answer to his own question. "You had to leave. You ran out of food."

She nodded. "It was time to get the hell out of there. I thought my brother was going to come back for me," she paused and swallowed hard. Her head dropped as if yanked down by an anchor. "But he never came."

"Maybe he couldn't. Maybe he tried." He made his voice sound as reassuring as possible, but he didn't fake it well. Her brother had done as so many other brothers had done after the Ejection. During the first few days, they were the concerned sibling, the concerned son or grandson. Those first few days, they tried to be the hero. Maybe they searched. Maybe they tried to find their way back to their families.

Then that hunger coiled in their bellies. The call of family is strong. The call of survival is stronger.

For whatever reason, she was left alone. He admired the way she made do with what she had. She was mature for her age and many as young as she perished quickly. In many ways, she was stronger than he was; braver, for sure.

"He's probably just waiting for me to come to him," she said as her head shot back up and she grinned. "I'm sure he's in Halcyon expecting me to make it there."

Shep blurted, "I wouldn't hold your breath."

Her eyebrows furled. She was quite cross with him. She could hate what he said all she wanted, but it was true. If he hadn't come back for her by now, he never was. If he was waiting for her somewhere, even in that place called Halcyon, if it existed, he must have given up hope.

It was irresponsible of her brother to think a teenage girl could make that kind of trek. If he was as important as she claimed, he would have found a way to get her, to bring her to safety. He did none of those things. Instead, he left her in a shelter with limited provisions and hoped she could find her way to him.

She was thinking wishfully.

Shep could hope for a baseball game, a slice of sizzling bacon and a Mustang convertible with an open road ahead all he wanted. He wasn't getting it. Ever. And she wasn't getting her brother back.

"Fuck you," she said softly before her voice rose and filled with vitriol. "Fuck you!"

"I'm just tellin' you the truth. Did you really think he's out there in this … this magical place where birds sing, butterflies flap their wings and kids play on swings? It's not real and you better get used to that."

Her face turned a deep crimson, much like the color of Red Dye No. 2. There was spittle when she spoke. "Oh, yeah, you're the one to talk to me about …"

Her diatribe was interrupted by a beeping noise coming from a speaker fastened to the wall above the entrance to the shelter. He knew what that siren meant and he held his breath, hoping it would stop.

It was a piercing sound. It needed to be. He was a sound sleeper. The volume on alarm clocks had to be turned up to maximum for him to hear it. He slept through fire trucks, lightning storms, and even heavy steps from the neighbor upstairs.

The shrieking tone continued and he resigned himself to the fact it wasn't going to stop.

"What the hell is that?" She was still mad and her voice was getting hoarse.

"It's not good."

He raced into the main chamber with Antigone following closely behind and turned on the television. A movie began to play. He didn't know which one. He turned the channel to seven and the screen went dark, then flickered into a grid of nine screens, images from nine security cameras stationed around the outside and the inside of the house.

Shep scanned the images closely. He saw movement on camera three and punched three on the keypad of the remote and that frame filled the screen. It was Frail Man, his long dark hair slicked back and tied into a ponytail. His right hand was wrapped in thick white gauze and he was kicking violently at the front door. The microphone picked up the sound of his every boot.

Bang! Bang! Bang!

Shep noticed that Frail Man gripped a shotgun in his left hand as he took more kicks at the door.

Bang! Bang! Bang!

"You were right," he said to Antigone as he looked more closely at the image of the Frail Man. He looked different now, yet so familiar. Time had morphed the features of men since the Ejection happened, aging and thinning out most, weathering them, grinding them down.

No. It can't be. Frail Man turned to give the door a mule kick and that's when Shep saw it. It was grainy in the black and white and low resolution of the picture.

He didn't need HD to figure out the tattoo on the back of Frail Man's neck looked like a small 'n,' that it was the symbol for strength.

Part I
Chapter Six
Joe Pesci Before the Ejection

We're all killing ourselves, Shep reasoned. Any time we cross the street without looking both ways, any time we eat a Big Mac, drink too much, take a long drag from our Camel cigarette, we're shaving a jiffy here, a second there.

He was just trying to speed that up a little.

Cut out the middle man. That was his mantra.

He climbed the steel stairs, his hand running over the cold rail, and thought about what it would feel like when he hit the ground.

Would he even feel it? Would he linger in a painful pile of flesh until he lost consciousness and eventually expired?

Would he shit himself? He'd hate to die with crap in his pants.

He reached the top of the five-tier parking garage and peered over the edge. In the distance he could see main street bustle with activity. He could even see the spot where Skye had died all those years ago. He pulled a flask out of the pocket of his faded jeans, unscrewed the cap and took a swig. It burned as he swallowed. He chuckled as he thought he had just cut another few seconds off his life with that gulp.

He peered over the edge again, down to the red brick alley below, and concluded he just wasn't high enough, that he'd probably just break his legs or his hip or his neck. The fall, at worst, would paralyze him, and then he wouldn't even be able to make another sounder attempt on his life.

That was just no good. That simply would not do.

He thought about the Glock pistol he had purchased as part of his survival gear. But he was squeamish about putting a bullet in his brain. It's such a messy way to go, he thought. He didn't like the idea of someone scrubbing the pieces of his skull and grey matter off the wall when he was through. That was just too mean to do to someone.

He was stuck, a man who wanted to die, but didn't know how to do it.

Strange things come into a man's mind – and he was sure the same thoughts crept into a woman's mind at these times – when he wants nothing more than to sleep forever.

He wished for an easy button.

He'd hit that button now and be done with it.

But there is no such thing as an easy button.

That's why he wanted to kill himself to begin with.

He was too ingenious for his own good. Ninety-nine percent of suicides involve pills or guns or jumps from great heights, or convenient gas leaks, or jumping in front of a moving car, or ramming a moving car into a telephone pole – all really nasty ways to go, he thought.

He had a better idea.

Sure, the premise is tried and true. Carbon monoxide poisoning.

It's clean. It's painless. No muss. No fuss. The closest thing to an easy button as there is.

There was only one problem.

He didn't have access to a garage.

This plagued him for some hours. He had more money than he knew what to do with, but no house – Anna lived in it now – and no garage. He snickered at the irony of that. Carbon monoxide poisoning was the way to go – out with the good, in with the bad, that was his new mantra.

•••

The wind slapped against his face as he drove down a winding country road in his cherry red Mustang convertible when he rolled past a row of storage lockers.

Most people wondered how many boxes of their useless shit they could cram into one of those.

His thought was, "Could I fit my Mustang convertible with the top up in there?"

As it turns out, he could.

•••

Strange things come into a man's mind – and he was sure the same thoughts enter a woman's mind at these times – when you are waiting to die.

We're all waiting to die. Every time we seize the Doritos instead of seize the day, we are just punching a clock until Death comes.

He was cheating. He was going on his own terms. He was checking out early.

He looked into the rearview mirror and his eyes stared back in the faint light of the dashboard.

What happened to you? How did you get to this point?

The answer didn't really matter.

He was here.

This was it.

He looked in the rearview mirror again, only this time she was there. She sat in the back seat with that blank gaze of hers through those dark eyes. He didn't know why her appearance startled him; she had been popping up for years now. But it always gave him a jolt.

"Here to see me off, Skye. Cool." He said. "What? Got nothing to say? All this time and you still won't say a single word that I can hear. This is your last chance. Say something."

Nothing. Just that blank stare.

He turned away from the mirror and leaned his head on the rest.

It won't be long now.

His eyelids were already growing heavy.

No, it won't be long now.

He heard a high, raspy voice hiss in his ear, "It's not time."

Before he could turn to see if she was still there, the door to the storage container rolled open and the bright beams of headlights flooded in and blinded him. He covered his eyes with his arm, heard the car door swing open and felt the grasp of two hands pull him out of the vehicle.

"He's still alive." It was the deep voice of Bray, yelling back to a pair of paramedics and a police officer who had pulled up in a cruiser behind him. "Shep, you crazy motherfucker. What are you doing? We'll get you some help. Don't worry."

•••

The man in the bed next to him was unconscious. Sedated. His left wrist was handcuffed to the bed rail. His head was shaved, but stubble covered his face. He looked weak and frail.

Shep felt sorry for him, but not as sorry as he felt for himself.

Shep lay on his back and counted the tiny holes in the ceiling. He was up to 262 when the nurse entered the room.

"Dr. Hale will see you now."

He looked like Joe Pesci, Dr. Hale did. He was short – really short – and wore a black sweater over a white dress shirt and black dress pants over black boots.

His hair was parted in the middle and feathered and obviously dyed charcoal. When he talked, Shep almost expected him to say, "Two yutes."

But he didn't say that.

"How long have you felt this way?" He asked in a completely non-Joe-Pesci-like way.

"Well, let's see … probably since I started to see a dead girl popping up everywhere I go." Shep stared at a Beatles poster hanging behind Dr. Hale. It was that famous one of the band crossing Abbey Road.

"Why do you think you are seeing her?" Dr. Hale had a soothing voice. Shep rather liked that about him.

He stared at George when he answered, "Because I'm batshit crazy."

"You're not crazy," Dr. Hale voice was even more soothing now. "Sometimes a traumatic experience like the one you had years ago with that young girl triggers emotions and feelings about other aspects of our life that we didn't know we had."

It was all very plausible and textbook psychobabble. Of course he knew she wasn't real. This wasn't *The Sixth Sense* after all. He wasn't Haley Joel Osment going around seeing dead people. That still didn't make him feel any better about the marbles he had rolling around in his head.

"It's a good thing your friend, Bray, was keeping an eye on you," Dr. Hale continued.

"He's not my friend," Shep snapped, his eyes were fixed on Paul now. "Why does everyone think he's my friend?"

"I don't know, Billy. He was concerned enough about you after your encounter in the bar to follow you. He saved your life. That's what I'd call a friend."

Shep hated when people other than his wife called him Billy. His eyes focused on Ringo.

"He was probably following me around looking for the right time to kill me. The dude is a psychopath. He shoots a girl, kills her, and just goes about his business like nothing happened. Who does that?" He gazed at John.

"Billy, I'm sure he grieved in his own way."

And Shep grieved in his.

"Just before Bray pulled me out of that car, I saw her again. This time, though, she talked to me," Shep moved forward in his chair. He was no longer looking at John. He was looking at Joe Pesci, Psychologist Man, and his words were earnest.

"She said it wasn't time."

Dr. Hale smiled and nodded as he crossed his left leg over his right. He tapped his pen on the arm of his chair and said confidently, "She was the manifestation of your subconscious telling you that you didn't want to die. That's all. And that's a very good thing, Billy. Very good. Just in case, we'll do a complete work-up to rule out schizophrenia. We'll also get you started on an antidepressant and get you set up with weekly therapy sessions. I think talking this out will make it easier for you to cope. You have been carrying around a lot of guilt with you. You have to let her go."

•••

They had been reduced to making small talk now. Shep asked Anna how her heart was – she was afflicted with Mitral valve prolapse and had been having increasingly severe episodes. She told him she was fine, that the doctor had increased her dose of Atenolol and it had mitigated the symptoms.

They were using words like "mitigated." That was never a good sign.

Anna sat across the conference table from him. Her eyes looked everywhere but into his. Her lawyer sat next to her. Shep couldn't remember her lawyer's name, but he knew it was impressive-sounding from an equally impressive-sounding firm. Shep's lawyer sat next to him. He was told Richard Morrow was the best divorce lawyer in the state of Pennsylvania and he was sure someone told Anna that hers was the best, too.

"Well, let's get started, shall we?" her lawyer, Whatshisname, said as he opened his fancy briefcase and pulled out a bunch of fancy papers for him to sign.

They had decided on a standard agreement, a fifty-fifty split. The sticking point was that she wanted the house, and the shelter that lay below it. That was unacceptable to Shep.

"Where will I go when the zombies come," Shep's voice was condescending. His suicide attempt months earlier didn't help his cause and his flippant jokes only made things worse. He knew that from the disapproving glance shot at him by Richard Morrow, Esquire.

"Billy, you are better off without that tomb," Anna pleaded. "Please, I'll give you a sixty-forty split. Just let the house and shelter go."

"How about this. You take it all and I get the house?" Shep thought his lawyer's head was going to spin off. Richard Morrow, Esquire, let out a nervous chuckle and shook his head from side to side with uncommon vigor.

"No. No. No," Morrow raised his right index finger and waved it. "That's not a serious offer."

"Doesn't matter," Anna said coldly, staring at Morrow. "Under no circumstances does he get that house."

Her eyes turned to Shep. She had that look in them again, that look she got when she was about to break down and cry. Shep had seen that look a lot lately. He figured he had a lot to do with it. They had dreams, Anna and him, big dreams. They had everything planned out. A house. A family. They were going to travel. He was going to compete in archery competitions all over the world. She was going to write masterpieces of literature – her true passion. It didn't matter if her manuscript sold one copy or a million. She had the means to put it out there and he was going to be proud of her.

They were going to be happy.

They weren't.

"I humored you with that shelter. I humored you when you stocked it. I even accepted that it was just something you felt you had to do to protect us. But you're obsessed with it. You're obsessed with death and destruction. You think the world is going to end so you want to end it for yourself. And you are obsessed with that dead girl. You have to let her go."

She must have been stealing from the book of Joe Pesci, Psychologist Man.

She stood. "For all they that take the sword shall perish with the sword."

•••

He sat in the dark in his small hotel room, the room he had called home for longer than he cared to admit.

He was drunk again. He knew this because he had trouble keeping his eyes open and what he could see in the near blackness spun slightly. Drool dripped from the right corner of his lip.

The same thought that had pried its way into his head as he sat in that storage container waiting to die wiggled into his consciousness now: *How did he get to this point in his life?*

Joe Pesci, Psychologist Man, was correct. He needed to get over it. He needed to let her go.

He could still win Anna back. He could stop drinking, be the man she married. He could do it. *Why not? I can be strong enough.* He could put his pride aside, his fears. He could take his medicine and get well again. He could maybe go back to work. *Structure. That's what I need. Structure.* He needed something to occupy his mind other than the thoughts of the world going to shit.

That was the problem with instant wealth. He had these feelings before when he was poor and scraping by on a reporter's salary. Once his pockets became flush with millions, he was able to indulge his darker side, his fears and phobias, his addictions.

No more.

He would sleep this one off and start fresh in the morning. For the first time in years – God, he thought, has it been YEARS? – he felt a wave of optimism crash over him. Anna would take him back. She had a kind heart and she still loved him deeply. He knew she did. He could even see it from across that conference-room table. She quoted a Bible verse out of context. She only did that with people whom she loved.

His heart thumped in his chest, he was so excited. He loved it when his heart rattled about like that. It made him feel alive.

Then she was there. Again.

"No. No. No. Dammit. No." He said no and dammit a few more times. What was his subconscious trying to tell him now? Or maybe it was just the booze talking.

Her hoarse voice murmured, "It's not time."

Just then, there was a rap on the door. Then another, much louder. He yelled, "What! Who's there?" and Bray's deep voice answered, "Shep, you better come with me."

Part I
Chapter Seven
The Birth of Bray the Beast

Frail Man wasn't so frail after all, it seemed. Bray the Bastard was back. And he was pissed.

"He can't get down here, can he?" Antigone asked nervously.

"Not right away. He can do a lot of damage up there, though. And he's determined."

Bray always was. Time had not been kind to him; that was certain. His shotgun was not going to be kind to them if he had a chance to use it.

His mule kicks had finally knocked the front door off the hinges and Shep switched to the living room camera. "Where are you, you fucker?" Bray's voice boomed through the speakers of the TV. It was hard to make him out in the dark, but he stood right in the middle of the room, pointing and waving his shotgun about in a haphazard pattern.

"I'm going to have to go deal with him," Shep said through heavy breaths as he hurriedly grabbed his bow made of yew and a quiver packed with arrows. "Keep an eye on the cameras. If something happens to me, there's another exit hidden behind the shelves in the pantry through the kitchen. There's a lever near the floor that will open the door and lead you down another tunnel about a hundred yards or so and up a hidden hatch into a field. He won't think to look for you that far away."

She nodded. He could tell she thought him foolish for engaging Bray like this and that she thought it a very bad idea. It probably was. In fact, it probably was a terrible idea. There was no other choice, though. This was not Frail Man stalking about in the middle of the living room;

Shep could handle Frail Man. This was Paul Bray and he was angry, motivated and out for blood. A switch had been flipped in him after their first encounter, creating a beast.

Bray the Beast.

Bray was many things: loud, obnoxious and brutish to name a few. But he also was clever. He would eventually find a way down into the shelter or, at the very least, a way to make them flee it.

"Don't die, okay," she said, squeezing his arm while leaning in to kiss his cheek. Her lips were cold and she pushed them hard on his skin, so hard he thought they might even leave a mark.

He chuckled. "That's pretty good advice." He put his hand on her left shoulder and rubbed it gently. "I need to get him out of the living room and upstairs. There's a panel on the wall in the kitchen. Open it. It's an intercom. There's a series of buttons. They're marked. Wait about two minutes after I leave, press the one that says upstairs bedroom and say something. Scream. Call him a douche. Anything."

He grabbed the wheel on the door, turned it clockwise and pulled it open with a groan. Air rushed in and mussed his hair. On his way out and up to an unknown fate, he stared into Antigone's deep blue eyes, fearing that he may never see them again, and said, "If I don't make it, take care of Anna for me. Tell her I love her."

He reached the entrance to the house and waited. He counted in his head. One. Two. Three … *She was probably at the panel now.* Four. Five. Six … *She was opening it* … Seven. Eight. Nine. … *She was calling Bray a douche or an asshat or a motherfucker or some other derisive name.* She had a colorful vocabulary; Lots of kids her age did. Vulgarity was very popular among the youth, he had observed, and Antigone loved to swear. That was one of the things he had learned about the girl.

He figured he had waited long enough. He lifted the door bar and gently pushed on the bookshelf. He always marveled at how little force he needed to swing the heavy door open. He crouched and carefully poked his head into the breach. Bray was nowhere to be seen.

He licked his fingers, grabbed an arrow out of his quiver and readied it on his bowstring as he crept through the living room. He looked for a good place to set up, a place of ambush, and he found it just inside the archway near the fireplace. He crouched and aimed toward the landing of the stairs.

He could hear Bray's clumping steps above him.

Stomp! Stomp! Stomp!

Some things never change.

Stomp! Stomp! Stomp!

He heard those feet pounding down the steps now. He pulled the arrow back and held his breath.

Height? Bray was about six-feet-2. Distance? About 25 feet. It was dark. Almost black as pitch, save for some dim moonlight painting the floor and walls in stripes, and his eyes hadn't yet adjusted.

He heard another pounding step and saw something move near the stairs. He released the arrow and heard the thwack of it penetrating something.

It wasn't Bray, though. It was a football and air hissed out of it loudly, an arrow cut right through it.

"I'm not stupid!" Bray yelled. Shep saw a flash of light and heard the boom of the shotgun blast. The spread punched a hole in the edge of the arch not more than two feet from where he crouched. Chunks of plaster slid across the hardwood floor.

He could smell the gunpowder and see the smoke waft through the shard of moonlight that streamed through the window into the room.

Shep scurried into the kitchen and ducked around the corner. He licked his fingers and quickly grabbed another arrow.

Bray's heavy feet crunched the plaster under his weight as he prowled. Billy Shepard had a decision to make now. In all those archery competitions, he never had to draw his bow, aim and shoot without calculating.

It was a terrible way to operate.

That's what I get for bringing a bow to a gunfight.

Bray's steps brought him closer to the kitchen now. Shep took a deep breath, readied his bow and twirled around the corner. Before he could aim, before he could even think to aim, he released the arrow and it whooshed through the air.

Shep heard a grunt and the sound of the shotgun knocking on the wood floor. It was hard to see, but he could make out the dark figure of Bray, on his knees now with an arrow sticking out of his left shoulder.

He drew another arrow, pulled it back as far as he could and hooked the tip of his middle finger into the corner of his mouth. He held his breath and aimed for the foggy outline of Bray's head when he heard something small rolling toward him. It sounded like a bowling ball on an alley when it curved toward the pins.

Shep wasn't sure, but it sounded like a grenade.

He heard the thrum as the arrow hissed through the air, missing its target. *It was difficult to shoot accurately with a grenade at your feet.* He dropped the bow and lunged for the door to the cellar, breaking through it. While he tumbled down the stairs, he heard the explosion and felt the heat from the flames. When he came to a stop on the cold cement floor, he could see the fire's flickering light.

It took him a moment to stand. Everything was spinning. He staggered to the steps leading up to the bulkhead doors, carefully climbed and thrust his shoulder into them. They opened and he spilled onto the ground, his face slamming into the dirt.

Blood trickled down his nose from where the bridge of his glasses had cut him and he dabbed it with his fingers as he struggled to stand.

He walked briskly at first, then jogged, then sprinted across the field toward the hatch.

The light from the full moon glistened off the dew that had formed on the tall grass and weeds, dampening his jeans as he ran. He reached the hatch in time to see it open and Antigone crawl out.

"We gotta go!" she yelled. "He made it out. He's still alive."

She had his large bug-out bag slung over her shoulder. It was enough food and water for a week, two if they rationed it properly.

"I have to go back for her," he said in a raspy voice, "before that fire spreads to the charges and the whole thing goes up." He turned to leave but she grabbed his shoulder and spun him around with what seemed like superhuman strength. He almost fell, the force was so great.

"You can't go back!" Antigone screamed. "She's gone, Shep."

He wrenched free of her grasp and shook his head.

"No. No she's not." Before she could grab at him again, he had already flung the hatch door open and was sliding down the stairs to the hard floor below. He gathered himself to his feet and sprinted down the corridor. His legs burned and cramped, but he kept running anyway. He heard her follow, her Nikes squeaking on the floor like high-tops on a basketball court until the sound finally stopped.

She was fast, but he was much faster.

When he reached the shelter, dark smoke already had begun seeping through the air vents and he could feel the heat rising in the room. He quickly swung open the cream door and burst into the bedroom. Anna lay, staring ahead at the wall.

He sat on the edge of the bed and cupped her head in his left hand, pulling it ever so slightly toward him so she would look at him. His eyes moved to the nightstand and he reached out for where the Glock pistol had sat, untouched for years. But it was gone.

"Anna!" He shook her. "Anna, we have to go."

She came to life. Her eyes blinked and she wet her lips.

"I can't go with you."

"Yes you can."

"You have to let me go."

He began to sob. "I won't lose you again."

"You already lost me."

She pulled the comforter down to her waist. There were nine slits in her white tank top, one just above her left breast, one high on her sternum, one below her right breast and six more, making an inverted triangle from the middle of her stomach down around each side of her navel. Blood began to ooze out of them, deep, dark and red.

"No!" He shook his head and closed his eyes tightly, as tightly as he could ever remember closing them, so tightly his cheeks and forehead throbbed with the strain.

"You have to leave me."

He swore he could feel her skinny, tender fingers comb through his hair like they used to when she tried to comfort him.

"I will never leave you."

Tears escaped his shut eyes. He could feel the water crawl down his skin and felt the wetness as it dripped on his hands that tightly clutched the comforter.

"Let me go."

Memories of her played on the inside of his eyelids: The way her lips tasted when they kissed. The way her soft hands felt when they brushed his skin. The way her sweet perfume smelled. The way she looked on their wedding day in her white dress with the long train that flowed down marble steps. The way she peered at him through those kind, loving eyes and the way she smiled at him with those soft, adorable lips.

Those things had been gone for quite some time.

He had to let go.

He knew this day would come, the day when he would have to leave the comfort of the shelter and the comfort of his delusion.

What a happy delusion it was.

"Better is the end of a thing than the beginning," he heard her whisper.

He opened his eyes. She was no longer there. She never was.

Part I
Chapter Eight
Nine Wounds Before the Ejection

The gruesome details were laid out before him in the form of graphic pictures. The nine stab wounds. Her dead eyes. Her mouth open with a column of dried blood pasted to the side of her face. He tried to veer his eyes way, but detective Cam Knott made him look.

Anna Shepard was found in an alleyway that ran next to the hotel where he stayed. Her car was parked out front. That made him the prime suspect. Maybe the only suspect.

"Just confess, n'at. It'll be easier on all'a us," Knott barked in thick "Pittsburgese." It was one of the quirks of this region and Shep usually enjoyed hearing the dialect. Not so much now. Now, Knott was the bad cop and he looked the part. He had a jutting square jaw and razor thin lips. His dark hair was buzzed and his gray eyes were cold, dulled by images like the ones he was making Shep see now. "We know ya did it, n'at. She took the house. Why'd you want that house so badly? You knew she was gunna demolish it tomorrow. The charges were already set. So you killed her. You get the house and all the money. No better motive than'at."

Shep sat motionless, catatonic really, starring at himself in the reflection cast back at him by the one-way glass. He wondered how many people were on the other side, peering in to watch one of his darkest hours unfold. *Did they feel sorry for him? Did they think he was capable of taking a blade to the woman he loved, the woman he cherished, and jam it into her flesh nine brutal times?*

He knew Bray was one of the spectators. He could almost feel his beady eyes looking through at him. Bray was arrogant, short-tempered, and crass. He wouldn't miss this. Shep also knew he was an unfeeling bastard. He had watched him sit on the bumper of that squad car that night, not like a man who had just taken the life of a fourteen-year-old girl, but as a man who felt no remorse. It was as if he messed up a cappuccino order at Starbucks, not put a piece of lead through a girl's heart.

Knott slammed his hand on the table with such a force that it snapped Shep out of his trance. "Come on, you jagoff. Confess. It'll make you feel so much better."

Shep said nothing. It felt like there were a million drums in his head pounding in unison. Everything was blurry, which he considered to be a gift from God. He never wanted to see those macabre pictures of Anna in focus. His breath still smelled of alcohol and his throat was raw.

"If you won't talk to me, maybe you'll talk to your friend." Knott smiled and winked as he left the room.

Bray lumbered in. Shep could hear his heavy feet banging on the floor. *Did he ever walk quietly?*

"Shep, dude, this is some crazy shit." Bray sat across from him and crossed his arms on the table. "Those are some pretty nasty pictures, huh? I didn't think you had it in ya."

Maybe he was wrong. Maybe Bray was the bad cop. "What did it feel like when you plunged that knife into her?" Bray made a stabbing motion with his muscular right arm. "I bet it felt good."

Shep pursed his lips and swallowed hard. "What did it feel like when you realized she only had a candy bar?" He spoke with a soft, gravelly voice. "Did you feel anything?"

Bray leaned back and slouched in the silver metal chair. "Wow, man," he shook his head. "You had it bad for that girl. Did you take her home and fuck her? Do you have a thing for little girls? I thought maybe you did."

Shep was too tired and still a little too drunk to react with any kind of fury. What was the point? Anything he did now was futile. "I feel sorry for you, *Detective* Bray. You don't *feel* anything. I mean really *feel*. Do you even have a little bit of guilt? Any at all? She was just an innocent little girl who got dealt a lousy, lousy hand."

Shep didn't even flinch when Bray slammed both fists on the table. The alcohol had dulled his reflexes, he thought. "What do you know about a lousy hand? A lousy hand is having your father go out for cigarettes and never come back. A lousy hand is watching your mother whore around so you can eat. A lousy hand is working double shifts to make something better of yourself. What do you know about a lousy fucking hand? You got lucky and won the lottery. You have more money than you know what to do with."

All true. Shep didn't care.

Just then, the door swung open and Robert Morrow, Esquire, walked in with his lawyer walk and his lawyer talk. "We're done here. Unless you are charging my client with something, that is."

They weren't.

The sun peeked above the horizon and cast a strange glow as Shep and Robert Morrow, Esquire, walked out of the police station. Throngs of reporters lined the sidewalk. News trucks from CNN, ABC, NBC, CBS, FOX and from other random assortments of mashed up letters lined the street.

Under normal circumstances, he would have been standing among them in an attempt to coax an answer out of the suspect.

A millionaire allegedly stabbing his estranged wife to death was big news, after all. He didn't begrudge them. They were just doing their job.

Morrow's job was to keep him quiet. That didn't work out so well.

A voice cried out from the crowd. "Did you kill your wife?"

Shep couldn't tell who it was who yelled the question. It didn't matter. They were all there to ask it. That was the crux of the issue. It was quite simple, really, and the only question that needed to be posed.

To Shep, the answer was obvious.

"I didn't kill my wife."

Morrow pulled him close and whispered, "I told you not to say a damn word."

Another voice rang out from the crowd. "Who do you think did?"

"I don't know," Shep answered, a wry, mischievous smile creeping on his face. "The one-armed man?"

A smattering of laughter billowed from the flock. Morrow was not chuckling. "Great. Just great," the lawyer groused as he stuffed Shep into the back seat of the black Suburban and sat next to him, commanding the driver to step on it.

Shep could hear the blades of the helicopters chopping overhead as the car moved through the streets. "Take me home," Shep murmured.

"That's where we're going, to the hotel. We're going to have a long talk there, you and I."

"No. My home. My house."

Shep had barely gotten the words out of his mouth before

Morrow launched his protest. "No, Shep, that's a bad idea. I advise against it."

"Call me Billy or Mr. Shepard. Only my friends call me Shep."

"Dammit, I'm trying to be your lawyer and your friend here."

"Take me home."

•••

This place was a tomb, Shep realized. And it would be his for an eternity.

He grabbed the Glock pistol and stuck the barrel in his mouth. It tasted foul and metallic. He hated that was going to be the last thing his tongue was going to touch. He closed his eyes, inhaled air through his nose and then pushed it back out.

Billy Shepard was ready to die.

He paused and darted his eyes about, expecting to see Skye standing there, muttering "it's not time," but she was nowhere to be seen. That oddly irked him.

His finger twitched on the trigger, and then things went dark, not from a bullet in the brain, but from a power outage.

It must not be time. Maybe Skye is here after all.

The shelter's power system kicked on and the room was bathed in light again; the gun was still shoved between his lips.

He was always a curious sort. That's what made him such a good journalist and his curiosity had gotten the best of him once again.

A few more minutes on this Earth won't matter much.

He stepped outside and marveled at what he saw. Ribbons of reds, purples, yellows and greens rippled through the dark sky. They were so bright he could make out where the tree line began five-hundred yards away. Then a burst of red set the sky ablaze. He felt the hair on his arms and his neck rise and tingle.

In Finland they called it "Revontulet," which translated meant "Fox Fires."

The ancient Saami, who once lived north of the Arctic Circle, believed the lights were the souls of the departed.

And the Vikings thought they were merry dancers.

Shep just thought they were beautiful. And they were here. *How were they here?*

He climbed into his Mustang, started it and switched on the radio. All he heard was buzzing as he drove into the city. He barely needed his headlights, it was so bright. Every house he passed was dark. Every street light idle.

People spilled into the streets, gazing up to the sky and then at each other with looks of profound awe. The red was gone and another aurora streaked across the sky even brighter than the last. He saw fires burning in the distance and could hear sirens wailing. Every now and then an explosion shook the ground.

A squad car drove slowly down the street and an officer announced over a bullhorn, "Go back to your homes. Power will be restored shortly."

He knew that was a lie.

The sun was pissed. And probably God, too. If Anna were here, she'd surely have a Bible verse to pull out for this occasion, something like hellfire and brimstone and the wrath of God coming down upon us for our evil, evil ways.

Most of the people heeded the officer and shuffled slowly from whence they came. They probably huddled in front of candle light, using whatever battery life they had left in their mobile devices and laptops in an attempt to find out just what was happening.

They probably had faith that the power would indeed be restored soon, that their lives would go back to normal like nothing had happened.

They were so wrong.

Shep recalled a story he did – it must have been four years ago – on the fragile state of the power grid and how one cataclysmic event could fry the entire network. When he asked the Allegheny Power Company spokesman, a dodgy man with a mustache, how long it would take to fix the grid should a widespread failure happen, his face turned grim and the first honest word spilled from his lips, "Never."

That sent shivers down Shep's spine then. Those shivers had returned now.

Shep stopped the car and looked at himself in the reflection of the rearview mirror. The light from the aurora danced on his face, sprinkling it with soft, changing hues.

His life had changed just as quickly as those colors that danced off his features. The things he wanted, he no longer desired. The things he feared, he no longer dreaded.

It wasn't an easy button that was punched, but a reset button.

It would take time, lots of time, and death, lots of death, but things were going to be irrevocably altered. Shep wanted to stick around to see what those changes would be.

Always curious.

He drove back through town, through the eeriness that was both wondrous and frightening, and back toward his home.

He would take refuge in his shelter for as long as he could.

Part I
Chapter Nine
Nigh Meals

The light from the fire lit up her face. It was such a pretty face. It was a young face, a face that should have been full of glee and wonder, a face that should fall in love with a handsome boy, a face that should be wet with happy tears as she said “I do,” in her white dress with a long train flowing down over marble steps, a face that should have babies with faces a lot like hers.

None of that was going to happen. Well, at least it was very unlikely to happen, not as long as she stuck around with him.

They were a good five football fields away from the burning house, yet he could still hear the cracking of the wood and see the embers zip off into the night sky like tiny shooting stars.

Antigone tugged on his shirt. “We better get going. He may still be around.”

Shep just watched the fire. He always liked the way the flames flickered and changed shape. He always liked the way they licked at the darkness.

Suddenly a ball of fire rose and the ground shook with a rumble. *That was the demolition charges going.*

“There’s an abandoned trailer about a mile into the woods. We can stay there tonight.” He could barely squeeze the words from his lips. His head throbbed. His eyes watered from the smoke and from the pain coming from his knees and hips and, well, everywhere.

He began to walk, pushing through the branches of the tree line. He shuffled very much like Frail Man did when he stumbled away from

Shep's home that day with an arrow sticking out of his hand.

Antigone followed beside him. He would catch her stealing concerned glances at him from time to time as they slowly made their way through the thick brush.

The trailer sat in a small clearing. The light from the setting moon glistened off the metallic roof and made a perfect outline of the rickety structure. He thought a large sneeze would surely knock it to the ground.

He pushed the door open and heard the sound of mice feet scurrying across the floor. The stench of animal urine was strong. *It's going to be a long night.*

He slumped onto the floor, resting his back against an old bookcase that was left behind, and Antigone sat across from him and folded her legs under her. He heard her rustling in the bug-out bag and then saw a beam of light shine at his face.

"That cut on your nose is pretty deep."

He put his arm up to shield his eyes. "Don't waste the batteries. I'll be fine."

The light went out and he could hear her rummaging through the bag again. Once his eyes adjusted to the darkness, he could see her move closer to him and could smell alcohol.

She removed his glasses and dabbed what felt to him like a piece of cloth on his cut. It stung deeply. He would have flinched and pulled away if he weren't so exhausted.

"That's better," she said as she slid back across the floor and sat, legs tucked under her again.

In the silence he tried not to think about what was to become of them. This was not the plan. The plan was to live in that house and in that shelter indefinitely, until either things in the outside world got much better or until things in the outside world got so much worse it would purge anything that could possibly threaten him.

That was Plan A. He didn't have a Plan B.

They were going to be fine for a night, maybe a week. Then, well, then things were going to change. They would be no better off than Frail Man and his wife.

"I miss …" Antigone broke the silence with a peppy voice. "music. I miss Lady Gaga."

He surely would have snickered if he didn't hurt so much. He was sure that was what she was trying to coax out of him, but he was in no giggling mood.

How can she be so flippant? She was acting as if she were at a slumber party with a girlfriend, swapping stories about boys and what color short shorts they should buy at the mall the next day. Maybe she didn't understand the trouble they were in now. *No. That wasn't it.* He was sure she knew. Maybe she was stronger than he. Maybe he could learn something from her.

He lay down in the fetal position, propping his head up under his clasped hands. He couldn't see her eyes, just the faint outline of her head in the near pitch-black darkness, but he could feel them drilling into him.

"I don't miss her meat dress," he groused. She cackled loudly. He thought he may have even heard a snort. "I miss the Beatles," he said softly before falling asleep.

•••

He awoke the next morning to her tapping on his forehead. Even that pained him.

"You need to eat something before we go." She dropped a tube of jerky meat on his chest. He tried to sit up, but everything ached. His forty-four-year-old muscles were barely equipped to play a pick-up basketball game, let alone escape a shotgun-wielding, grenade-throwing psychopath.

On the second attempt he was able to steady himself. He grabbed the jerky, chomped down on it and pulled off a chunk. She did the same.

She had a knitted hat pulled down over her ears and her dark hair spilled out from under it. She managed to find clothing, a grey sweatshirt, and gloves with the fingers cut out. She had found some warm clothing for him as well; a heavy wool jacket was draped over his lap.

She took a bite from her jerky and swallowed it. Her face grew earnest.

"What was that about last night? Going back the way you did," her voice was tinged with nervousness. "I mean, you know there was no one in that room, right?"

He knew now. For so long he didn't, though. He figured it must have been grief or psychosis or loneliness that made him spawn Anna. His therapist who looked like Joe Pesci would have had lots to say about this if he was here.

He sighed and searched for words to explain it to her. She deserved at least that much.

"When you miss someone who is gone so badly, I guess you can fool yourself into believing they are actually there." It was kind of the truth, he reasoned. More likely was the fact that the stress of living in this life, the death that surrounded him, broke him and made him see and believe what he wanted to see and believe.

There was no guarantee that it wouldn't happen again. *That makes me a pretty piss-poor guardian.*

"You are better off without me, Tig. You should just go. Find your brother. Find Halcyon."

"You're such an ass, you know that?" Her voice was incredulous as she glowered at him. "I mean, you saved me from that shithead – twice. You fed me. You gave me water and a place to stay. You helped me when no one else would and you say I'm better off without you? Um, no. You saved my life. Maybe one day I can save your ass."

She took a frustrated bite out of her jerky and chewed it animatedly. *Yes, there was something special about this girl.* He knew it more than ever now.

He shrugged his shoulders and made a funny gesture with his face. It must have looked very odd because it stopped her in mid-chew.

"Who am I to argue with that?"

She smiled, finished off her jerky and slid closer to him. "What do we do now? You got a car hidden away somewhere?" She lightly punched his shoulder.

There was no car. Any vehicle was a magnet for trouble. *Might as well throw some flesh into a pool full of piranhas.* The goal was to be inconspicuous, to blend in. That's why his house was so unkempt. That's why he scarred its exterior and interior. *A car? That would be inviting trouble.*

It pained him when he had pushed that Mustang into the lake, watching it float and then sink into the murky water. That car was his baby, the only material thing he had really desired with his newfound riches – other than the lavish shelter, that is. It had to be done. An automobile wasn't worth much in the new order of things. In fact, it was a liability.

Without a Mustang convertible at the ready, this journey was going to be done mostly on foot. It was going to be a long and arduous one, fraught with all sorts of peril. There was no protection provided by a comfy shelter. No security system. No electricity. No curling bare toes on plush carpet. No soft bed or couch on which to slumber.

No SpaghettiOs.

There were bands of marauders out there, praying on the weak. And most everyone was weak. At their base, people are just animals with an impulse to survive.

Sleep. Feed. That was it.

He knew that. He needed her to understand that, too.

"This is going to be hard. This is gonna suck."

Antigone frowned. "It may be even harder. Bray knows where we are going. When I was with them, I told them about Halcyon. Do you think he'll follow us?"

Shep had known Bray pretty well in that other life, but that meant little now. The Ejection had changed people profoundly, some for the better, most for the worse. The Bray that had come looking for vengeance was a new kind of Bray.

Bray the Beast.

He rubbed his temples as he answered. "He might. He obviously found some weapons and food. We'll have to be careful. We have a long way to go."

"We better get moving then, if you are up for it?" She stood and held her hand out to him. He grabbed it and she helped pull him to his feet. His legs still burned and his back was stiff. The pounding in his temples was still severe, but tolerable. The pain didn't bother him as much when she looked at him with those optimistic eyes and flashed that crooked grin.

He met the morning that had dawned clear and cold with lungs full of chilled air. It was almost fall now. Had to be. The leaves on the trees were beginning to turn deep reds and dark browns. It would be winter soon. The prospect of trudging nearly a thousand miles in the cold did not make him feel any better.

"I think I missed my birthday," she said, tilting her head back and closing her eyes. The warm sun bathed her face.

"Happy birthday. Sorry, I didn't get you a card or a cake."

"That's all right. You can hook me up next year." She winked at him and began to walk through the clearing. She strode as if she hadn't a care in the world.

He followed. For that one brief moment, he hadn't a care, either.

Part II
Chapter One
The Nine Commandments

Shep's eyes strained to open. All he saw was gloom and desolation. The trees carried no leaves. The sun offered no warmth. The wind smelled stale and cold.

It already was an awful day.

There were many of them in succession now. They came one after another, each just as bleak as the last. His stomach ached so. His head always throbbed. *Maybe the trap would work this morning. Oh, God, please let the trap work this morning.*

Antigone still slept as he forced himself to rise off the unforgiving ground. It took more and more effort each day for him to make his arms and legs move, but he was able to rise again. He cinched his belt tight. He hadn't been at this notch since he was in college, maybe high school. His black thermal shirt, once snug around his shoulders and chest, hung loose now and his once round face was drawn and gaunt.

He trudged through the mud and the dead leaves to where he had set the trap the dusk before.

His heart leapt and he laughed aloud when he saw the deadfall had been triggered, the large, flat rock pressing down against another.

Shep didn't know how he mustered the energy to run, but he did. It was a sprint, really, as if he were a little boy running into his mother's arms after a week away at camp.

He reached the stone and lifted it, trying to peek under to see what kind of animal lay dead under its weight. He couldn't see one. He lifted the slab of rock higher and flung it to the side and stared down with great despair. *Nothing. Absolutely nothing.*

He slumped to his knees, sat on the back of his heels and stared at the nothing that was to be his breakfast. He felt the anger well up inside him. It rose and rose and he clenched his jaw tighter and he felt his face flush with blood and his hands, now fists, shake, and he slammed them hard onto the rock, pounded them down in frustration and wretchedness.

And he cried. Hard. He bawled, really. He hadn't blubbered like that in – how long? He couldn't remember – not even when he contemplated killing himself, not even when Bray had told him Anna was dead.

He was numb in those times, however. He wished he could be numb now.

Shep plodded slowly back to where they had made camp. The fire they set the night before to keep warm and to boil the clovers and burdock roots in a salvaged tin can still smoldered. Antigone lay by it, curled up in a ball. She still looked healthy and strong, but the same could not be said for Shep.

He was about to wake her when she stirred. She looked up at him through sleepy eyes and gasped. "You look terrible."

He grinned. "Well, thanks. You sure know how to make a fella feel good."

"Nothing in the trap, huh?"

"Nope."

She slowly pushed herself up from the cold ground and brushed the dirt off her worn jeans and green parka. "We'll get something soon. And when we do, you get it all, okay? We both need to keep up our strength, not just me."

A frigid wind blew in and his teeth began to chatter. He grabbed the wool coat he used as a blanket, slung it over his shoulders and zipped it up as high as it would go. He buried his hands deep into the pockets, sighed and looked at the position of the sun, which was just a dim orb in the overcast sky.

"We need to head over that way," he pointed through the bare trees at a shallow creek. "That water should be fresh."

Their journey had been a slow one. They were able to start an abandoned car, but it only took them so far before it sputtered and stalled on a rural road somewhere in Ohio. Shep knew it was going to be near impossible to find another that would groan to a start. The gasoline left in these automobiles was breaking down and their batteries were all but out of juice after years of sitting idle. It was a miracle they were able to coax the Nissan Versa to life.

Shep had told Antigone as much and she replied with her usual optimism. "No. We can find another that will start."

"Not likely."

She didn't believe him. "Are you a car expert or something?"

"No. I saw it on the Discovery Channel."

Now they were on foot and he took every labored step with dread. Travel was slow and grueling, especially as malnourished as he had become. If the increasingly chilly days and bitingly cold nights didn't retard their pace, avoiding the traveling gangs did.

So far they were able to stay unnoticed, even if it meant driving a day out of their way in that dying car, or marching through thick woods and brush. Shep feared, though, that it was just a matter of time before they would stumble upon trouble – or trouble would stumble upon them.

He had set up some rules for their travel. Number one was to stay alive. All the other rules were designed to make sure that prime directive was realized. An important theme of the *Post-Apocalyptic Travel by Shep Playbook* was to stay away from people because most, if not all of them, were not to be trusted.

He would have felt a lot better about their chances had he had a bow, but all they had was a pistol with one bullet in the magazine.

He figured he only needed one when he stuffed the barrel in his mouth that night that seemed so long ago. Now that's all they had – a gun with one bullet and a prize-winning archer with no bow.

Antigone grabbed the bag and smiled. "Let's get to that creek then."

He marveled at how positive she always was, even amid these circumstances. She acted as if they were hiking through a wildlife preserve as part of a camping trip, not scrounging for food and fighting for survival.

He thought if it were not for her, he surely would have gone mad by now.

They reached the creek and he scooped up some water in his cupped hand and slurped. It was fresh and he nodded at Antigone, who snatched a canteen out of the bag and sunk it into the flowing stream.

"Where are we?" she asked, taking a swig from the canteen before placing it back into the water.

"Somewhere in Indiana I'd guess, probably pretty close to the Illinois border. We still have a long way to go and the weather isn't going to get any better. It's going to get much worse. A few more hard freezes and a good snow cover and there goes our clovers and roots."

"Just think of that nice hot meal you're gonna have when we get to Halcyon." She smiled big and patted his flat tummy. "You're gonna get fat again."

He simpered. "Again?"

She chuckled, handed him the canteen and he took a big gulp. At least the water quelled his hunger pains a bit.

"Let's go, schmo," she said, trudging through the creek to the other side.

It became harder for him to walk. His legs were as stiff as iron and his temples throbbed. He had trouble focusing on Antigone, who walked a few feet in front of him. He felt jittery and light-headed and he fell farther and farther behind her pace.

Antigone slowed, looked over her shoulder at him and stopped, waiting for his ponderous steps to bring him to her. She grabbed his face with each hand at the cheeks and examined his glassy eyes.

"We have to change our plan. You need food. Real food." He was too weak to argue. "Come on. Just a little longer. Let's get you something to eat."

He wasn't sure how he was able to keep going, but he did. He whispered "left foot, right foot, left foot, right foot." It kept him focused on the task and he thought it was the only thing that kept him from collapsing.

They emerged from the thicket onto the shoulder of a main road. It stretched for miles in both directions. A few abandoned and rusted cars sat on both sides of the road and in the distance they could see a crop of buildings rise into the foreboding gray sky.

It took about an hour more for them to reach the garrison that was made up of two minivans, one sapphire blue and the other brush aluminum, and parked front end to front end in front of a gate. Two men stood with rifles on the each of the hoods.

She had done what the playbook had said not to do: sought out people, and a lot of people, judging by the activity beyond the minivans. *She had no choice, really. I can't last much longer like this.*

The garrison guarded a fortress of walls made of old chain-link fence. Barbed wire weaved along the top like vines. Old buildings of varying heights and states of decay rose up into the ashen sky.

A stop light in an intersection in the middle of the town swayed in a gust.

The man on the sapphire blue minivan seemed to be in charge. He was a burly man with barely a neck poking out above his coat. His black hair was thick and wavy and his face was dotted with dark stubble. Antigone walked slowly toward him, holding her hands up, and spoke, but Shep couldn't hear what she was saying. She was too far away now and it was all he could do to just remain standing.

Her arms flailed and she pointed back at Shep a few times. The gruff look on the man's face slowly melted away. He grabbed a walkie-talkie and mumbled a few words into it, then swung the gate open for them to pass.

Antigone excitedly waved for Shep to come, yelling: "You're gonna get that meal a little early."

He forced his legs to move until they carried him through the gate. The residents stopped what they were doing and stared at them as they followed closely behind the man who stood on the sapphire blue minivan.

Shoots of grass and weeds sprung up through cracks in the asphalt and defaced storefronts lined both sides of the paved street. One of the stores, its windows boarded, appeared to be a pizza shop in that other life, another looked like it once was a drug store, the shelves inside toppled. The other side of the street once housed a clothing store with a sandwich shop next to it. All the signs were ripped down from the facades, with just a faded square and a growth of ivy left in its place.

They walked to a building that was the tallest in the town, one that Shep surmised was once the city's courthouse. They entered through a revolving door and under the broken frame of a metal detector that was a relic of that old life. The man hurried them through a pair of double doors that swung open into a courtroom.

Sitting on the bench was a middle-aged woman, her hair, equal parts black and gray, pulled back in a bun. The skin on her face was tight around her jaw and cheek bones and was flush with color. Her green eyes were sharp and bright.

Antigone took a few sheepish steps forward as Shep hung back, swaying as he stood.

The woman crossed her arms on the elevated desk and looked down at them with an odd smile. "It's not every day a couple of wanderers can talk their way in here." She spoke with a thick Welsh accent. It was odd to hear such a dialect in the Heartland. "I hear this man you are with needs help. Sure looks like he does."

Antigone nodded and looked back at Shep with a smile. "He saved my life more than once. He took me in and fed me and kept me safe when he didn't have to. I figured I'd return the favor."

The woman spoke proudly. "That's awful brave of you to approach our perimeter like you did. Other places and people may not have been so accommodating."

Antigone nodded in appreciation. "I had to try. He's the most important person in my world right now."

Shep shuffled closer, standing next to Antigone. He moved his lips to speak, but the words were so silent even he could not hear them. He tried again. “We don’t want any trouble.” His voice was hoarse and weak. “We just need some food and then we’ll be on our way.”

The woman leaned back in her large black leather chair and smirked, alternating her gaze between Shep and Antigone. He didn’t know what to make of this. He hoped it wasn’t a bad thing because he had neither the strength nor the will to fight.

“You and this lush thing stay as long as ya like.” She stood and motioned for the man who was on the sapphire blue van to come closer. “Wynn will take you to get something to eat, and then find you a place to stay.”

Before they made it through the double doors again, her words cast an echo in the chamber. “Don’t make me regret this hospitality.”

•••

It was the first time he had chewed and swallowed solid food in months. He ate so fast he didn’t really taste what he was consuming – it was some kind of beef, *real beef, not that canned crap,* in dark gravy with greens mixed in – but he figured it was palatable. He frowned every time he spilled a little on the gray molded plastic table, one of many in the cafeteria where they sat, or when some trickled down his beard, which was long, thick, coarse and more gray than black.

Antigone sat next to him and ate a bit slower, her eyes locked on the man they knew as Wynn. He stood by the entrance to the cafeteria with his rifle ever ready in his grasp and his slit eyes never wavered off of them.

“So, what’s the deal with boss bitch?” Through it all, Antigone had retained her bluntness. “What’s her name anyway?”

Wynn frowned. “Rhian is her name and you’d be wise to respect her. She’s putting food in your bellies.”

By the time Shep had finished his bowl of whatever it was that slid down his gullet – it certainly wasn’t SpaghettiOs – he already felt a world better. His limbs were stronger and his eyes more focused. For the first time since he could remember, his stomach wasn’t barking at him. He could even feel the color coming back into his face. Antigone smiled at the change.

He took a gulp from a bottle of water. “Please thank her again for us, Wynn.”

Wynn shook his head and the bass of his voice boomed. “The name is Ward. She insists on calling me Wynn. It’s Welsh or some such shit. I let her call me whatever she wants because she feeds me. She can call me shithead for all I care.”

Shep took another big gulp of water. Some seeped from his lips into his beard. "What is this place? Is this Rhian in charge?"

Ward's eyes narrowed and his grip on his rifle grew tighter. He rang his hands around the shaft and handle in frustration. "I would offer you something more to eat, but you need to pace yourself. Eat too much too fast and you're likely to perforate your stomach, then it won't matter who is in charge." Ward opened the door behind him and waved his arm. "Let me show you where you're going to stay."

They walked down the middle of the street, right down the double-yellow lines that were still as bright as if they were painted yesterday. The road seemed to stretch for miles over the flat landscape beyond the fence. There were three windmills off in the distance. The sails spun rapidly in the brisk wind.

They reached what looked to be an old apartment building, not dissimilar to the one in which Shep and Anna once dwelled. It brought back good – and bad – memories.

Ward opened the front door to the building and pointed. "You'll stay here. There's an open apartment straight ahead on the first floor. There are a couple of mattresses in there and blankets to keep you warm. We'll try to scrounge up some more clothes for you tomorrow. It'll be dark soon. I assume you are pretty tired. Get some sleep."

Shep nodded and smiled. "How do you do it? How do you keep this place from getting overrun?"

"Guns," Ward said as his eyes turned cold. "We have lots of guns. You'll be wise not to forget that. And Rhian always gets what she wants. You'll be wise not to forget that, too."

The apartment was small and spartan. A mattress lay against the wall to their left, while another was pushed into a corner to their right, thick wool blankets folded on each. Set against the far wall was a round table, scuffed and chipped. A wicker basket stacked high with fruit sat on it and a piece of crisp white paper was wedged under the basket.

Antigone rushed to the fruit, grabbed an orange and quickly sank her ragged thumbnail into the peel. Juice squirted as she did. Shep grabbed a plump red apple – he never thought he would see one of these again – and bit into it.

It took until his teeth reached the core to wonder where this fruit had come from.

Shep was solemn. "There is something not right about this place."

Antigone sat on the mattress, her back resting against the wall, and shoved a wedge of orange into her mouth. "Yeah. This place is pretty creepy."

"How do they have fruit? Oranges? We're a long way from

Florida. They must have a greenhouse or a hydroponics bay somewhere. Maybe those windmills I saw power it? And that meat, they have to have livestock on a farm somewhere near here."

Antigone shrugged and popped the last orange wedge into her mouth.

Shep pulled the piece of paper out from under the basket and squinted to read the words in the dim light. It was a set of nine laws, punched out on an old typewriter, some of the letters darker than the others. It was the usual fare, laws one would expect any society to keep: No killing, no assault or theft. There was a curfew stipulated and a table of the rations each man, woman and child was to receive. It was the ninth commandment at the bottom of the page that was particularly unique and he read it aloud.

"No interference with or objection to the chosen pairings for selective breeding." Printed in bold capital letters at the bottom of the page was a sentence that jumped out at him, too, and he read it with a booming, authoritative voice. "All lawbreakers found guilty by a tribunal of their peers will be punished by death."

A terrible feeling came over Shep. *Nothing comes without a price.* The people of this town paid for their food with strict obedience.

And who knows what else.

He began to slip the paper back under the basket when he saw something chiseled into the table. The letters were ragged and misshaped, but he could make out enough of them to figure out they read, "She will kill us all – Gwynn."

Antigone lay on her back on the mattress and pulled the blanket up to her chin. "These people are batshit crazy."

"Yes, they are batshit crazy … and they have lots of food. As long as we follow these laws, we'll be all right."

Antigone crowed. "Just don't shoot anyone in the eye if you find a bow and some arrows lying around somewhere."

Shep lay back on his mattress now. The room was dark and quiet. So quiet he could hear the thumping of his heart.

"I miss," Antigone said, and then let out a loud chuckle, "bowling."

Shep covered himself with the thick wool blanket. It was the first time in weeks he was warm before sleep. "They probably have a bowling alley somewhere, probably leagues. You could join a Thursday night one."

Antigone snorted. "We could get corny bowling shirts with our names stitched on them. After we're done, we can stuff our face with pizza."

For that moment, all his worries melted away. Without a care, he faded into slumber.

Part II
Chapter Two
The Million-Dollar Apple

They awoke to a clamor.

When Shep hit the outside and the cold mist of rain, he could see people cramming into a building across the street.

It was an old pub, probably the place where people of this town once went to knock back a few beers, talk about their day and feel better about their mundane lives.

Shep and Antigone pushed past a throng of people trying to wedge in through the narrow doorway. The bar stretched almost the entire length of the room and Rhian sat at a table in the corner near it. Ward stood to her right, menacing and ill-tempered as ever, and another man, equally gruff and brutish, flanked her on the left. Both were holding rifles as a show of force.

Sitting before them, slumped in a chair, was a balding man, his chin buried in his chest. Three more townsfolk sat at a small table to his right and faced him. They looked everywhere but at him.

People spilled into the pub and crowded around tables and sat on stools. Shep looked up and noticed a length of rope draped over a support beam above a stairwell that steeply climbed to a seating area on the second floor. An uneasy feeling crashed over him.

"You have been found guilty of stealing," Rhian said with a loud, booming voice and a hush fell throughout the pub so profound that Shep could hear the man's anxious breaths. "Do you have anything to say to the court before we pass sentence?"

The man lifted his head, licked his lips and swallowed harshly.

"Just that I am sorry."

Rhian nodded and motioned to Ward, who pulled the man out of the chair and dragged him up the stairs.

"So be it," Rhian bellowed. "There is only one punishment for crimes against this community."

Ward pulled the rope toward him, revealing a noose, and gently put it around the man's neck. The man wept silently in the moment before Ward pushed him over the railing. Shep could hear his neck snap as he swayed several feet above the stairwell.

Antigone grabbed Shep's arm tightly. He could hear her heavy breaths.

"What the fuck?" She whispered.

"Gwynn knew our laws and broke 'em," Rhian's voice boomed again, and Shep held his breath for a second when he heard the dead man's name. "Without law there is no order. Without law, we are no better than the hoodlums out there who roam the wastes and take what they want, no matter who they hurt. There are people out there who would slit our throats to take what we have. Will we let 'em? No! They can't, not as long as we stand together. Every man, woman and child has an obligation to this town, to make it the shining jewel in this dark and desolate land. When those like Gwynn threaten what we have built with our raw hands and our blood, they must be punished. It is only justice."

It was an eloquent speech – Shep gave her credit for that much. But it was also self-serving. He had been around enough politicians to know she was a seasoned and experienced one. Her punishment was brutal, but he figured it was an effective deterrent and an efficient way to maintain order.

Food was currency in this new world and Rhian, obviously wise to these things, had positioned herself well in it. She had access to enormous stores of food, and with it, enormous power, and she wasn't shy about wielding it.

A million dollars or one apple, it was all the same.

They blended in among a herd of people moving toward the cafeteria building. Shep stared straight ahead as he walked with Antigone at his side. "We have to get out of here."

Antigone's voice was tinged with desperation. "We can't. You're not strong enough yet. We leave now and in a couple of days you'll be right back where you were yesterday."

She had a point. He still felt weak and malnourished. "As soon as I feel stronger then."

Townspeople flooded into the cafeteria much like they did into the pub to see the execution of Gwynn. By now, the solemness of that event had worn off and a hum of conversations mixed with a few bursts of laughter filled the room. Shep suspected executions were nothing new here and that they had become numb to it all. *More rations for us, they probably thought.* It was a small price to pay for the food that was on their plates.

And what glorious food it was.

Shep could see the draw. It was going to be difficult for him to leave this bounty. He held up a piece of bacon and stared at it, in awe, really. *Pigs. They must even have pigs, and a lot based on the amount of people who savored the crisp slices.* Milk filled his glass and a scrambled egg sat on his plate. The milk was probably from powder and so were the eggs. *But the bacon? Oh, that bacon was real all right.*

Shep could tell Antigone savored every bite – her eyes closed with each slow chew and swallow.

She smiled through closed lips. "I never thought I would eat bacon again."

Shep wondered what it would cost them. When it came to fight or flight, he usually chose fight. Not this time. This time he knew he couldn't possibly win one, unless something radically changed. Rhian had said they could stay as long as they like through that Welsh accent of hers. He wondered about that, too, how a woman from Wales ended up running a post-apocalyptic Midwestern town?

There were men and women with rifles at her command, guarding an oasis in this desert of a world. *Are those guns more for show?* Their determined faces told him otherwise.

He wondered just how free they were to leave.

Shep looked up to see several people in the cafeteria staring at him and Antigone. He was so preoccupied with his bacon that he hadn't taken notice until now. It was unnerving. Antigone had figured it out, too. Her eyes darted about the room and it was the first time in a long time he had seen a scared look on her face.

She whispered, "Why are they looking at us like that?"

"We're the new kids in school, I guess. Maybe they're curious. I have to believe they don't see many visitors here."

"Guess not." Antigone leaned forward so no prying ears could hear. "They're giving me the heebie-jeebies."

He caught her stealing another glance at a young boy sitting two tables over. He was young – it looked like it would take him a hundred years to grow even one whisker on his chin – and his raven hair was mussed, but in a hip, purposeful kind of way. His eyes were dark and brooding.

"That boy over there doesn't seem to be giving you the heebie-jeebies. You like him."

Antigone's face flushed with embarrassment. "Shut up."

That was girl-speak for yes. "I don't know. He kind of looks like a Backstreet Boy reject to me."

The corner of her lip curled in confusion. "Who?"

If Shep didn't feel like an old man before, he certainly did now. "Really? Okay. Let me give you another more contemporary example. He looks like a One Direction reject."

Antigone snorted. "Shut up. He kind of gives me the creeps, too."

No, he certainly did not. He knew that look. Anna had flashed it to him when they first met. He knew that look anywhere. He also knew the Backstreet Boy was as smitten with her as she was with him.

The rest of this crew, though, gave him the heebie-jeebies, too. They were also giving him food. *Yes, everything comes with a price*. If the heebie-jeebies were the only cost, he'd gladly accept it.

•••

Shep picked up the bucket and peered inside. It smelled foul and he could make out a strange mixture of grasses, rotting fruit, worms and mashed-up rodents. The pigs in the pen grunted and squealed. They knew it was feeding time.

Shep slung the bucket toward the pen and the contents flew out in a wave of nastiness. It sloshed on the muddy ground and the pigs flocked to it and snorted as they ate.

Everyone in the town had to pull their weight and this was his contribution. Manual labor never appealed to Shep, but he was surprised by how much he enjoyed this work. He had even named one of the swine "Miss Piggy."

Shep wiped the sweat off his brow with the back of his hand and peered up at the windmill that rose high above him. On a balcony near the top stood a man with a rifle, looking out over the horizon. He wondered if he was up there to guard the windmills, the greenhouse and the farmhouse that sat far off in the distance, from trespassers, or if he was there to make sure Shep didn't sprint off.

The energy from the windmill sails was enough to power three hydroponic bays and the large greenhouse. They produced an ample supply of fruits and vegetables for the entire year.

It was quite the setup, Shep thought. He admired how they had carved out such an existence, a throwback to simpler times when people lived off the land. That was how things had to be now. There was a time when Shep would have been lost on a farm, but he was adapting quickly.

He heard footsteps approach from behind and looked over his

shoulder to see Ward stomping his way toward him. "Rhian wants to see you."

Shep's brow rose. "I'm not done yet. I have to check the greenhouse and the other two mills."

Ward groused. "Call it a half-day."

Rhian sat on her throne like always. She pushed around some papers on the bench and ran a pen over one vigorously before whisking it to the side. When she noticed Shep standing there, her head shot up and she smiled. "Shep, nice to see you. You're looking well."

Shep nodded as he looked up at her. "Thank you, Rhian. I'm feeling much stronger, and I have a little more meat on my bones. Let me express my gratitude again."

She shook her head and waved her hand in front of her face. "No thank-yous necessary. You've done a fine job tending to the livestock and making sure our bays are running. I heard you had a little bit of experience doing the same in your shelter. But that's not why I brought you here. I want to talk to you about that lush thing you're with."

Shep clenched his jaw. He was hesitant to ask why. "Oh. What about her?"

Rhian leaned back in her chair and bit down on the pen before she spoke. "Antigone's a beautiful girl and Padrig has taken a liking to her. Unfortunately, another has been promised to him. I need you to put a … light foot down. I'd hate to see things get knobbed up."

He assumed that was Welsh slang for "make her stop flirting with the boy or she'll end up hanging from a rafter."

"I'll do my best," he said.

"I know you will."

•••

Shep looked a sight better than he did a month ago when he could barely stand. He looked at himself in a full-length mirror he had found stashed in a closet and marveled at how much fuller his face appeared now. His thick beard was gone and only black stubble flecked with gray took its place. He buttoned up a flannel shirt. It kept him warm and fit snug to his body.

Antigone looked as healthy as ever in the reflection as she stood next to him. She pulled that knitted cap over her long dark hair and tucked a few stray strands behind her ears. She had even found some lipstick – Twilight Nude was the shade – and she made it a point to repeat it over and over again with a giggle when she applied it to her plump lips.

"Got a date with the Backstreet Boy? What's his name, Padrig?" Shep's quip was met with a quick jam of her knuckles into his ribs. "Oh, that's right. That's what 'the queen bitch' calls him. What's his real name? Patrick. I wonder what your Welsh name is? I don't think there is a Welsh equivalent for Antigone."

They shared a laugh and for a moment Shep had forgotten just how different the world had become. For a moment, everything seemed normal, seemed as it once was. For a moment he thought he was late for work and Antigone late for class and they had better get going if they were to beat rush-hour traffic.

That moment passed. It always did.

Reality is a sonofabitch.

Things weren't normal. Anything but. Antigone and Patrick had continued to steal moments together. She insisted they were being careful, that it was harmless and in no way a violation of the law. He trusted her. He really had no choice. But he still feared for her. She was taking an awful risk, but she always returned from her rendezvous with Patrick with a gleam in her eye and a smile on her face.

Shep approved of anything that made her grin like that.

Antigone slipped a brown wool sweater over her head and pulled it down past her waist. She was wearing black yoga pants and those same Nike shoes. She looked beautiful, stunning really, and happy.

"You look really pretty, Tig," Shep said, putting his hands on her arms and rubbing the soft wool of her sweater. "You look really happy."

He took delight when he saw those lines around the corners of her lips when she smiled, big and beaming. She tried to say something, but the words just didn't quite come out. He figured it would have been some clever retort, or some snide remark, but he was surprised when she threw her arms around him and hugged him tightly. He felt her hands rub up and down his back and her head jam under his chin.

"Shep, I don't know if I could ever thank you enough." She sniffed. "I mean … you have been so great to me. I love you."

Shep placed his hand on her head and hugged her even more tightly.

He spoke softly. "Tig, I love you, too."

•••

It wasn't long after Antigone had bounced out of the apartment to meet Patrick when Shep heard the pounding of knuckles on the door. He swung it open and Ward stood before him, his eyes cast with ruefulness. "Shep, you have to come with me."

Ward wouldn't say why as they walked down the sidewalk, their strides long and purposeful. He hadn't known Ward all that well, the husky man was a difficult fellow to be chums with, but he recognized the look that was etched on his face all too well.

It was the look Ward got when he was frustrated, when he was asked to do something unseemly, like put a noose around a poor soul's neck.

Shep wondered if it was his neck that was destined for a length of rope.

They glided quickly past the courthouse – *I guess it wasn't Rhian who summoned me* – and into a building tucked away in the corner of town. Crystal chandeliers hung a few feet apart, dangling over a long corridor. Doors marked with numbers lined each side the hallway. It was apparent this was a hotel in that other life.

Now, it appeared, it was a brothel. An old man, his white hair pushed across his pink scalp to hide a bald spot, exited a room, adjusting the belt on his loose-fitting trousers. A young girl, perhaps no more than fifteen, exited behind him, her face flushed and wet and her red hair a tangled mess.

"What is this, Ward?" Shep asked, knowing full well the answer.

Ward's words were couched in disgust. "You have been *promised*."

They came to a door on the other end of the corridor and Ward swung it open. Sitting on the edge of the bed, her hands clasped and her thumbs twiddling was a young girl, her light blond hair combed straight and bobbed around her ears, her white dress cut low to reveal ample cleavage. She stared at the floral pattern on the green carpet.

"This is Ginny," Ward said. "Ginny, this is Billy Shepard." With the introductions concluded and his duty met, Ward beat a hasty exit and closed the door.

That left Shep to stand there, awkwardly, before the girl.

He was frozen in place, as if cast in stone. He peered wide-eyed at her.

She lifted her head and gazed at him, her lips quivering. She was quite beautiful, stunning really. Her face was smooth and waxen as if it were carved perfectly in ivory. Her mouth was covered by a shimmering shade of bright red lipstick and her blue eyes looked at him through lush lashes and dark mascara.

She looked like a porcelain doll – and just as fragile as one.

The girl, while breathtaking, couldn't have been more much more than eighteen. Shep's stomach turned and he felt nauseous.

The words stumbled out of his mouth. "We, um, we don't have to do this."

Her thumbs were doing rapid somersaults. "We have to."

Shep was finally able to move and shuffled over to the bed, sitting next to Ginny. She leaned away from him slightly and cast her eyes back down to the carpet. She smelled like lavender.

"We don't *have* to do anything we don't want to do," he said. "I won't do it."

Her eyes shot back to him and her mouth gaped. "But we have to!" She exclaimed. "If we don't, she'll hang me!"

"No one's hanging anyone," Shep reassured her. "I promise. I'm not going to touch you."

"But you have to. She'll have Wynn check to see if we did it. She'll know and she'll hang me!"

Shep sighed and pressed his face into his palms. This was an untenable situation. There was no way he could do what Rhian wished. There was no way he was going to defile this young girl. Yet if he didn't, he would be putting both of them at risk. *And maybe Antigone, too.*

He wondered how he kept finding himself in these situations with young girls. Maybe Bray was right. Perhaps he did have a thing for them.

He glimpsed her cleavage again and quickly looked away. "I'll talk to Wynn. Maybe he can lie for us. I don't think he's too thrilled about this anyway. Just a gut feeling."

"I don't know," she said, her voice trailing.

"Hey. Trust me. Nothing is going to happen to you."

She smiled and smoothed out her dress on her thighs. "What should we do, then? You can't leave yet. They'll know we didn't … you know."

"Let's just talk."

She spoke of her life before the Ejection. She was just a little girl then, growing up near Indianapolis with her parents. Her mother had survived the chaos in the aftermath. Her father wasn't so lucky.

He had stolen food from children. He had beat women. He had killed men who had clung to food and water to keep their own families alive. Ginny's father didn't care. He did it for them. That was always the justification. He only did it for them.

At the time, Ginny had not known where the sustenance came from, nor did she much care. It wasn't until later when her father was wounded trying to murder a man for his fresh deer kill that she came to know the full scope of his crimes.

And her mother's.

Her father lay there, bleeding from the gut, dying. He had managed to wound the man from whom he stole. His final words were, "Kill that sonofabitch. Take his deer. It'll feed you for days." Ginny's mother grabbed her husband's knife, stalked over to the man and stabbed him. Over and over and over again. Then spat on his corpse.

It was a scene Ginny would never forget. She still relived it in her nightmares, waking most nights with a ring of sweat around her shirt and her heart pounding.

Just retelling the story made her chest heave with heavy breaths and sweat bead on her skin.

"Those stories are common," Shep said.

It was unfortunate, but true. Her father was probably once a good man, a good father. He most likely thought he was still being a good man and a good father when he murdered and frightened and stole from people to keep his family alive. *Who's to say he wasn't?*

Perhaps it was Ginny's say.

"My mom and I ended up here," she said, sniffling. "I hate it here. I hate it so much. I hate her, too."

Shep had no good reply to that. He searched his brain for something comforting to say to her as her thumbs circled each other like two planets locked in an orbital dance, but he came up empty. Instead he told her of his struggles, of Anna's brutal murder, of Skye, of the psychopath that hunted him and Antigone and how, if he had a daughter, he would want her to be strong and brave like her.

He told her of his transgressions and how, when it came down to it, he was no better than the man who sought to destroy him, and perhaps, no better than her own father.

Ginny reached out her hand and squeezed his. "You are a good man. You are nothing like that jerk, Bray. You are nothing like my pop."

Shep smiled at that sentiment. He wasn't sure if he deserved it.

They spent the next hour sharing stories of their triumphs and their losses, of the way things had become and the way they wished they could be.

It was a very pleasant way to spend an evening.

Part II
Chapter Three
The Trial of Billy Shepard

Shep's body ached from a day of slopping pigs and tending to the hydroponics bay. It was hard work, but he had grown to enjoy it. The labor made for some fitful nights on that hard mattress, but he managed.

The sun had already dipped below the horizon and darkness was invading the apartment as he lay there, staring across the room at the empty mattress where Antigone slept. Only on this rapidly approaching night she wasn't under those blankets, and her shallow breaths were absent in the quiet.

There were many nights when he stayed awake, feeling his muscles seize, and listened to her breathing. He often wondered if she were dreaming and what they were about. *Were they disjointed scenes from her past life with her parents and brother? Were they dreams of a future with Patrick? Were they dreams of me?*

Right now all he wondered was where the hell she was.

Shep gathered himself to his feet with a groan and a whimper and paced the room. He thought this must be what if feels like to be a nervous father. It was well past curfew and there was no wiggle room when it came to the laws on that typewritten manifesto. Each time his worried steps took him to the window he peered out and hoped to see Antigone creeping down the sidewalk on her way home.

Finally he heard the door crash open and he turned to see who it was. Hulking in the doorway was Ward, breathing heavy and hard.

"You better come with me," he said between heaves of his chest.

Shep knew better than to argue. He followed Ward, his feet crunching the freshly fallen snow, to the farm and through the entrance into the closest windmill. Patrick and Antigone sat huddled by a ladder that led up to a landing above where the gears of the mill ground loudly.

She held her right hand, knuckles swollen and bleeding, delicately in her left.

"What the hell happened to your hand?" Shep asked.

"She punched one of my men when he caught them together. Knocked him out cold. Lucky for them I was the first one to catch up to 'em. I dragged them here," Ward said gruffly and loudly so he could be heard over the knocking of the wooden cogs above him. "You don't have long, Patrick, so you better hurry up and talk."

Patrick just stared sullenly at the floor. He didn't say a word.

"What's going on, Tig?" Shep, his jaw clenched and his eyes narrowed, only looked to Antigone for answers.

"Tell him, Patrick," Antigone said. "Tell him what you told me."

Patrick's head bounced up and his eyes stared at Shep with a mix of fear and anger. "They're coming for her."

Shep knew what coming for her meant. They were coming to accuse her of some violation of Crazyville law, either a breach of curfew or a breach of messing with the wrong boy. Whichever, the punishment was the same.

"We have to get out of here. Now!" Antigone said, panic rippling in her voice. "I packed a bag already. I stuffed as much fruit and clothes in it as I could. If we leave now, we could be miles from here before the sun comes up and they realize we are gone."

Shep knew it wasn't going to be that easy. He could see that much in the glumness etched on their faces. "I'm sensing a catch here."

"You won't make it very far. They're already looking for her," Ward said, then looked at Patrick. "And you, too, you little dumbass."

"They're not looking for me," Shep said.

Antigone was a smart girl, Shep always knew that about her, and she was catching on quickly to where he was going with this.

"Oh, no! No way," she said, standing. "We all go together. We're not leaving you behind!"

Shep took a deep breath, so deep the air hurt his lungs, exhaled and bit his lower lip in thought. He knew what needed to be done. They were coming for her, and no matter how much he wanted her to stay, he had to let her go.

"Tig ..."

"No!" she cried.

Shep glanced at Patrick. "There's no other way, is there?"

He shook his head, staring down at the floor again.

"I'll figure something out. I'll catch up to you in Halcyon." He forced a smile. "I'll bring a card and a birthday cake."

She slammed her face into his chest and grabbed him tightly. He could feel her heaving cries as he combed his fingers through her hair. He wondered if she thought it as soothing as he did when Anna did the same for him, but he supposed nothing was comforting to her now.

"We have to go," Patrick interrupted.

Antigone pulled away and wiped her eyes. "What will they do to him, Pat? Will he end up hanging in that pub?"

"I'll plead ignorance," Shep said. "There's no law against that and Rhian is all about the law, right, Patrick?"

He tried to say it as believably as he could, but he failed miserably. He could tell when Antigone's bullshit meter buzzed and it was wailing now. He saw it in her eyes, but she let the fib go, more for his sake than hers, he supposed.

Patrick grabbed her hand and squeezed it tightly. Before they passed through the door into their unknown future, she gazed over her shoulder at Shep. He realized then that this was probably the last time he would ever see that face, the one he had risked everything to save. It was a face that deserved so much more than this life could give and that made him more heartbroken than the fact he would be so alone without her.

He hoped she would find some kind of happiness, some kind of life without fear or hunger with Patrick. He hoped the boy with the mussed hair and brooding eyes was up to that challenge.

Billy Shepard thought he just might be.

"Take good care of her, Patrick."

Patrick didn't look back. "I will," he said, pausing. "And say hello to my crazy mother."

•••

Shep said, "Sooie, sooie," in a hushed yell. He wasn't even sure if it would work and he felt silly for even trying. Surprisingly it was indeed effective as the pigs scattered out of the pen, Miss Piggy leading the way. It was a laughable sight and it even brought a strained smile to Ward's face.

"So, what did you do before?" Shep asked Ward as the last of the pigs oinked his way out of the pen. That, too, was a common query after the Ejection. "A bouncer? A farmer? A construction worker?"

Ward put his hands on his hips and watched the pigs scurry. "Doctor," he said.

Ward closed the pen door and waved for Shep to go. "You better get back to your apartment before anyone sees you. I'll sound the alarm and round up the others. Chasing down all these pigs should keep everyone busy for awhile and give those two the time to get far away from here. Get some sleep. You're going to have a tough day tomorrow."

That much was true.

Shep got home clear enough, the men and women with guns more concerned about baconless breakfasts in the near future than him wandering the streets after curfew. The apartment seemed so empty without her.

Shep lay in bed and stared at the empty mattress again. He hoped she was miles from here by now and he hoped she would forget him. It would not be as easy for him to forget her.

He rolled over on his back and stared into the darkness, whispering, "I miss … you."

•••

Morning came and Ward right along with it. He was accompanied by two men just as large and menacing as him. Rhian made her entrance a moment later. They surrounded him as he sat up in bed.

"Where is that lush thing?" Rhian asked. *Her Welsh accident is as Welshy as ever.*

"I don't know," Shep said as convincingly as he could. "I'm worried. She didn't come home last night. I was going to come find you or Wynn to go look for her if she wasn't home this morning."

He could tell Rhian was not buying the fiction he was spinning. "Thick as thieves, you two are, so forgive me if I don't believe you have no idea where she could have gone."

"Maybe they went to Vegas to get *promised*."

Rhian nodded at Ward, who gave Shep a swift kick to the ribs. Pain shot up to his shoulder and down to his hip. He gasped for air as he caught a glimpse of Ward mouthing, "Sorry."

"Jesus! I told you. I don't know," Shep forced the words from his mouth, trying to take in air as he did. "She has a mind of her own, you know. I can't keep tabs on her any more than you can on your own son."

Rhian squatted and grabbed Shep's hair, pulling it so his eyes would meet hers. "What did you say? You best be careful what comes out of that munting of yours."

Shep still gasped for air. "Boys will be boys, I guess. You have as much control over him as I do over Antigone. I guess we both got fooled."

Rhian let go of his hair and pushed his head down hard on the mattress. "Take him," she said and walked out.

Ward helped Shep to his feet, grabbed his arm firmly and began dragging him out into the frigid air. "Sorry about the kick. I had to make it look good."

It was snowing again and white blanketed the sidewalk, road and the rooftops. Shep's dragging feet left a canal in the snow behind him as people stopped and watched. Ward pulled him along like a corpse into a building that was once the police station and tossed him into a jail cell. As the doors clanged shut, Ward gave him a subtle nod. "Man, she wants to kill you, but she knows she can't. At least not yet."

Shep grimaced and sat on the hard cot, his arm pressed tight against his ribs. "That's what I'm counting on. Why did you help Antigone and Patrick, anyway? Why are you trying to help me? You're risking a whole lot."

Ward grabbed the bars firmly, as if he were the one on the inside of the cell. "I took an oath once to do no harm. I'm tired of dropping people over stairwells. I'm tired of escorting old men to have sex with young girls – no offense. I'm tired of doing bad things so I can eat. At first, we were all just happy to have food in our stomachs and a warm place to sleep. That's all we cared about. We didn't see what was happening right in front of our eyes."

Ward pressed his forehead onto the bars and closed his eyes. "Absolute power corrupts absolutely. We see that now. We're the ones with the guns. We're the ones who have given her this power."

He opened his eyes and rung his hands on the bars, gritting his teeth in anger. "It has to end. The cost of that food is too high for us now."

"How did she get this power anyway?" Shep asked.

Ward told the story of Rainie Longwell, the wife of a farmer and mother of three boys. They raised livestock and had two hundred acres of fertile Midwest land just outside of the small city of Attica. They grew crops as varied as corn, soy beans and wheat.

Walter Longwell, her husband of twenty years, had become weary of the way things had become, weary of scratching and clawing and watching the profits of his large operation dwindle. His hands were raw and callused from years of working them hard on the land, and he had very little to show for it. The stress of such a life had worn him down and he became increasingly paranoid. He hated the government, disliked most outsiders and feared the end was near. He was determined to protect his family and land from what he thought was an inevitable doom.

He invested in windmills to power three hydroponics bays and a greenhouse that allowed them to produce crops on a limited basis year-round. It also gave them a means to survive should his fears be realized.

When they were and the Ejection burned the sky, Walter Longwell took up arms to protect his wife and three sons, Walter Jr., Joseph and the youngest, Patrick, the best he could, but his best wasn't good enough. The town of Attica was soon overrun by desperate masses, searching for food and shelter. His nearby farm, flush with such things, was an easy target.

Walter Longwell fought them off the best he could. Bones of those he had slain were still buried there under the corn fields. He could only fight them off for so long. Only Rainie Longwell and Patrick survived the onslaught.

They lived only because of a doctor who knew he was just days from death stumbled onto their land in the middle of another attack. Ward Webster, a skilled rifleman and survivalist as well as a surgeon, quickly quashed the invasion.

Rainie Longwell fed him and in return, he protected the farm. More people wandered in, hungry and cold, and she welcomed them with food, a smile and a new persona she had invented of a Welsh immigrant. She had traveled to Wales as a schoolgirl on a class trip and became fascinated with the people and their culture. Her new identity helped her escape the horror she had seen and allowed her to feel special and important. Ward didn't mind the fallacy. Food was ample and they needed as many hands as they could to tend to the farm.

When the population grew too large for the farmhouse, Ward Webster brutally cleared out the town so people had places to live and thrive. He went door to door, murdering the squatters, eliminating them with the surgical precision he once used to cut out tumors or pluck out an appendix or a gallbladder. They were easy pickings and he did it because he didn't want to go hungry again.

Ward was ashamed of what he had done.

"People do things they never thought they would do when they are desperate," Ward said. "We all have done things we're not proud of."

Shep knew that all too well. *Human life wasn't worth much. It wasn't worth much before the angry sun and it was worth even less after.*

Shep grimaced again. Each breath he took felt like another kick to his side.

"You'll be okay," Ward said. "I made sure I didn't kick you hard enough to dislocate any ribs that could puncture your lung. You have bigger things to worry about."

"I suppose I do," Shep said.

•••

Shep saw her face, cold and white, again in his dream.

Smile. White teeth. Wrinkles around the corners of her mouth.

White dress, train flowing down red steps. Altar. Patrick in a black tux, holding her chalky hands.

Noose around her neck. Crimson blood flowing from her eyes. Terror.

"Help me, Shep! Save me, Shep!"

Gray sweatshirt. Crimson blood blotted like ink, stab wounds, nine of them, in her chest and stomach.

"Help me, Billy! Save me, Billy!"

Falling, raven hair blowing up. Snap of the neck. Dangling lifeless.

"It's time," Skye whispers. "It's time."

•••

"It's time." Ward poked Shep in the forehead with the butt of his rifle. "It's time for your tribunal."

Ward escorted him into the pub and sat him down in the chair where Gwynn squirmed not so long ago. It was an uncomfortable seat and his tailbone already had begun to ache. He peered to the right to the table where the "jury" sat and was stunned to see Ginny wedged in between two men with clean-shaven faces and short cropped hair. She looked at him through those blue eyes of hers with shame and sorrow, her thumbs spinning wildly again.

Rhian sat smugly at the table in front of him and banged a clear paperweight shaped like a stone on the desk. The pub, packed with people all around him and even some peering down from the balcony above, hushed. She smacked her lips, wetted them with her tongue and bellowed, "William Shepard, how do you plead?"

Shep had no idea how these proceedings worked and he imagined it didn't really matter.

I wish Robert Morrow, Esquire, was here. He knew enough from looking at Ginny that his fate was already decided, that this tribunal was just for show to keep the good townsfolk believing Rhian was benevolent, just and a worthy leader. She had constructed a very careful illusion and the people gobbled it up much like they gobbled up the fruit and the beef and the bacon she was feeding them.

Rhian had gotten to Ginny, probably promised she would be spared for not "mating" with Shep. He didn't hold a grudge against the girl. He looked at her and mouthed, "It's okay." Ginny whimpered and tears streamed down her porcelain cheeks.

Shep looked around at the throng of people peering at him, at the rope that dangled over the support beam, and then stared right into Rhian's eyes and said boldly, "I am innocent."

Rhian smirked and nodded to a man he knew as Rhys, but could only imagine what his real name was. Shep could tell he was a lawyer in that other life by the way he stood, rolled up the sleeves of his crisp white dress shirt and looked confidently at the "jury."

Before Rhys could speak, Shep asked, "Do I get a lawyer?"

A wail of laughter rose in the pub.

Rhian chuckled silently. "Only the guilty feel they need someone to speak for 'em."

Rhys stood in front of Shep and looked down at him with a smirk. He was a rather tall man and a commanding presence in a courtroom, even a makeshift one like this. That's probably what made him such a good lawyer in that other life and it most likely served him well in this one, too.

Rhys strutted to the jury table and acknowledged each with a simple nod. His first question was already spitting out his lips before his saunter carried him back in front of the chair where Shep squirmed. "Did you know Antigone and Padrig were in a relationship?"

Shep's back was aching now. He figured the chair was uncomfortable for a very good reason. It made him shuffle about, appearing uneasy and very guilty.

He tried not to grimace when he answered. "They were friends. Nothing more."

"Is that right? Nothing more, you say? You didn't encourage their relationship?"

"Yes, I encouraged it. A young girl needs friends. She can't hang all the time with an old guy like me." Shep looked at Ginny and winked. "What would people say?"

He could hear a smattering of laughter from the spectators. Even Ginny cracked a smile. *That had to be a good sign, at least.*

It knocked Rhys off his game a bit. The lawyer looked about the pub with a small frown, before he refocused his attention on Shep. "Is it not true that they were involved romantically? Intimately?"

Shep raised his brow as he flashed a sly smile. "Well, I wouldn't know *that*."

He made it a point to look at Rhian as he continued. "What parent knows, *really knows*, what's in their child's heart?"

Rhian squirmed in her seat. *Perhaps her chair was as unforgiving as mine.*

"Isn't it true you helped them run away together, even

though Padrig and Antigone were both promised to others?" Rhys asked.

That revelation caught Shep off guard. *Antigone was promised to another, too? Who?* He peered about at the masses, many of whom were taking delight in his trial. His eyes stopped on every male face, the handsome ones, the ugly ones, even the old ones, and he wondered each time if that was the man who was to be Antigone's mate.

Shep stammered before he answered. "I … I had no idea she was to be *promised*."

Rhys leaned against the corner of Rhian's desk, crossing his arms on his chest. "You didn't answer the question, sir. Did you aid in their escape?"

"She wasn't home before curfew, so I went out to try to find her. When I couldn't, I returned to the apartment to wait for her there. She never came home. You know about as much as I do about the whereabouts of Antigone and *Patrick*."

All the faces in the pub had confusion drawn on them. That was the point. He purposely called Padrig by his real name, Patrick, to see what kind of rise he could get out of Rhian and the onlookers. The reaction he received pleased him. Her eyes narrowed and her jaw clenched. She summoned Rhys over to her and whispered something emphatically into his ear.

Rhys returned to his perch on the corner of the desk. "So, you claim you went out looking for Antigone and then when you could not find her, you returned home and waited. Can anyone vouch for this?"

"Just the mice."

There was another smattering of laughter, a bit louder and of longer duration this time. This did not amuse Rhian, whose lip curled with disdain.

Rhys' words hushed the crowd, "Were you not promised to another as well?"

"Yes. I was."

"Did you consummate the pairing?"

"No, I did not."

Rhys clapped his hands and looked around the pub with a smile. "So, you admit to another breach of the law?"

"The only thing I admit is being a decent man and not some heathen who has sex with a young girl just because he is told to."

"But that *is* the law," Rhys exclaimed. "Did you not read the laws on your first night in town?"

"I read them."

"So," Rhys paused, circling Shep like a predator does his prey, "you willfully disobeyed them. These laws are clear. The punishment is clear. But you chose to ignore one of them. You *chose* to break the law."

"No," Shep said, smirking. "I chose to challenge the law and the one who made it."

The crowd gasped in unison. Shep caught a glimpse of Ward, who nodded subtly at him. He wanted this charade to end. The man who had defended this place so brutally was done with the theatrics and the killing just so he could remain fed. He had told Shep as much the night before and his nod was a sign to set the end of it in motion. Most of the others in attendance at this farce of a trial wanted change, too, Shep sensed.

Even Rhys.

And especially Ginny, who had watched her parents compromise so much of themselves. She, too, had given in to fear. It was time to make a stand.

They all had grown weary of life under Rhian's thumb. They were waiting for an impetus of change and, as it turned out, Shep was that force.

He was happy to serve that role.

Shep continued: "I really don't know how this works, but I'm wondering when I get to ask some questions? Why isn't Padrig's mother held to the same standards of the law? For all we know she helped them escape."

Rhian again squirmed in her chair.

"She's not on trial here, sir," Rhys said. "You are."

"And why is that exactly? Why am I the one sitting on this god-awful chair and not her? Is it because *Padrig's* mother runs this town?"

A hush fell. Not so much as a sound was heard. All the eyes in the room had suddenly swayed from a stare at Shep to a stare at Rhian, whose face was as flushed with red as one of those juicy apples she traded for fealty.

"I think that is all for today," she said.

People were hesitant to move. Shep's words made sure they didn't. "No! Let's get this over with here and now. They don't know, do they *Rhian*?"

She stood and her hand trembled as she pointed at him and yelled, "Get him out of here!"

"They don't know about Rainie Longwell, do they? A life-long resident of Attica, a wife of a loving man and mother of three sons, two of whom she saw die along with her husband, a woman so consumed with grief and anger that she whipped up a false identity and hid her son from everyone, a boy who you all know as Padrig, whose real name is Patrick."

Shep turned to the jury, their eyes wide and fixed on him, and he pointed a finger at the man on the far left. "She is no more Welsh than you." Then at the man on the right. "Or you." Then at Ginny, who smiled as Shep winked. "Or you."

Shep's eyes scanned the onlookers and his words were cast with zeal. "She's been misleading all of you. She was a small woman who was afraid and alone and wanted to feel big. She took advantage of a terrible situation to grab power and to lord it over you masked as law and honor. You all know deep down that all of this is wrong. You don't have to live under her rule. You don't have to attend trials, watch people hang and allow your children to get pawned off to a stranger."

Shep stood and commanded the room. He was just happy to be out of that torturing chair. "You don't need her or her laws. There is ample food. You have guns to protect yourselves. Ward would make a fine leader. You have the barbed wire fence you built to keep people out. You have everything here you need to survive. Why subject yourselves to this?"

Rhian fumed and slipped out of character, bellowing in a decidedly un-Welsh accent, "He's guilty. The sentence is death. Take him! Take him now!"

No one moved. "I said take him!"

There was an eerie quiet in the pub as the population of the town looked at Rhian not with anger or malice, but with pity. They all owed their lives to her, but not their souls.

"Do you know what I have given you? I gave you a haven and I can take it away. There are people lining up outside these walls to get what you have. Ward. Shoot them! Shoot them all!"

Ward dropped his rifle and it hit the wood floor with a loud thump. The other men and women who held weapons took their cue from Ward and let go of their rifles, too. They knocked on the floor loudly when they hit.

Ward walked slowly to Rhian, who stood sobbing and motionless. He rubbed his hand on her arm gently and spoke with great mournfulness. "Rainie, it's over."

"No," she said, shaking her head. Her eyes squinted and her lips shook with rage. "I'll have all of your heads. I'll put them on spikes around the fence as a warning to insolence. Anyone who doesn't take up arms to defend me will die. Mark my words."

"No one is going to die today. Or tomorrow." Ward put his arms around her. She tried to fight him off, punching at his chest weakly with her fists until she finally surrendered. She was Rainie Longwell again. Rhian, the Welsh ruler of Attica, died at that moment as if it were she dangling from the rope.

"I just wanted to keep them safe. I didn't want what happened to my Walt and my boys to happen to them," she cried.

Ward rubbed her back and whispered, "I know."

People began to leave the pub now, filing out sorrowfully. Most stared straight ahead as they exited. Some glanced quickly over to Rainie who bawled into Ward's chest.

Ginny approached Shep, a rush of tears filling her eyes. "I'm sorry, Shep. I'm sorry."

He hugged her. She still smelled of lavender. "You have nothing to be sorry about. You can repay me by helping these people, and your mother."

She laughed as she pulled her head out of his chest. Shep lightly punched her on the soft skin of her shoulder. "Keep 'em in line."

"Are you leaving? You can stay here, you know."

"I have to go," Shep said. "I made a promise to Tig."

Rainie slumped now in her chair, the one in which she sat determined to rule mercilessly, and stared straight ahead. No emotion. No expression. Blank. Ward shambled over to Shep, who looked at Rainie with deep sadness.

"What will happen to her now?" he asked.

Ward looked back at Rainie, and then to Shep. "I'll take care of her. I'll always take care of her."

Shep could see she meant a lot to him, that their bond had gone much deeper than ruler and hired gun. He had saved her life and she had saved his. It wasn't unlike Shep's relationship with Antigone, and that made him want to reunite with her and Patrick even more.

Shep loathed himself for a thought that crept into his mind, the thought that if things had gone differently and he had the chance to kill Rainie, he most surely would have. No second thoughts. No regrets.

Billy Shepard knew all too well that sometimes people have to be put down.

Part II
Chapter Four
The Days After the Ejection

Bodies lay in the street, flies circling them. Billy Shepard could hear the flies buzzing and feel some of them land and scrape against his sweaty neck.

Like everyone else, he just walked over the corpses. *Nothing he could do for them now; nothing anyone could do for them.* They had stopped burying the dead weeks ago, the numbers growing too fast for them to keep up.

What little authority that remained was eroding. It wouldn't be long, Shep thought, before order crumbled all together.

Glass was thick as sand on the sidewalks and in the streets, and his feet crunched over the shards as he walked. Cars burned. A man, his shirt ripped, pounded another man with a sledgehammer. A woman, mumbling, huddled under an awning and asked for God to take her. Others went into and came out of stores with nothing but angry expressions.

There was nothing left to loot.

The desperate just became bent on destruction, feeling that setting a car ablaze, pulling down a light post or taking a sledgehammer to someone's skull was better than waiting to die. At least it gave them something to do, something to focus their energies, as futile as it was.

The city was still dark – *hell, everywhere was dark* – and Shep knew it would stay that way, perhaps even for the duration of his life. He hoped that would be a long, long time.

He chuckled at that revelation. Just a month ago he had a gun stuffed in his mouth, seconds from pulling the trigger. Now, he wanted to live … in this, where people slaughtered people for whatever food and clean water they had, no matter how little, where people destroyed things just so they could feel like they were in control, where people simply stepped over the rotting flesh of a corpse as if they were stepping over a piece of gum stuck to the sidewalk.

Human life was now worth no more than a stick of Wrigley's Spearmint.

Shep had seen enough of the city that burned. The flickering light of the many fires was the only thing that lit up the midnight sky when he drove toward what once was his tomb, but was now his sanctuary.

•••

Cheese Ravioli, Beefaroni or SpaghettiOs? That would be his choice on special occasions. Other times it would be canned stew mixed with the vegetables he was able to preserve and jar. Or the fish in his aquaponic bay that he carefully balanced. He figured he had enough to survive for years. *That would be a good start.*

He had stored as much as he could in the shelter, but had the rest stacked on shelves in the cellar. He stood there now, in front of the towers of cans, and picked out his meal.

He still liked to eat his lunch in the dining room. He enjoyed the natural light that spilled in through the window and he savored the smell of the fresh air that blew through it when it was open. He liked looking out over the yard and reliving the good times, the better times.

It made him feel a little bit human. It made him feel normal, if for a fleeting moment, or a fleeting meal.

He swallowed the last spoonful of Dinty Moore Beef Stew and set the dish in the sink when he saw three figures approach, two men and a woman. Shep walked briskly out the door and onto the porch and watched them as they stumbled closer. He could tell they were weak and hungry and desperate. The man was in his forties and wore a button down shirt, the kind worn by mechanics with the name sewn on the pocket. The sleeves were rolled up and a ring of sweat darkened the fabric under each arm. He looked average in every way, height, weight, looks. His beard was scruffy, gray on the chin, yet brown everywhere else, and his face was weathered by the sun.

The woman was also in her forties and very thin, almost skeletal. She was constantly pulling the dishwater blond hair that whipped into her face by the wind out of her eyes. She wore a white sweater over a pink shirt and Capri pants that were extremely loose around her calves. She too appeared ordinary. She was pretty, but not necessarily a stunner.

Her face was red, beaten by the wind, and her eyes were big and round and tired.

The other man was young, perhaps twenty, and he looked the strongest and in the best health of the three. His light-colored hair was closely cropped, almost buzzed, and he had tufts of a beard on his chin and around his jaw line. He was helping the woman along, holding her arm.

As soon as they saw Shep standing on the porch, they stopped about ninety feet away from his home.

"Hello, sir," the man yelled, lifting his hand and waving his knobby fingers. "We're just looking for some food. We mean you no harm."

Shep wondered if it was wise to let people into his home. After all, the night before he had just seen some of the worst the human race had to offer not ten miles from here. But they looked harmless and hungry and pitiable and he had enough food and water to spare, at least for the short term.

Someone had to be a hero in what was turning into a land of villains. "Come in. Get out of the heat. Looks like you could use a nice meal."

As they walked up the porch steps, Murdock smiled. Shep knew his name because it was stitched on his shirt. "I'm Murdock," he said, pointing to his pocket, "and this is my wife, Bethany, and my son, Ben. Thank you so much. We had to get out of the city – it's a madhouse – and we have no place else to go."

Bethany stood behind him, her eyes staring at the floor. Ben burst into the living room and looked around in wonder. "That's a lot of trophies," he said, analytically. "You're pretty good with a bow, I gather?"

Shep smiled. "It took a lot of hard work and practice, but, yeah, I'm pretty good."

"Did you know humans created rudimentary tools 2.5 million years ago, but it took them another two million years to invent the bow and arrow?"

Shep's eyes bulged as he looked at Murdock, who just smiled and shrugged.

"Sorry about Ben. He's always been very smart and curious." Murdock's eyes shot around the room. "This is a gorgeous home you have here. Is it just you?"

"Yes. Just me. My wife … passed not long before the Ejection."

"Oh, I'm so sorry," Murdock said. "Then you could probably use the company. Sorry to be impatient, but we haven't eaten in a couple of days ..."

Shep smiled and patted Murdock on the back. "Beef stew, coming right up."

•••

They gobbled it down quickly and Shep could see the relief they felt. His relief was palpable, too. He was able to help a family in need and he had someone to share a meal and a conversation with. It was a welcome change to the solitary life he had been living, even before the Ejection turned everything upside down.

Murdock wiped his thin lips. "Well, I don't know about you, but that hit the spot."

"I'll be sure to send a letter to Dinty Moore," Shep joked, prompting an odd look to pass over Ben's face.

"There is no Dinty Moore," Ben said. "You'd have to send the letter to Hormel, which introduced Dinty Moore Beef Stew in 1935."

Shep chuckled. "Good to know." He noticed Bethany staring down coldly at her empty bowl. "Bethany, are you still hungry? Can I get you more?"

Her eyes darted up to meet his and she bit down hard, bracing against something that deeply bothered her. She shook her head in short, quick bursts.

"I'm sorry, Shep, it's been tough on her. She hasn't been feeling well for a few days now, probably because she hasn't had anything solid in her stomach. She'll come around now that she's had something to eat and after she gets a good night's sleep. We haven't had much of that lately, either."

"I understand completely," Shep said. "You can stay here. There's a guest room upstairs and I can get you some pillows and blankets if you need them. I have a First Aid Kit if Bethany is hurt."

"No. She's fine," Murdock said abruptly. "Just tired from our long journey." Murdock put his hands together and looked up in prayer. "I knew God looked kindly down upon this house. I knew you were a man of faith when you invited us into your home. Many thanks, Shep. Many thanks."

•••

Shep decided to sleep on the couch in the house instead of retiring to his shelter. His recurve rested near his head, leaning against the coffee table, the quiver lying next to it. He had no reason to distrust his guests upstairs – they seemed nice enough – but he had no reason to trust them, either. He hoped when he fell asleep he would wake up before Ben plunged a knife into his heart. Then again, Ben would probably wake him to give him a history lesson about when the knife was first invented before he tried to slice him open. *That will give me plenty of time to protect myself from that oddball.*

The thought sent Shep into slumber with a smile on his face.

He awoke to Ben nudging his arm with his foot. "Hey. You awake?"

Shep recoiled, startled. It was still dark and Ben stood over him with a goofy look on his face.

Shep wiped the sleep from his eyes. "Yes, Ben. What is it?"

"Will you show me it?"

Shep was confused, perhaps because he was still half asleep. "What are you talking about?"

"The underground shelter you have. Will you show me it?"

Shep sat up on the couch and examined Ben, trying to figure out how this boy knew there was a sprawling shelter dug deep under this home. He decided to play dumb. "A shelter?"

Ben nodded. "I was thinking about the layout and where the house was in relation to the land. It just didn't seem right. Then I saw you, how healthy you looked and the Mustang convertible parked out front and inferred you were mostly likely very wealthy. From those deductions, I concluded that you have a shelter, and a big one at that."

There was a moment of awkward silence before Ben broke it with an excited query. "Will you show me it?"

What the hell? No use hiding it now. He walked over the bookcase and pulled out the copy of the *King James Bible*, then over to the trophies and grabbed the marble base of the golden one that was set aside. The blast door swung open and Ben let out a long, "Ahhhhh."

"Clever," he said.

They walked down the long corridor to the other blast door and Shep punched in the code. The door jerked open. "After you," Shep said.

Ben entered and eyed the room with awe. "I didn't expect this. I underestimated your wealth by two-hundred percent. Your house is nice and all, but this is spectacular. I assume this is all powered by solar panels, probably camouflaged several hundred feet away from here?"

Shep crossed his arms on his chest. "Yep. You got it."

Ben pointed to the air ducts near the ceiling. "Recycled air through those vents. Nice. Walls are probably ten feet thick, cement and lined with steel. There's probably an emergency exit on the other side. An intercom system for communicating with the house. Very nice. Very well designed and thought out. You should be able to live down here indefinitely."

"Glad you approve."

"Did you know the first bomb shelters were just concrete walls built in a corner of a basement?"

Shep slumped on the couch and yawned. "No, but I figured you would tell me. So, Ben. How do you know all of this stuff?"

Ben paced around the room, touching every surface, examining every nook. "Well, I've always been fascinated by things. Lots of things. I have an eidetic memory, so everything I read or learn kind of just sticks up here." He tapped a finger on the side of his head. "My IQ is nearly two hundred. A lot of good that will do me now. As intelligent as I am and as intelligent as other scientists and scholars are, they saw this coming but didn't do anything to prevent it. So shortsighted. It's mind boggling to think something as simple as a CME would destroy civilization. Truly fascinating."

Shep had no answer to that. Everything Ben had said was correct. *For as smart and as evolved we think we are as a human race, we are still extremely weak and fragile. It only took a couple of weeks for everything we had built over centuries and millennia to disappear.*

Following his thorough examination of the room, Ben sat down next to Shep and looked at him, emotionless.

"You're going to die soon," Ben said as matter-of-factly as when he uttered useless tidbits about Dinty Moore and the first bow.

Shep's eyes narrowed as he peered warily at Ben. *What was that supposed to mean? Maybe the history lesson on all things knives was about to come.*

"Unless you protect yourself," Ben continued. "I assume a bow would be your first choice?"

Part II
Chapter Five
Slaughterhouse

Shep tightly clutched the upper limb of his bow. The sun was just peeking above the horizon and cast a warm, yellow glow to the living room. Bands of sunlight glistened off the trophies in the case.

He could hear footsteps striking on the floorboards above him. Ben stood shielded behind him. "There's a good chance they're both going to come after us. Did you know the fastest time to shoot ten arrows is one minute, seven seconds? How fast can you shoot ten arrows?"

Shep hoped he wouldn't need to find out.

Murdock burst into the room. He stopped quickly and stared at the bow that Shep clutched. "Hey, guys. What … What's going on?"

Shep quickly changed his disposition. "I was just showing Ben here my bow. He wanted to see it. You hungry? Let's get you something to eat." Shep didn't see Bethany. That worried him. "Murdock, go get Bethany and we'll chow down."

Murdock frowned. "No. She's still not feeling too well. Sleep is what she needs. Let's let her sleep."

Shep looked at Ben, who shrugged, and they made their way into the kitchen. Shep had brought some canned goods upstairs and placed them in the cabinet where they once stored such things. He grabbed three cans of stew and tried to pry up a pull tab on one, but couldn't get his thick finger under it, his nails too short. It was a nasty habit, but he had picked and bitten his nails since early childhood. He reached for a knife in the cutlery block and noticed one was missing. He grabbed another one, popped the tabs up with the tip of it and pulled them open, pouring the stew into the bowls. "Sorry I can't heat these. The reason is obvious."

"Cold stew is nothing compared to some of the things we've been eating," Murdock said.

Shep figured they had a less discriminating palate in recent weeks. Anything was fair game: insects, rodents, even dogs and cats. *The drive to survive is strong, very strong.*

Murdock spooned the stew into his mouth slowly. Shep could tell he was preoccupied with something – *the best way to cut my throat, perhaps*.

Shep tried to take Murdock's mind off of whatever was troubling him. "What did you do before the Ejection?"

Murdock's head bounced up and a smile came upon his face. Shep could tell it was a subject he quite enjoyed talking about.

He told the story of Murdock Lynch, born and raised in Mars, Pennsylvania, and into a brood of mechanics. He gladly joined the family business and was a wizard with a wrench. He met a lovely woman named Bethany while he was very young and they wed soon after high school. Their first child, Benjamin, came soon after, but he wasn't born with motor oil in his veins. He was born with an insatiable thirst for knowledge and spent all his waking hours with his nose in a book.

Murdock and Bethany Lynch tried to have other children, but she miscarried five times before doctors told her she could not carry a fetus to term. It was devastating at the time, but they chose to focus on what they had, not what they couldn't. They had a bright young boy and a thriving business. Murdock had a Sprint car he raced at local dirt tracks on the weekends and he was quite successful, winning point championships nearly every season and earning the nickname, "The Mars Missile."

It was a good life. And in many ways, it still was. Even after the Ejection forced them from their home and made every day a struggle, they still chose to focus on what they had, not what they didn't.

"And now we're here, among a new friend," Murdock said. His smile was bright and harmless.

•••

Shep lounged on the couch, picking at his nails. A few of them bled and stung. *I need to stop that, but old habits ...*

Ben had his head buried in a book – *The Great Gatsby* – and turned page after page with a look of contempt on his face.

Bethany was still upstairs. A few times Murdock climbed a couple steps on the way to check on her, but stopped and instead paced the living room. This worried Shep much more than what state Bethany was in on the second floor.

Shep, growing weary – and dizzy – of watching Murdock stalk about, pushed himself off the couch. "Want me to check on her?"

Murdock's head snapped around. "That would be kind of you."

Shep looked at his bow, resting against the side of the couch. He thought about taking it, but wondered what reaction Murdock, already tense and on the verge of snapping, would have to that provocative action.

Ben slammed the book shut and contorted his lips strangely. "I don't get it. This book is lauded, and I've read it five times now, but I still don't get it. The writing is fine, but the story is rather boring. I can see now why only twenty-four-thousand copies were printed in F. Scott Fitzgerald's lifetime and why copies were stacked in a warehouse at the time of his death."

Shep had read the book a long time ago. He was probably in high school when he last turned those pages. As he recalled, he didn't get it either. At least that gave him one thing in common with Ben. "I'm going to go check on your mother. Read another. *Slaughterhouse-Five* is quite gripping. I'm a Vonnegut man myself."

In fact, so was Shep's mother. She had named him William – or Billy – after Billy Pilgrim, the protagonist of the book. Shep was nothing like his counterpart, although sometimes he wished he could get "unstuck in time," too. *How different things would be. So many things I would change.* But he knew such thoughts were futile. What happened has happened. He just hoped that in the end what he had done and what he would do would be forgiven, because like Vonnegut wrote: in Hell the "burning never stops hurting."

Shep walked slowly up the steps, wondering what he would find up there. He heard nothing from the guest room as he pressed his ear against the door. *Was she sleeping? Was she dead? Or was she just lying in wait for him to open that door?*

Shep turned the knob slowly and pushed the door open silently. He was glad the hinges didn't creek like others in the house and in the shelter. At least he would maintain some modicum of surprise should Bethany try to attack for some reason.

He peered in to see her spread out on her back, her arms and legs dangled over the edge of the small single mattress. Shep crept closer and stood over her. Her face was pale and a white crust was stuck on her skin at the corners of each of her eyes, which suddenly opened and were bloodshot and red.

She screamed and Shep backed away quickly. "Bethany, are you okay?"

She sat up and stared at him through those discolored eyes. White foam spilled from her lips and Shep could see bite marks made from a dog on her forearm, exposed by the rolled up sleeves of her white sweater.

Bethany Lynch charged at him and he quickly pulled out the knife he had stashed in his pocket, the one he used to pry open the pull tabs of the cans of stew, and stuck it into her neck as she dove at him. Blood squirted out like water from a sprinkler and she lay there, bleeding to death all over Anna's favorite throw rug.

It happened quite quickly. It took no more than a minute for Bethany to draw her last breath. Shep marveled at how rapidly the blood emptied from her body. *Such a strange thought at a time like this.*

Murdock and Ben had heard the commotion and raced upstairs, flying into the room to see the horrific scene.

"What the frig?" Murdock bellowed, falling to his knees and crawling over to his wife. *He must have never said a swear word in his life to say a thing like, "Frig."*

Such a strange thought at a time like this.

"Bethany. My poor Bethany." He rubbed his fingers through her hair. "You are free now. No more pain."

"Murdock, I didn't have a choice. She was crazy and she attacked me. I was just protecting myself. There was nothing we could do for her."

Murdock continued to brush her hair with his fingers. "I know, Shep. I know. I wanted to come up here so many times to do what you did. But I just couldn't do it." Murdock dropped the missing knife on the floor. Ben picked it up and stared at it oddly. "You did what I couldn't do, and I thank you for that."

Ben was as emotionless as ever. "Did you know rabies was eradicated in the United Kingdom?"

Shep closed his eyes and tried to slow his breathing, which was a difficult chore. Murdock had set him up, but that didn't much matter to Shep right now. What did matter was he had taken a life and, even though it was justified, it affected him more profoundly than he ever thought it would.

He feared he was going to have to kill again soon. "Murdock, I have to ask you. Were you bitten?"

Murdock's hand stopped moving with Bethany's hair still twined around his fingers. "No. We pulled the dog off of her, Ben and I, and I beat it with a branch until it ran away. It never bit us. I swear."

"Even a small scratch can spread the virus," Ben said.

Shep wanted to trust Murdock, wanted to believe what he was

saying to be true. He decided to give him the benefit of the doubt. "Let's give her a proper burial."

"Wait until the saliva dries first, to limit exposure," Ben said in his monotone voice. "The virus is transmitted through saliva, and Shep, you have cuts on your fingers from picking at them. A terrible habit. You should stop. When the saliva dries, the virus dies."

Shep shoved his hands into his pockets. "Good to know."

•••

Shep understood why they did not want to sleep upstairs; Instead Murdock and Ben lay on the floor in the living room. Shep sat on the couch, his bow on his lap, and tried to stay awake.

Inhale. Exhale. Inhale. Exhale. The room began to shake as Shep desperately tried to keep his tired eyes open. *Inhale. Exhale. Inhale. Exhale.* His breathing became slower and his lids shut.

He had another dream, a glorious one, of Anna, her hand in his, walking on the sand of a beach by the ocean. The cool breeze on his face and the smell of the salt water was so real and so soothing. So was the way she smiled and pecked him on the cheek, placing her head on his shoulder, the squeeze of her arm around his.

He wanted to stay there, stuck in that moment in time. But he became unstuck.

Murdock thrashed about on the floor, enraged, waking Shep with a jolt. Murdock was yelling, "Bethany, my sweet Bethany" over and over again. Shep feared he was becoming rabid. There was only one thing left to do.

He drew the arrow back and pointed it at Murdock, who was now wide-eyed and staring at him in the flickering light of the candles.

Shep fired an arrow into his chest. Murdock flailed, grabbed the stem of the bolt with both hands and attempted to yank it out. Shep grabbed another arrow, aimed and fired it into his chest again. This one brought to an end Murdock's desperate thrashes.

It took Murdock much longer to expire than Bethany. Shep watched as he squirmed a bit, his eyes big and staring in disbelief before the life escaped from them.

Shep slumped back onto the couch, dropped the bow and slammed his head into his palms. He wept for Murdock.

He heard Ben rustle. Shep pulled his head out of his hands to see what he was doing. Ben pulled his father's shirt, tearing around the arrows, up to his chin, and then rolled up his pant legs one at a time. He pushed his father on his side, the bolts holding him up like the kickstand of a bicycle, and continued his examination before saying, "Shep. I don't see any scratches or bite marks."

Shep fell to the floor on his knees, crawled over to Murdock and looked him over, too. Like Ben, he found no visible scratches or bites.

"Oh, God," Shep said.

"You didn't know, Shep. He could just have easily been infected. You just never know. Rabies can present with rage or with lethargy. They call that 'dumb rabies.'"

Who cares what it's called! He had needlessly murdered Murdock. "He was agitated. I thought he was going to attack me or you. He was just having a bad dream. He was just having a nightmare."

"Easy mistake," Ben said. "I guess I'm an orphan now. Did you know there are approximately one hundred and twenty three thousand orphans in the United States? I suppose those numbers are much higher now after the Ejection. Or smaller, since most orphans probably died. Calculating the number now is near impossible."

Shep envied Ben. He was incapable of feeling. He was a robot, an android. *He was Data from Star Trek with better skin.* He marveled at how he could watch both of his parents die within hours of each other and not shed so much as a tear. It was a blessing these days to be able to pull off such a feat, to be incapable of emotion, of empathy, of warmth.

His parents were dead and he might as well be, too.

"You're not alone, Ben," Shep said. "You can stay here as long as you like."

•••

Morning came and with it the cold and gruesome reality of what he had done. Murdock lay in a pool of blood and Shep's feet squished on the soaked carpet.

Shep peered down at Murdock's open eyes, still frozen in shock and fear, and hoped he would forgive him. Someone had to grant Shep some solace; if not Murdock then maybe his son.

Ben was nowhere to be found. His bloody footprints led from the living room toward the kitchen. Shep followed them, yelling, "Hey, Ben," as he walked.

Shep's eyes met the back of Ben's head. He stood at the sink, peering out over the yard that was drenched in sunshine. Ben scratched at his back vigorously.

"Ben, about your father …" Shep said, pausing to try to find the right words to say next. Ben didn't give him a chance to show off his vocabulary. He twirled, his eyes red and bloodshot, holding the knife his father had dropped.

"You have to kill me." Ben scratched again at his shoulder. "I'm infected."

Shep shook his head vigorously. The prospect of killing again made him feel ill. "No, Ben. I can't. There has to be another way. A treatment. Something. Come on, you're smart. Dazzle me with something we can do to fix you."

Ben bit his lower lip. A small amount of white foam leaked out of the corner of his mouth. "There's nothing that can be done. I'm already dead. Killing me now is merciful. It's only logical."

I was wrong. Ben is more like Spock with better ears.

Strange thought at a time like this.

Shep retreated to the living room and grabbed his bow. He stared at it remorsefully. He plucked an arrow out of the quiver, but before he could turn, Ben came barreling into the room, swiping at him with the knife.

Shep put his right arm up as a shield and felt the blade slice into his forearm. He kicked Ben, pushed him, then reached for his bow and backed away.

"You have to kill me, Shep," Ben pleaded. "Shoot me through the eye. The arrow will go right through my temporal lobe, and if your aim is as good as those trophies suggest it is, the arrow will hit my brain stem. I'll die instantly."

Shep quickly readied the arrow on the string, blood dripped from his arm as he pulled the bolt back and aimed at Ben's right eye.

"Do it now. You may not get ...," Ben fell to the floor. The force of the arrow so great, it punctured the rear of his skull, the tip poking out through the back of his head as he crumpled.

Shep dropped the bow. It hit the floor, causing a splash from the blood-soaked carpet. He slumped down on the couch again, staring coldly forward. Ben had rubbed off on him. He felt nothing.

•••

Shep dug three holes in the hard and rocky Western Pennsylvania earth, each of similar size and depth. It had taken him the better part of the day in the scorching sun, but he had finished.

He rolled Bethany into the first hole and covered her with dirt. Then Murdock, shoveling the clay full of tiny pebbles and rocks onto him.

Then he rolled Ben's body into the last hole and began covering him with soil. Every shovel full of dirt Shep poured on him came closer to erasing him from existence. Too bad he couldn't erase him from his memory as easily.

"And so it goes," Shep mumbled to himself.

Part II
Chapter Six
Parker's Pecker

Shep trudged a day through the hard, thick snow and kept warm the best he could. He had enough food provided by the new leader of Attica, Ward Webster, to last a few weeks if he was careful. He melted snow for drinking water and heated his bones by a fire he started at night.

He also had the bow Ward had scrounged up for him in what used to be the sporting goods store of Attica. It was a compound bow and cheaply made, not like the hand crafted ones he used in competitions, and he only had a six-pack of equally cheap aluminum arrows as ammunition. But they were going to have to do.

His thoughts often wandered to Antigone and Patrick. He wasn't much for prayer, but he looked toward God often lately, hoping He would guide them to a better life, to Halcyon if it existed – he prayed hard for that, too – and to her brother, food, shelter and happiness.

Shep kicked snow over the smoldering fire. The sky was a burnt red to the east and black to the west. That's where he was headed, into the black.

He came upon a road lined with poles that held up wires that had been long since rendered useless. They used to buzz with power. They were the veins that brought blood to that old life and now they were clamped and dead, just like that old existence. Shep beat down that road, icy and cold, for miles until he saw a figure leaning against a pole in the distance.

He hesitated at first, wary to approach. *It could be a raider looking to pick off wanderers like me*. He approached anyway. As he got closer he determined it was not a person propping himself up against the pole, but one bound to it. As he drew nearer, he could see the body was limp and pale, blood dried and blotted on his coat. There was a lot of blood. His face was red and nearly unrecognizable, until he looked more closely.

He gasped and his stomach turned. It was Patrick. A piece of barbed wire dug deep into his throat, which was also slit from ear to ear. His face was bloated and crows had pecked out his eyes and left nothing but the empty sockets. His hands, skin filleted to the bone and a few fingers missing on each, were bound behind him.

Shep turned and puked, the site so grizzly he could not keep down the water and jerky he had consumed before he began his march on this day. It colored the snow a putrid yellow.

Shep spat out the last hunk of vomit still stuck in his mouth. "Jesus," he said. "Oh, Jesus."

Panicked, he looked around at the surrounding poles to his right, and then twirled with uncommon speed to peer back to the left. He was relieved to not see Antigone tied to one. There was nothing but snowy fields on either side of him. Large footprints cut into the pack led away over the road and through a field. He stuck his foot in one and determined whoever made them must have worn size thirteen or fourteen shoes. Another smaller set of prints led away from the pole across the other field.

He resisted the urge to yell Antigone's name for fear whoever had done this to Patrick was still nearby.

He had no idea which sets of footprints to follow to look for her and his mind produced only terrible scenarios of her fate. He could feel his heart pounding and his desperate eyes well with tears. Images of Antigone, lifeless and hanging on a pole, filled his head. He quickly expelled them.

Shep didn't know what to do and it was an uncomfortable feeling. He always knew what to do.

He vomited again as he searched Patrick for clues. The hideous sight of him was bad enough, but the stench of rotting flesh was worse. He rooted through Patrick's pockets, first in his coat, then in his green cargo pants. Finally, Shep sunk his hand into the front pocket of Patrick's flannel shirt and felt something cold and round. Shep hoped it wasn't one of Patrick's missing fingers when he pulled it out, but it was a tube of lipstick marked "Twilight Nude."

Shep stuffed it into the pocket of his wool coat and eyed his surroundings again. *Where could she be?* He hoped she had escaped. He thought about praying for it, but decided God wasn't listening.

He chose to follow the small prints that led away from the poles.

Each step he took in the hard, wet snow sounded like the crunching of bones. He thought about the pain Patrick must have endured in his final moments and his stomach began to turn. He surely would have vomited again had there been anything left in his stomach.

He trudged on until he saw a house, smoke billowing out of the chimney. *Either Antigone had sought shelter there, or the ones who slaughtered Patrick had. Someone had walked here from that pole.*

The sun broke through the clouds and reflected brightly off the white roof of the dilapidated home. The snow had begun to melt, revealing crumbling brown shingles. The house itself looked to be barely standing. The wood was rotting and the aqua blue paint peeling. The wooden porch was leaning profoundly to the right and brown grass poked up through the snow cover throughout the large property.

The wood creaked under his feet as he climbed the rickety steps onto the porch and the door groaned when he pushed it open. He could smell firewood burning and heard it crackle and he could already feel the warmth it generated.

The light of the fire flickered off the walls, some of them littered with holes. He peered around the corner into an empty living area. A mattress was strewn on the warped floor in front of the fireplace where the flames licked and clothes were haphazardly piled next to it.

Shep crept inside, trying to be quiet, but that was made impossible by the floor board that whined with each of his steps.

A voice called out from behind him. "That's far enough."

It was an older man, his white hair so thin the skin of his scalp showed through. He was frail looking – *wasn't everyone these days* – and he pointed what looked to be a shotgun as old as he in Shep's direction.

Shep raised his hands. "I mean you no harm. I'm just looking for someone. Maybe you've seen my friend."

The old man thrust his shotgun at him angrily. "I haven't seen anyone, except for you, in weeks. You better get going before I make a twitch and blow a hole clean through you."

Shep sensed something was wrong. Maybe it was the way he looked at him, not as a man protecting his property, but as a man protecting a lie.

"There were footprints in the snow leading here from the ..." Shep said, hesitating, "road. I'm just trying to find my friend."

He was unmoved. "I told you I haven't seen her. Now go. Go now."

Sunshine broke through the windows and glistened off water droplets on the floor that lead through a doorway behind the old man, whose eyes narrowed and wrinkled face contorted angrily. "Are you deaf? Git."

Shep hadn't said he was looking for a girl, yet the old man said he hadn't seen *her*.

"Okay. I'm going. Once again, sorry for intruding."

Shep hit the cold air and raced down the steps of the leaning porch, fearing it may topple down on top of him. *She's in there. Maybe hurt. Definitely his prisoner.*

He hoped she could hang on for a few more hours.

•••

It was a nearly moonless night, only a shard of it hung in the darkened sky, and Shep struggled to make his way back to the house. He could see the faint glow of a fire and candlelight in the windows as he approached.

He made his way to the bulkhead that led down into the cellar and pried the doors open. The wood was brittle and the lock broke with just a few tugs.

Shep felt his way around the dark basement. He could hear his feet squish on something he didn't care to identify as he finally made his way to the stairs that led up to the first floor. He could hear a muffled conversation through the boards and hear several sets of feet pace above him. He could not make out if Antigone was one of the voices he heard or if a set of clumping feet belonged to her.

He drew his bow, felt for an arrow in his bag and put it between the index and middle finger of his right hand. The door swung open silently and he could better make out the conversation.

A man spoke, "She's just a girl. Don't go sticking that thing in her."

Another chimed in, "I just want to have a little go at her. I won't hurt her. I swear."

He heard what sounded like a punch, then a loud thump on the floor. "You so much as touch a hair on her head and you are going to be pissing sitting down for the rest of your sorry ass life. You hear me?"

At least someone was looking out for her.

Shep crept closer, hunched down into a shadow and peeked carefully around the corner of the crumbling wall. He could see a man on the floor looking up and another hulking over him. The man on the floor was a boy, really, with a straggly beard and wearing a bright orange hunting cap. The man who stood over him appeared older, thicker, and also wore a hunting cap, his camouflage.

Shep stood, took a deep breath and spun into the room, pulling back on the arrow as he did. "Where is she?"

The men turned their heads, startled.

"Who the fuck are you?" the man on the floor asked.

"Shut up, Parker. Let me do the talking," the other man said. "I don't know who you are talking about, friend."

Parker pushed himself up off the floor. "Yeah. You're in our house, motherfucker."

Shep pulled the aluminum bolt back farther. He feared the cheap bowstring would snap. "One of you better start talking."

Parker pointed and waved an angry finger at Shep. "Don't say shit to this fucker, Sam."

"I heard you talking about a girl. Where is she?"

Sam shrugged his shoulders. "Girl? What girl?"

Shep laughed incredulously. "Don't play dumb. Ol' Parker here wanted a go at her after all. Isn't that right, Parker?"

In the flickering light of the fire, Shep could see Parker reach for something behind his back. Shep didn't give him a chance to grab it. The arrow lodged in his crotch, just where Shep had aimed, and Parker screamed as he fell to his back and grabbed at the bolt.

Sam gasped. "Shit! Shit! What did you do that for?"

"I guess Parker will be peeing sitting down for the rest of his sorry ass life after all." Shep grabbed another arrow and readied it against the string. "This is fun. You wanna go next, Sam? Where is she?"

Shep could barely hear Sam over Parker's cries. "Okay. Okay. I'll take you to her."

The barn had long been empty, but the stench of animals was still strong. Sam, his hands held high so as not to provoke an attack on his genitals from Shep, walked him to the back of the barn to a stack of hay piled high. A lantern, burning brightly, hung from a rafter in the corner. She lay on top of the bales, her back to them, but Shep could see her flowing raven hair.

"Tig," Shep bellowed, shaking her. "Tig, it's Shep."

She awoke, trembling, and rolled over quickly, pulling her knees tight to her chest. The light from the lantern filled her face and Shep sighed and gritted his teeth.

It was not Antigone. This girl was all of fourteen, her lip cut and swollen and her eye puffy. *Probably from a jab of the fist from Parker.* Her eyes were big and round and stared at him timidly.

"You can take her," Sam said. "We didn't mean her no harm. She wandered onto our property yesterday scared and crying. She said she had seen a man tied to a post dead and just ran until she got here. Parker got to her first. He has a … problem."

Shep turned to Sam and bristled. "Not anymore."

"I tried to protect her, but my brother has drives that pop up that I never understood," Sam pleaded. "Just go. We don't want any trouble."

Shep held his hand out to the girl. "Don't be afraid. I'll help you. What's your name?"

She pulled back as far as she could and shook like a leaf in a stiff wind. A tear rolled down her bruised and swollen cheek. "I know you don't trust me, but I promise I'm not going to hurt you. I'll take you anywhere you want to go. Do you have family?"

The girl nodded and her voice crackled. "Skye. My name is Skye."

The lump in Shep's throat was so big he thought he would never be able to swallow again. "I knew a girl named Skye once. She was pretty like you. I wasn't able to help her, but I can help you – if you'll let me." He held out his hand to her again. She reached out hers, but then pulled it back under the loose sleeve of her coat. She hesitantly reached it out again and placed it in his. It was cold and smooth.

He helped her down and she squeezed his hand tightly. "I don't live far from here," she said. "I just want to go home."

Sam stood aside and let them pass. "This is over, right? I mean, I protected her from Parker and I led you to her. No grudge?"

Just then the old man with the shotgun burst in. He pointed it at Shep, who held his pose … and his breath.

"What the hell is going on," the old man said. "Parker is lying in there with an arrow sticking out of his pecker."

Sam stood between the old man and Shep. "It's all right, Pop. They're leaving."

"Did you put an arrow in Parker's pecker?" the man asked. Despite the direness of the situation, Shep nearly burst into laughter. He held back his chuckle. "Yes, sir."

The old man lowered his shotgun. "About time someone stopped him. He thinks because the world ended he can stick that thing into anything that moves. Just go. Get outta my sight."

Shep and Skye left the barn, hand in hand.

She wasn't lying when she said she lived close. It took just thirty minutes of a leisurely pace to reach a large house surrounded by tall red pines. A man, his face drawn and his eyes sunk and circled by deep dark bags burst out of the house, pointing a gun at Shep. He was thin and his arms looked disproportionately longer than they should be. But he held the gun, an old revolver, steady and true.

I am growing very tired of people pointing guns at me.

"What are you doing with my daughter?" The man's voice was deep and booming, the kind of voice that carries and hits like a hammer.

That also did not sync with his slight frame.

"Daddy, stop," Skye yelled. "He saved me. He rescued me."

The man lowered his weapon. "He did, huh?" His tired eyes looked Shep up and down and up and down again before the next words boomed out of his lips. "Then I guess I owe you my gratitude. Name's Cyril. Come in. Let me give you something to eat."

The inside of the house was immaculate. The floors were rich parquet. The windows were large, beveled and stained glass and were framed with white sash. Plush couches and chairs covered every inch of the available space in the living room and flower pattern wallpaper hung on every wall.

The dining area was also stunning. A large oak dinner table sat in the middle of the room under a crystal chandelier. Five ceramic bowls were set at the table on top of cream colored doilies. Shep sat on an oak chair, its back rising much higher than his head.

Cyril sat across from him with Skye to his left. She smiled at Shep almost freakishly, unnerving him a bit.

"Mia will be out with the food shortly," Cyril said. "How did you come upon my daughter?"

Shep cleared his throat. "I was looking for a friend of mine. I thought she had come that way. I saw tracks and followed them to that house. That's where I found your daughter. I was glad to help, but I must ask Skye about something she might have seen before they got her."

Cyril turned to Skye, whose unsettling smile had turned to a frown. She whispered, "I don't want to talk about it."

"I hope you like stew," Mia charged into the room, carrying a steaming kettle. She set it in the middle of the table and stirred it with a ladle, plopped in the chair next to Shep and said, "Dig in."

"Where are our guests?" Cyril asked.

Mia scooped up some stew and sloshed it into her bowl. "I think some of them might have left. The strange one is still sleeping. That's probably for the best."

Shep poured a ladle full of the stew into his bowl and took a spoonful into his mouth. "This is delicious."

"Thanks, dear."

Skye stared somberly at her bowl.

"Don't you want any, honey?" Mia asked with a concerned voice.

"I'm not hungry."

Shep figured she had been through a lot today and the sight of Patrick lashed to the pole was still singed in her mind. It haunted him as well. He also figured she may have seen who was responsible and perhaps even knew where Antigone was. But she wasn't talking, at least not now. Shep couldn't afford to waste any more time.

Before Shep could speak again, he heard feet banging loudly on the floorboards above.

Stomp! Stomp! Stomp!

Then he heard the pounding of feet coming down the stairs.

Stomp! Stomp! Stomp!

Then through the living room.

Stomp! Stomp! Stomp!

Bray stood in the doorway with a devilish smile. "What's for dinner?"

Part II
Chapter Seven
Charming Billy Boy

Bray sat next to Skye and grabbed the ladle with his right hand. The scar was big and discolored on his palm and he struggled to get a firm grip on the handle. "This hand isn't what it used to be," he said, squinting angrily at Shep.

Suddenly, Shep had lost his appetite.

Bray slurped some stew from his spoon loudly – *Bray never did anything quietly* – and set it down with a clank on the table and patted his stomach, "Shit, that was good. Nothing like a good home-cooked meal, eh, Shep?"

Cyril cocked his head. "You two know each other?"

"Know each other? We were practically best bros,'" Bray cackled. "Boy, we have some stories we could tell, huh, Shep? Like the time you stabbed your wife nine times in the chest and stomach."

Bray held his scarred right hand up high. "Or the time you shot an arrow through my palm and then through the eye of my fucking wife!"

Cyril leaned back in his chair and began to stand, but a whimper from Skye stopped him. Bray made a tsk fall from his lips. "I wouldn't do that, Cyril. I have a gun in little Skye's ribs and, as Shep will tell you, I'm pretty good at killing Skyes."

Cyril pleaded to Shep with his eyes, but there was little he could do now. There was no reasoning with Bray – *he was out for blood, anyone's blood, and he was going to take it.*

"Bray, let these people go," Shep said in a voice as calm as he could make it. "We'll leave together and we can sort all of this out."

"Sounds good. There's a post out there with your name on it." Bray motioned for Shep to stand and he did, slowly, holding his hands up so Bray could see them. Bray marched him out to the road and each step Shep took brought him closer to his end, he thought.

"I'm going to enjoy this," Bray said.

"As much as you enjoyed killing Patrick?"

"Who? Oh, that Backstreet Boy? I have to give him a lot of credit. I had to skin his hands to the bone and then take a finger until he told me you were in that crazy town. It took a few more fingers until he finally told me where that little bitch was, though. Love. So powerful and shit. Imagine my surprise when I came down those stairs and you were in that dining room. It was like Christmas morning, dude. I guess there are no coincidences. This is fate, man."

They were getting nearer to the spot where Patrick hung. Bray was following so closely, Shep could feel the heat from his breath on the back of his neck. Shep stopped. He wasn't going to walk a step farther.

Shep turned to face Bray. "If you're gonna kill me, just do it now. I'm not gonna play your little game."

"That's not how this works, man. Move."

"Sorry. I'll die here."

Bray's eyes narrowed and he shook his head. "Maybe this will change your mind." He pointed his gun, aimed and fired. Shep could feel the bullet burn through his left hand and could feel the bones in it split. The pain snaked all the way up his arm as he slumped to his knees, grasping his wrist as the blood trickled down onto the white snow. He tried to stand, but his legs gave out on him and he stumbled back down to his knees. "I was nicer than you were. I picked your left hand. Now get the fuck up."

Shep was defiant. Even if he could stand, he wouldn't now. "No, Bray."

"Jesus Christ, you are thick," Bray barked. "Fine. Have it your way." He leveled the gun at him and Shep could see right down its barrel. He closed his eyes and thought of Antigone. Her smile, her eyes, her laugh. That was the last thing he wanted to see before the end.

His eyes shot open when he heard groans coming from Bray. Someone rode him and poked a finger knuckle-deep into his right eye. Bray bucked wildly, like an angry horse trying to throw a rider attempting to break him. He flailed his arms and was lucky enough to make contact with the side of his attacker's head, flinging his foe onto the snow. In his desperate attempt to get free, Bray had dropped his gun and Shep reached out for it with his right hand, getting enough of it with his fingers to pull it close enough to grab. He pointed it at Bray, who galloped away into the darkness. Shep fired a shot, and then another. He pulled the trigger again, but only heard a click. He had no idea if either of the bullets he fired found the mark.

He crawled over to the figure lying in the snow and rolled it over. It was Antigone, her eyes glassed over, a large cut above her right eye.

"Tig!" Shep shook her, leaving a bloody handprint on her coat. "Tig!"

She stirred and cupped his face in her hand. "I saved your ass again," she smiled. "You owe me one."

•••

Mia met them on the porch with a towel that she wrapped tightly around Shep's hand. Skye pressed another white towel on Antigone's brow as they made their way into the living room and slumped onto the plush antique couch.

By now, the pain pulsating through his hand was nearly unbearable and he felt like vomiting, but he choked it down.

Mia peeked under the towel at Shep's hand and cringed. "This looks bad. Really bad."

Skye continued to press her cloth on Antigone's head. Bray's blood stained her swollen index finger.

Cyril sat slumped in a chair, frowning. A shotgun lay across his lap. "Was what that man said true?"

Shep gritted his teeth against the pain. "Yes. Except for the stabbing-my-wife-to-death part. I didn't do that. The other stuff I did, though."

Cyril fumed, but spoke quite calmly for a man who just had chaos break loose in his home. He probably fought hard and long to keep such things away from his family and in the course of a day, his young teenage daughter was kidnapped, beaten and nearly raped and a psychopath had eaten stew and threatened to kill them in their home.

Yes, I am not his favorite person right now.

"I want you gone. I want you out of my house. Now."

Mia protested. "Cyril, we can't just throw them out. He's badly hurt. That hand looks terrible and I think the infection is already setting in."

Cyril pushed himself up out of that chair and stood over Shep now. His thin finger pointed right at his eyes. "Sounds to me like you deserved what was coming to you. I'll give you tonight, but in the morning, you're gone. You hear me? Both of you."

•••

Shep's hand ached and his fingers tingled, like a million needle pricks. It was an uncomfortable feeling and nothing like he had ever experienced before. The only thing that made him forget about the pain was the pounding in his head.

Antigone felt his forehead with the back of her hand. Her index finger, twice its normal size and probably broken from the force of jamming it into an eye socket, was turning bright purple. "You have a fever."

Shep felt like he did. He remembered the feeling well from when he was a little boy, stricken with strep throat and scarlet fever more times than he dared count. It always started the same: the chills, the aches from his joints, the way things looked oddly shaped to him, like they were skinnier or fatter than they should.

Antigone sat next to him on the bed, rubbing her hands through his damp hair. "Did you see Patrick?"

Shep didn't know what she meant by that. *Did he see him, as in on that pole, dead and mutilated? Or did he "see" him, alive and well.* Shep chose the latter interpretation. He loathed lying to her, but he would have loathed telling her the truth profoundly more. *How do you tell someone her love has been brutally murdered and displayed on an electric pole? You just don't. There had to be a written law somewhere, perhaps in Rhian's commandments. I'll have to check when this fever breaks.*

"What? No. I didn't see him, Tig. I didn't see Padrig."

Antigone's face became somber. "He's been gone for days now. He went back to help you in Attica. He said his mom wouldn't kill him, she wasn't that crazy. I thought that's how you got out."

Damn, it's cold. He shivered and Antigone covered him with a warm blanket. *Wow. There are dolphins on this comforter. Anna liked dolphins.*

"How … how did you find me?" Shep asked.

"I was here the whole time. When Bray came, I heard him say that stupid line he always said when he begged for food, so I hid in the cellar. It was so hard to stay down there when I heard your voice. I was so happy to hear it, but I knew Bray was up there and I prayed he wouldn't just kill you on the spot."

Bray, that arrogant ass. I should have shot him through the eye with an arrow, too. Through both eyes. Given him glasses made of fletching. Why didn't I shoot him through the eye with an arrow? Or through the back of the neck as he walked away, through that hair and through that stupid "n." It was an "n," a fancy "n," but it was still an "n." Symbol for strength, my ass. It was a fancy "n."

"Why are you crying?" Antigone asked, feeling his head again. "Oh my God, you're burning up."

Anna stood beside Antigone. Her hair was short and dyed red, just like when they met. She looked beautiful and peered down at him lovingly. Behind her were all he had slain, Murdock and Bethany, Ben and Bray's wife, the fletching still poking out of their eyes. They stood there and smiled.

"The Lord our God is merciful and forgiving, even though we have rebelled against him," Anna whispered.

Why have they come to me now? Why have they forgiven me? I do not deserve it. I am no better than Bray the Beast. I have murdered and maimed. I have thought of only myself. How many more lives will I take? How many more souls will suffer because of me?

He sobbed and Antigone tried to shush him. She sang to him, a song her mother once hummed to her, he thought, and one his mother did to him when he was a little boy, sick with strep.

"*Did she ask you to come in, Billy Boy, Billy Boy? Did she ask you to come in, Charming Billy?*"

Antigone kissed his boiling cheek.

"Yes she asked me to come in, there's a dimple on her chin ..."

He felt her lips on his. They were cold and tasted sweet. "Looks like I'm going to have to save your ass again."

Part II
Chapter Eight
From Old Comes New

Red rain ruining her white dress.
Blood flowing over her veil, dripping on the white marble floors.
"Why?" Antigone whispers. "Why did you not tell me?"

•••

The walls were striped like a zebra in alternating patterns of moonlight and darkness. Shep held up his left hand, wrapped heavily in gauze. His fingers no longer tingled and the pain no longer shot up his arm like an electric current.

Antigone sat on a chair on the other side of the room, her knees pressed up to her chest, her arms crossed on top of them, her chin dug into her forearms.

"Look who's awake," Antigone said.

Shep tried to sit up to get a better look at her in the pale light, but the room spun too fast and too violently, so he thought it best to lay his head back down. "What happened?"

"I did what I said I would. I saved your sorry ass again," she said as disdain flooded her voice.

"I don't believe you used the word sorry the last time," Shep joked.

"No, I added that after I found this in the pocket of your coat." Shep felt something land on his lap and he lifted his head just enough so he could see it. It was the tube of Twilight Nude lipstick. "I gave that to Pat when he left to go to Attica to help you, so he had something of mine on his trip. You said you hadn't seen him, but that obviously was a lie.

Where is he, Shep? You owe me that much."

There was no getting out of this one. His lips began to quiver and a rush of tears blurred his vision. He blinked them away and searched for words, any combination of syllables that would lessen the blow of what he was about to tell her, but he knew there just weren't any. There was no language, no order of speech that could soften this message.

"Tig, I didn't want to tell you. How can I tell you?"

Antigone bolted out of the chair and plopped on the mattress next to him. She thrust her face close to his. Her breath was hot on his. "You better be careful what words come out of your mouth right now, Billy Shepard! You tell me the truth. Don't sugar-coat it. Don't try to make me feel any better, because you won't be able to."

Antigone began to cry now. Shep could feel warm tears fall on his cheek. "I just want the next thing you say to be what happened to Pat and where I can find his body."

"He's tied to a post, tortured and mutilated," Shep sniffed snot back up into his nostrils. "Bray killed him. He was trying to get Patrick to lead him to me and you."

Antigone put her head on his chest and sighed. She had known Patrick's fate deep down for days now, he thought. She was just holding out the slimmest amount of hope that she was wrong. That was what was so special about her – her capacity for hope. If she were to lose that, it would be an even bigger tragedy.

Shep put his right hand on her head and began to stroke her hair. It felt like strands of silk. She slapped it away, raised her head and peered at him, fuming. "Why?" she said, her chest heaving in anger. "Why didn't you tell me?"

It was for all the usual reasons, he thought. To spare her. To keep her from pain. At this moment, though, he knew that to be a lie. He withheld the truth from her to spare himself, so he wouldn't have to bring her such pain and loss. He had brought pain and loss to so many. He couldn't bear to do it again.

He told Antigone as much, and her scorn melted away. It was probably the most honest thing he had ever told another human being, even his wife, even himself. It was honest and pure and anyone would be lucky to have such a moment.

She placed her head back down on his chest. "What am I going to do, Shep?" She let out another long sigh.

He put his hand on her back and rubbed it gently. "Look for your Halcyon."

She pressed her head harder into his chest. "I miss … him."

•••

In the light of the morning, Shep could see the toll the last 48 hours had taken on Antigone. She had a large welt under her eye and her lip was swollen and bruised. She had a bandage wrapped around her right bicep with a blot of blood oozing through the gauze. She popped the cap off a bottle and shook out two pills into her palm. She swallowed one and gave Shep the other.

"Don't ask me how I got these antibiotics," Antigone said. "It'll only make you mad."

Shep had learned not to push Antigone for answers. She was not one to be interrogated. He let the matter slide. "I see Cyril lifted his eviction notice."

Antigone chuckled. "No, Mia did. The woman is always the sensible one. Don't you forget it."

She sat next to him on the bed and peered down at him with a smile. Those lines were back. *Oh, how I missed that grin.* "It's just temporary. As soon as you are well enough, we have to hit the road again, Jack."

Shep sat up. The room didn't spin like a carnival ride, it just teetered a bit – a huge improvement from the night before. "I hope you won't go to Patrick's body."

"Already did. It's gone," Antigone said. "Either wild animals tore it down and dragged it away, or someone else. It's okay. I already said my goodbyes."

Mia brought up some broth and Shep sipped it slowly. It felt good going down his throat and into his stomach. His hand throbbed a bit, but he could wiggle his fingers now without much discomfort.

"You almost lost that hand," Antigone said, running her swollen and bruised index finger over the digits that poked out from under the gauze. They both winced. "Cyril was sharpening his butcher knife. I think he would have enjoyed cutting it off."

"I'm glad he didn't get the chance."

"What are we going to do about Bray?" Antigone asked somberly. "I mean, he's still out there and he's more pissed than ever, I bet."

"He's also a Cyclops now." That coaxed a smile and a giggle out of Antigone. "Remind me never to go ten rounds with you."

"Seriously, Shep. He ain't gonna give up. He's a fucking psychopath."

Shep knew that better than most. He hoped that maybe his wound had become infected, or he bled to death, or one of his blind shots into the night had hit Bray, severing a vital artery, but he knew none of those things to be true. People like Bray rarely perish in such mundane ways. They don't crawl off to die somewhere silently. No, it takes an extraordinary feat, a grand measure to end them.

Shep feared he was fresh out of grand measures.

•••

Cyril hadn't slept much in the weeks since that night when Bray came, instead choosing to guard his family and his house vigilantly. Bray hadn't returned, but that didn't mean he was gone.

He could tell the desperation Cyril had to get them on their way. Shep was able to stand and keep down solid food now. His hand was healing, the infection gone. All that meant was it was time to go.

Skye hugged Shep tightly before they left, to the great displeasure of Cyril, who clenched his jaw. *And probably bit his tongue a little.* If his eyes were bows, Shep certainly would have two arrows stuck in him now. "Protect your father for me," Shep said to Skye, prompting a coo from her.

Mia packed them some provisions, enough to last a few weeks. "I wish you didn't have to go so soon," Mia said apologetically. "But you know Cyril."

Actually, Shep didn't really know Cyril. Probably never would. He did know enough to see he was a devoutly protective man. That got people pretty far in this new life. Skye and Mia would be well taken care of.

Shep and Antigone set out again on their journey to Halcyon, their eyes looking ahead with promise and hope – and back with anxiety and foreboding. Bray was probably out there somewhere, lurking, following and waiting for the right time to strike. They would have to be steadfast and alert.

Antigone's eyes darted about as they walked toward the setting sun. Every branch that jostled and cracked in a stiff wind and every howl of a coyote startled her.

Shep was on edge, too. He was just a little better at hiding it. He made his words sound as reassuring as possible when he spoke. "Maybe one of those coyotes mauled him. Or maybe a bobcat. Maybe he tripped and fell and banged his head and died. Accidents happen. He can't see very well, you know."

That made Antigone smile. It was a big one as they walked on a dirt path that weaved through the woodland. She stepped over a root that snaked in front of them as she spoke. "I just wish I could have gotten a finger in both of his beady eyes. Then we'd be safe."

The sun had dipped below the horizon and the chill had returned. Most of the snow had melted, but there still remained some random patches of white. They made camp, Shep with his flimsy bow on his lap as he sat in front of the fire. They ate some of the food Mia had packed for them and Shep fashioned more arrows out of sticks he whittled into fine, sharp points, charring the tips over the hot coals. He crafted the fletching out of feathers he had collected on their march.

It wasn't easy for Shep to make them, his left hand still ached and his fingers were stiff, but he managed. The arrows were by no means perfect, but they would work in a pinch. They would certainly protect them should Bray make an appearance. They also could be used to hunt game to keep meat in their bellies.

Antigone slept fitfully on the hard ground as Shep took the first watch. He reacted to every noise. Every sound seemed ominous. Every movement caused by the wind rustling branches or a small animal treading through the brown brush seemed threatening.

He was more concerned about when it was his turn to sleep. He trusted Antigone, but he slumbered so deeply, he feared he would not wake quickly or alert enough to take action should Bray show his deformed face.

They made it through the first night. And the second. And the third. They marched on, wary and guarded. At times Shep had the sense they were being followed, but he eventually chalked that up to paranoia.

Perhaps Bray wasn't out there after all. Maybe they were rid of Bray the Beast.

•••

The weather was starting to break now, the days longer, the sun staying higher in the sky. The air smelled fresh and new.

Shep opened and closed his left hand as they walked. It was getting stronger, but it would never be like it once was. The bullet had broken bones as it passed through and they hadn't properly healed. He had a rather large white bump in the middle of his palm and on the top of his hand where the calcium deposit had grown out of control. It looked almost like a golf ball was encased in the flesh. It had become convenient, though, his palm serving as quite an effective hammer to break the wild black walnuts they scrounged on their march.

They had made much better progress than the last time they set out for Halcyon. Shep was surprised at how few organized bands of gangs and raiders they saw on their journey. Perhaps things were getting better. Perhaps nature had done her job, weeding out the weak, weeding out the excess.

Survival of the fittest. That crazy Darwin.

It was a good thing, too, because there was a scarcity of places to hide. The landscape was flat and they often found themselves walking through fields of wheat and grain, no one left to harvest it.

It also made for some incredible star gazing. Most nights they lay, looking up at the sky, and almost every night they did, they would see another satellite lose its struggle with the Earth's gravity and tumble into the atmosphere in a bright fireball as it streaked across their view.

"There goes my cell phone service," Shep would joke, causing Antigone to snort.

"No more Snapchats for you," she would say as she nudged her elbow into his side.

On this night, they lay again, peering up at the heavens. He thought it very much the way people who lived thousands of years ago must have seen the sky and the world. It was pristine and unsullied, full of possibility and wonder.

He thought of fires that ravaged forests, an apocalypse at the time for the canopy, the understory and the forest floor and everything that thrived in those habitats. But once the burning and charring was over – once that world had ended – a new one sprung from the death and created a different forest, a better forest. Re-growth was more vigorous, the forest more lush than it had been before.

It was a pleasant thought that this world, too, could see such a rebirth. Shep would cling to that belief, for it comforted him.

Part II
Chapter Nine
The Way the Universe Wants It

The leaves were full on the trees and rustled in the wind by the time they reached Kansas. It had been weeks since Antigone slept in fear. He watched her almost every night as she curled up in a ball and tucked her hands under her head. He knew when she was dreaming – he could see her eyes flitter about under her lids and a smile sometimes creep across her lips.

She surely was dreaming of Patrick. Or of Halcyon and her brother. Or perhaps of him. Shep quite liked to think so, anyway.

As for Shep, he slept peacefully, too. He figured if Bray was stalking them, he surely would have attempted an attack by now.

At their current rate, it would take them no more than four weeks to reach the Colorado border and perhaps another week to ten days to reach Halcyon.

Shep was as fit as he could ever remember. He marveled at the definition in his chest and stomach and how he could see his bicep muscles extend and contract when he flexed. Antigone was always rugged, in spirit and in physique. She was the strongest person he had ever known for her size and the strongest person he had ever known for her will.

Shep was getting quite good at shooting his crafted arrows. He was able to kill small game with regularity and that kept their stomachs full and their hunger at bay.

They set out as soon as the sun peeked over the horizon, through fields with stalks that were silvery green and through other prairie grasses of crimson and gold that stretched up to their waists. The billowing clouds hung in the sky and cast moving shadows across the landscape that stretched as far as they could see.

The natural habitats were reclaiming their lost lands, the grasses swallowing tractors and automobiles and roads. Shep thought it oddly refreshing.

The Earth was erasing the scars of man.

Shep picked dandelions and popped them in his mouth on their journey. He had grown to love the texture and the taste. Antigone hadn't acquired a palate for them as of yet, making a foul face whenever he chewed one up and swallowed.

"How can you eat them?" she would ask, repulsed.

"They are good for you," Shep would answer, bending to pick another to chew.

•••

The clouds, dark and purple, looked ominous on the horizon. They couldn't afford to get caught in a storm as exposed as they were. They needed to find shelter.

Their brisk pace became more hurried as the storm approached. They could see the sheets of rain spilling out of the clouds and the lightning strike far in the distance, although they still could not hear the claps of thunder. That meant they had some time before the storm would engulf them.

Shep spotted a farm in the distance to his right, what was left of it anyway. The farmhouse had only two walls standing, and precariously at that, but the big red barn that stood next to an old grain silo still looked sturdy.

They made their way for the barn. They could hear the thunder now as the storm closed in and the wind had picked up, howling at their side as they raced toward the structure, the doors open.

The livestock had long since fled, but bales of hay were still stacked high in the back and an oil lantern still hung. Shep lit it and warm light filled the barn.

Rain beat down outside and lightning flashed. Shep liked storms. He found something beautiful about the fury of nature. He most liked how refreshing the air was after a good hard rain and he loved breathing it deeply into his lungs. It made him feel new and alive.

They sat, backs against the bales, and watched the flashing light outside and felt the earth shake from the thunder.

"Looks like we are bunking here for the night," Shep said.

Antigone wrapped her arm around his bicep. "Oh, wow. You are getting ripped." She squeezed it. "Look out Channing Tatum."

Shep looked at her, puzzled. "Who?"

She laughed. "Let me give you a more old-fogey example: Arnold Schwarzenegger."

"I wonder if they have body building competitions in Halcyon?" Shep gibed. "I wonder if I could compete."

Antigone punched him in the arm with her sharp knuckles. "Don't get full of yourself. You know what they say about overconfidence."

The storm raged on and Shep could feel his head nod down, then lurch back up. He yawned and looked at Antigone, who was also falling quickly into slumber.

"I miss …" Antigone said through a yawn. "Nothing. I don't miss anything."

"Not even Channing Tatum?" Shep caught another set of knuckles on his arm.

"Maybe this was the way it was meant to be," she said, smiling as wide as the Mississippi River they had recently crossed. "Maybe this was the universe hitting control-alt-delete, making us all appreciate what we have. The world is going to be such a better place now. I really believe that."

And Shep believed it, too. Who was he to doubt her? She was wiser than her years and more optimistic than she had any right to be. She was the most remarkable person he had ever met and he was better to have known her.

They both slipped into a peaceful sleep. No cares. No worries. No fears.

•••

Shep was never awakened by the sound of thunder – he usually slept straight through storms. It was a curse, really, to be such a sound sleeper.

It certainly was now.

Antigone was awake and trembling. Shep wiped his sleepy eyes and looked out toward the entrance to the barn to see Bray standing there, his gun pointed up and smoking.

"Jesus. This is too fucking easy," he bellowed. He hadn't even bothered to cover the grotesque hole where his right eye used to be. It was still puffy and red and the skin around it sagged.

He moved toward them slowly. He looked very much like Arnold Schwarzenegger at the end of the Terminator movie, his face malformed, but still pressing on to accomplish his goal, the one goal that would satiate his vengeance.

"I could have just popped two bullets in your brains while you slept, but what's the fun in that?"

Lightning flashed behind him. Thunder clapped.

Bray stood there, staring through his one good eye. "Nothing to say? You used to be a better conversationalist, Shep."

Shep slowly stood, holding his hands up. Bray caught a glimpse of Shep's deformed left hand and sniggered. "Holy, shit. Your hand. Wow, that's fucked-up."

"It doesn't have to end this way, Bray," Shep said, inching closer to him now. "Look what this lust for revenge has brought? You lost your eye. Your hand is messed up. When's it going to stop? It has to stop."

Bray shuffled closer. "Oh, it will stop, and soon. You took my wife from me and why? Because we wanted some food? That's all we wanted was some kindness and instead you wounded me and killed her. Why did you have to kill her?"

"She pulled a gun and pointed it at me, Bray."

"Only because you shot me with an arrow!" Bray clumped his way closer. "And that gun? It was empty. It was fucking empty. She wouldn't have pulled the trigger anyway even if it was loaded. She was the gentlest woman I had ever met. She accepted me with all my faults. She was a treasure and you took her away from me, you motherfucker."

Bray slammed the butt of his gun down hard on Shep's head and sent him staggering backward, falling against the bales. Antigone stood and charged at Bray, but he pushed her down to the ground.

Shep tried to stand, but wobbled and fell over again. Antigone crawled over to him and pressed her hand on his bleeding head.

Bray stomped his way over to Shep and jammed the gun against the right lens of his glasses. "I'm gonna kill her so you can watch, then I'm gonna kill you. I should cut your fingers off one by one. I should make you hurt, but my wife didn't feel a thing, so I owe you at least that."

"I'm the one you want, Bray. I'm the one who killed your wife. Antigone is innocent. Haven't you killed enough young girls? I believe even you have some decency left."

"No fucking way." Bray pointed the gun at Antigone and sneered. "I have been waiting for this for months, following you, biding my time for you to let your guard down, waiting for the right time. It's the right time, now. Oh, it's so right."

"Bray! Whatever you do to me, I deserve. Everything you said is right. All you wanted was food, a little help, and I didn't give it to you. I was scared and I let that fear control me. I've killed people. Good people. People who did not deserve to die, like your wife."

In that moment, Shep had forgiven himself. He felt the relief well up in him and a strange giddiness envelop him. For so long, he had blamed himself for things that were out of his control, and for the things he had done to survive. He let the guilt consume him until there was nothing left but his pain and loathing. Now, suddenly, it was all gone.

He was free.

The Lord our God is merciful and forgiving, even though we have rebelled against him.

"Antigone doesn't deserve to die," Shep said as he looked at her and smiled, and then peered back at Bray. "You have to let her go."

Someone like her could not be destroyed. Someone like her needed to exist. She had seen so much tragedy in her life, had people torn away from her in the most brutal of ways, yet she still fought to live, fought to see the best in other people, even him.

If the world was to ever get better, Antigone needed to be in it.

Bray lowered the gun and stared at her with an odd sympathy. It was as if he had taken pity on her. *Perhaps Bray wasn't such a Beast after all.*

Bray didn't share the same affinity for Shep. He raised the gun and pointed it at him now, the rage cast back on his face.

"Go, Tig," Shep pleaded.

She didn't as much as twitch.

"Go. Get away from here."

This time she moved, slowly walking past Bray, which prompted him to say, "Don't even think about jumping on my back to try to poke my other eye out. I'm ready for that shit this time. I'll snap your neck like a twig." She continued on toward the exit to the barn and looked back at Shep through teary eyes.

"It's okay, Tig," Shep said, smiling. "Maybe this is the way the universe wants it." Lightning flashed and he could see her still standing there. It flashed again, and she was gone.

"Well, you get to save the girl after all, fuckhead," Bray said. "Now stand up. I want to shoot you down like a man."

Shep rolled onto his knees, and then wobbled to his feet.

"You broke me when you killed my wife. I mean, I was always a little broken, but I was a different man after I left her there. You won't be the first I've killed since that day and you won't be the last. You taught me that. Kill or be killed."

Bray aimed the gun and once again Shep found himself looking right down the barrel. "You created this monster. I hope you have made your peace with that, motherfucker."

Skye Padme Walker appeared to Billy Shepard again. He had grown to miss her and was happy to gaze upon her one last time. She stood behind Bray, who was taking a moment to savor his victory with a lustful smile.

He could hear her soft voice as she said, "It's time."

Part III
Chapter One
Antigone

Antigone Raptis was born to a Greek father and an Irish mother, both immigrants to the United States. That unusual pairing produced exotic children. Antigone was quite the beauty, with deep blue eyes, thick pouty lips, milky skin and long raven hair that sparkled and shone in even the harshest light.

Boys flocked to her – it was the wrinkles around the corners of her lips when she smiled that really got to them, and she smiled often – but she showed only a tepid interest in most.

She had a brother named Niko, who was eighteen years older than she and a decorated pilot in the Air Force. She looked up to Niko, idolized him. To her, he was the epitome of a hero, everything she wanted to be. She had plans to join the military herself as soon as she turned eighteen.

Of course, she never got the chance. The Ejection saw to that.

Now, she was hunched over Billy Shepard, a hole made by a bullet from Bray's gun where his right eye used to be. Shep's thick dark-rimmed glasses, sticky and caked with his blood, lay with the right lens missing and the frame bent on the ground next to his head.

Words were scrawled in red by his feet: "I'll give you time to mourn before I kill you."

Thanks, Bray. You're such a sweetheart.

Antigone didn't know how long she had been there, looking after his corpse – an hour, maybe two – but she didn't want to leave him. Part of her thought he would spring back to life, make a jest about how it's all fun and games until someone loses an eye, or some other witty wisecrack, and they would share a laugh. He would run his fingers through her silky hair and everything would be all right again.

That wasn't going to happen, of course. The blood that spilled was already dry on the ground in a circle around his head. She cupped his head in her hands and peered down at his cold face. She wanted to say something, a grand goodbye, but she was terrible at such things. Instead she stood, grabbed a shovel that was once used to remove shit, and began digging a hole as the mid-day sun beat down on her shoulders.

She finished the shallow grave and ran the back of her hand over her forehead that was sweaty and gritty with soil. She tried to lift Shep and carry him to the hole she had just dug, but she was only able to ferry him a few feet before he flopped back onto the ground. Antigone kicked at the dirt and at the stray stalks of hay in the barn in frustration and cursed loudly, fighting back tears as the expletives poured out of her.

She always felt better after a tantrum. Not this time. Once her tirade had concluded, she dragged him to the grave and rolled him into it, standing to wipe more sweat from her forehead and trying to catch her breath.

She buried the tube of Twilight Nude with him. It wasn't much of a good luck charm, anyway. Two of the men whom she had loved in different ways had died while carrying that particular shade of lipstick. It was time to get rid of it.

Antigone spread the last shovelful of dirt on the mound and jammed the blade of the shovel into the ground as a makeshift headstone. She closed her eyes, felt a gust of wind on her grimy face, and again searched for words to serve as a fitting farewell.

But all she could think of saying was, "Bye."

It would have to do.

Bray had swiped everything that Shep had carried, including his bow, but he hadn't taken her bag, which still rested against the bales where they had slept. She thanked him for that. She slung it over her fatigued and aching shoulders and, on her way out, picked up his broken glasses, folded them and slipped them into the bag.

It was the only thing she had left of Shep.

The wind howled and jostled her hair about. She pulled it back and tied it in place with an old rubber band she had found. It was such an odd thing to come across, a relic of a life that no longer existed. There wasn't much need now for rubber bands. There wasn't much need now for many of the trappings of that old life. There was a time when she couldn't be more than a few feet away from her iPhone. Now, she couldn't imagine being tied down by it.

She slapped the dust off of her clothes and it billowed and blew in a gust and stared toward the western horizon. The sun was dipping fast, but she did not wish to stay here another second. She knelt and patted the fresh dirt under which Shep lay, in peace now, and she wept a little, not out of sadness for her loss, but out of sadness for the world's.

"And so it goes," she whispered, not knowing what that meant.

•••

Antigone had become very proficient at making a fire. Her brother tried to show her once when she was thirteen, but she had little interest in acquiring the skill. *What would I need it for?* Niko insisted that a situation could arise when she would need to know how to do such a thing, but she scoffed at that notion.

"That's what matches are for," she would say insolently. Niko would just shake his head in frustration. Antigone figured he knew better than to try to make her do anything she didn't want to do. She was stubborn and strong-willed. It was one of the qualities she was most proud to have. She learned quickly after the Ejection that sometimes being willful wasn't in her best interest.

Lessons learned, that sort of thing.

She knew how to make a fire now and it crackled and warmed her. The nights were still brisk and the heat thrown off was welcome.

She cooked a few roots in a tin can. The water bubbled and steamed. She even ate a dandelion, paying homage to Shep. She smiled, knowing if he were looking down upon her from heaven or wherever – she wasn't quite sure if she believed in such a place as heaven now – he would be smiling, too.

That gave her great comfort as she lay with the Glock pistol on her chest. She knew if she needed to use it, she would have to make that one bullet count. Shooting a gun was the one thing she wanted to learn from Niko. They would go to the shooting range and she would fire off round after round.

At most places she would have been too young to shoot firearms, but Niko was friends with the proprietor and, as a military man, vouched that she would be safe.

It was tough for Antigone at first because the gun was so heavy and cumbersome, but she quickly learned and it became second nature to her. She was quite good at it, too. Not as good as Niko, but few were. Niko could put a bullet right through the middle of an X on a firing-range target with ease, shot after shot after shot. Antigone would hit the X every now and then, but most of her shots punctured the target all around it.

She figured, how exact do you really need to be when shooting someone? Close enough would do.

Horseshoes and hand grenades, that sort of thing.

As she was drifting into sleep, she heard rustling from the brush. She sat up quickly, grabbing the Glock pistol from her chest and aiming it blindly at the woods. She almost fired as a head poked out into the clearing. It was a dog, a yellow lab, and it stared at her with friendly, warm eyes.

She reached into her bag, grabbed the one piece of jerky she still had left and broke off a piece. The dog took a few nervous steps forward.

"It's okay, boy," Antigone said in a high-pitched voice. She often found it funny how people talked to children and animals, as if they had suddenly taken a drag from a helium balloon to speak. But she was doing it, too.

The dog crept forward; his tail wagged. He was timid and fearful – he trembled like a buzzing iPhone on a coffee table – but he was hungry and he inched closer to her. She held out the meat and she could feel his wet nose on her fingers as he sniffed. He gently grasped the jerky with his teeth and chewed.

"That's a good boy," she said, her voice high and squeaky again. She reached out a hand to pet his head, but he backed away quickly, turned and galloped back into the brush.

She was sad to see her friend leave so soon.

She lay down again, sighed and closed her eyes. Perhaps tomorrow will be a better day, she thought.

How could it get worse?

•••

Weather was variable at this time of the year and the sun that had warmed her in the days before was gone now, obscured behind a low and foreboding cloud bank. When she exhaled, her breath froze in a chilled vapor and then dissipated. She zipped up her coat as far as it would go, gathered her things and began marching against the harsh wind.

Her legs felt weak, but she defied them by continuing. Her eyelids were heavy, but she defied them, too, by keeping them open and alert. If Bray was following her, she would need to stay sharp. If she were to elude him, she would need to keep moving.

She may have been young, but she knew men like Bray, the brutish types that once they got a thing stuck in their head to do, they would keep going until it was done. She knew the type because she was that type. And the thing she wanted to do most, next to reaching Halcyon and seeing Niko again, was to kill Bray.

Antigone thought of many ways to do it. Shooting him would be too mundane.

She thought about pressing her finger into his one good eye, pushing it as far as it would go and, God willing – if there was such a thing as a God – right into his brain.

She thought about cutting his dick off and watching him bleed out.

She thought about slicing him open from Adams Apple to navel and plucking his heart out and squeezing it. *That would be such a badass thing to do.*

She thought about slicing his throat from ear to ear and hanging him from a post, but that had been done before.

Cliché, that sort of thing.

Oh, the ways she would kill him for what he had done to her and those she held most dear after the Ejection. That's what kept her going on her traipse through the muck the hard rains had turned the fields. That's what kept her stiff and fatigued legs moving. That's what kept her eyes open and those frozen exhales escaping from her mouth.

Oh, there will be blood.

•••

Antigone had walked for days until she finally stumbled upon an old ranch house, this one in much better shape than many of the others she had seen on her journey. Most of the houses and buildings and trailers that were abandoned soon after the Ejection didn't hold up well against the passage of time and intruders that looked to loot and ransack them, travelers much like her.

This one, though, stood sturdy. It had shown evidence of some wear, the paint chipped and peeled and most of the shingles on the roof were missing. She was sure it leaked and could smell the mustiness as soon as she walked through the door. But otherwise it was in good condition and it would serve her purpose on this night.

Shep had warned about such structures. It was part of his code: stay away from buildings. They attracted the unseemly of this new world.

She was breaking the code by entering.

She hadn't had a real meal since Shep had died and her belly was bloating, perhaps from malnutrition.

The roots and dandelions she had gobbled weren't cutting it anymore and the nights were still cold, the wind biting across the flat plains. She had to find better shelter, at least for one night. She couldn't take another night of teeth chattering and body shivering.

A table was overturned in the middle of the room and broken chairs were strewn about. The laminate wood floor was curled from water damage. As she took a few more steps inside she could see flames flickering down a long hallway. She could also see candles burning from a kitchen through another archway.

For a moment, she thought about turning and leaving, forgetting this place. She heard muffled voices and a burst of laughter from down the hall and caught a whiff of cooking meat in her nostrils.

Her belly rumbled at the smell that charmed her, beckoned her against her will to walk down that hallway toward that room where wood crackled. She ignored the danger and the peril. Before her better sense could stop her, she was standing in the arch and three sets of eyes were staring at her, shocked.

Two were women, both wearing wool hats pulled down over their ears with stringy hair flowing out from under it. The other was a man, older with long gray hair and a white beard and deep wrinkles around his eyes that shone in the light of the flames.

He looked like Santa. She half expected him to laugh a deep "ho ho ho" and rub his belly that was like a bowl full of jelly. But he did none of those things. His belly was very much flat. *He was Skinny Claus.* The thought made her chuckle inside.

No one spoke for what seemed like forever. Antigone stood frozen, her legs wobbling a bit. It was too late to turn back now.

Point of no return, that sort of thing.

In the middle of the room was a fire, the smoke billowing out through a hole in the roof. On a spit spinning over the flames was a large slab of meat from some sort of animal, Antigone could not tell what. All she knew was it smelled very good.

One of the women finally spoke. "You look hungry."

That much was true. "Yes."

They looked at each other with troubled faces. Antigone could tell all three were wondering what they should do. Should they feed this poor girl who stood before them, or should they turn her away?

They made their choice.

"Have a seat," the woman said again with a strange, almost crazed smile on her face. "There is plenty."

What happened the last time she had encountered strangers wasn't lost on her. She hoped this time would be different.

Once the meat was cooked to their liking, the man stood and pulled out a large serrated hunting knife. It was intimidating, but Niko had one much like it when she was growing up, so she was accustomed to the fierceness of such things.

The man carved off a sliver of meat and handed it to Antigone. It smelled very different than anything she had ever sniffed before. She took a bite, chewed the tough meat and swallowed.

It most certainly doesn't taste like chicken.

"You like it?" The woman asked again and then looked at the others with a knowing, creepy grin.

"It's okay, I guess."

The man carved a few more pieces and they all sank their yellowing teeth into it, ripping off chunks and chewing excitedly. Antigone finished her piece more slowly, the meat going down hard with each swallow.

When they were finished, they all stared at her with heads cocked and strange simpers.

"Where did you come from?" The woman asked. She appeared to be the only one who spoke.

"Nowhere really." Antigone tried to be as vague as possible. She was getting the heebie-jeebies again.

"Here. Have more," the woman said again. "We need to fatten you up."

"No thanks. I should be going."

She stood and backed away slowly. Those three sets of eyes just stared at her, their yellow and rotting teeth showing behind their deranged grins.

"Help me! Oh, God! Help me!" She heard a voice scream from the kitchen. Part of her wanted to just run out the door and through the dark field and far away from this house as fast as her tired and stiff legs would take her, but the part of her that was noble and daring and heroic won out.

Lying bound to the kitchen counter was a man, thick and healthy. His left leg was missing below the knee, his right freshly cut at the hip. "Please! Help me! Kill me!"

She turned to see the man who looked like Skinny Claus standing in the arch. "He'll spoil if you kill him. We haven't even gotten to the rump roast yet."

The room began to spin violently and vomit spilled from her lips. The man laughed. "Yeah. I did the same thing, too, after the first time I ate whatshismane. You get used to it. It doesn't bother you so much after you keep a meal down or two and realize it is keeping you from dyin'."

"Please!" The poor man on the counter screamed. "Kill me!"

Antigone quickly pulled a pocket knife from the bag that was still slung over her shoulders and opened it with a click. Skinny Claus held his hand up. "Whoa. Whoa, little girl. Don't do anything stupid."

She turned to the man begging for death and held the knife with both hands, shaking, over his chest. She felt the muscles in her arms twitch and tried to thrust the blade down into his heart, but couldn't. It was as if she were paralyzed. Tears streamed from his eyes as he whispered, "Do it. Please. Do it."

The old man took a step forward and Antigone tried to slam the steel into the legless man's heart, but as her arms came down, she stopped. The tip of the knife barely poked into his bare and heaving chest. A drop of blood oozed out.

Skinny Claus took another step forward and Antigone twirled to point the knife at him. He had his hunting knife drawn and light from the candles reflected off its smooth surface. "You did the right thing, little girl."

Her breathing was heavy and labored now. She could barely steady her blade as she pointed it at him as he slowly advanced, grinning through that white beard of his. She could barely see through the panic.

Suddenly, Skinny Claus stopped as he choked up a crimson liquid. It spilled from his mouth and colored his ashen beard red. He looked down to see a makeshift arrow sticking out of his chest and dripping with his blood. As he clutched it, he fell and Antigone could see Bray's one eye looking at her, the bowstring still flush against his face.

"I always wanted to do that. Last of those arrows, too," he snickered as he dropped the bow and approached Antigone with his usual lumbering steps. "Shep wasn't the only one who could shoot an arrow, you know. I did lots of bow hunting in my youth. Got plenty of small game."

He grabbed the pocket knife out of her grasp. She was too shocked and scared to fight him. "Never shot a woman in the eye, though," he said, smirking, and pointed the blade at her chest.

In that moment, she thought she was surely going to die. She didn't want to die, but she figured if there was a heaven, she would see Shep and Patrick there. *Death wouldn't be such a bad thing, perhaps.* This life certainly was no place to be right now. In this place, people consumed people, both figuratively, and in this case, literally.

Bray gave a snort as he brushed past her on his way to legless man, who wept and whimpered.

He raised the knife high over his head and brought it down into the man's chest. Blood quickly seeped out of the wound, and he whispered, "thank you," as he died.

"Are there any more of these crazy fuckheads?" Bray asked as he turned to her, leaving the knife stuck in the man's torso.

Antigone pointed to the hallway and to where the poor bound man's leg roasted on a spit.

"Don't think this changes anything between us," Bray glowered. "I still have a bone to pick with you." He turned, crouched and crept away. As she pulled her pocket knife out of legless man's chest, she felt herself hyperventilating. Air barely pushed into her lungs. The room began to spin. Her legs quaked as she felt her way toward the door, her eyes losing focus.

She finally toppled face down onto the warped floor when she heard a scuffle and screams and moans coming from the room down the hall. She thought it was over, but she heard that woman's voice exclaim "You sure are ugly, but you'll make a nice stew."

Antigone crawled quickly now, pulling herself forward toward the door with frantic thrusts of her hands and arms on the floor. Finally, she spilled out onto the deck and then into the tall grass and stared up at the moonless sky.

Just then she felt a lick on her face. The yellow lab peered at her, licked her again and whined. He ran a few yards, then stopped and barked. She pulled herself to her feet and followed him.

The lab led her through the field and away from that house and Bray and the women who sought to consume him. She peered back, not knowing his fate. Her bet was on Bray, though.

When she turned back, the lab was gone. She missed him and wasn't entirely sure he had ever been there.

Part III
Chapter Two
A Girl's Best Friend

The image of the legless man still burned in Antigone's mind as she chewed on more dandelions and boiled more roots over another splendid fire she had built.

It had been days since she escaped that house of horrors. For as strong and daring and brave as she thought she was, she crumbled under the weight of fear and doubt in that house. Killing that man would have been the right thing to do, but she couldn't bring herself to do it. Bray had so easily and effortlessly brought him escape and peace from the horror. He didn't hesitate. He didn't weigh the moral implications of his actions. He just did it.

She almost admired him for his resolve.

Antigone felt it wrong to leave Bray there in that precarious position. He had saved her life. She found it odd to feel so guilty about abandoning her mortal enemy, one who had killed two of the most important people in her life and one who had vowed to kill her as well.

Still, she thought about going back to attempt a rescue. *Even a loathsome man like Bray didn't deserve that kind of fate.* She had thought better of it and instead pressed onward toward Halcyon and perhaps her own escape and peace.

She ate another dandelion. *Shep was right, they grew on you.* It was in these quiet times with the fire dancing and embers zipping that she missed Shep and Patrick the most. They were such different people, yet fundamentally so similar, both tender of heart.

She hated to cry, but often was a prisoner of her emotions. She cried now as she remembered the way Patrick held her, the way he pecked her on the forehead with his soft, damp and warm lips and the way his heart would beat a little faster in her ear when she told him that she loved him.

She grabbed a large, flat stone and rubbed the blade of the pocket knife on it, sending sparks into the darkness. The knife was already sharp, blood dried on the blade, but she figured it could be a little sharper. If she had the occasion to use it again, she would. *No hesitation the next time. I'll be like Bray and act, not cower like a little girl.*

Once she was satisfied it could cut through anything, she tossed the stone into the night as if she were skipping it across a lake, closed the knife with a loud click and lay on her back, balancing the Glock pistol between her breasts.

She had a dream of the old swing set in her backyard, the one that squeaked and squealed with each kick of her legs. She dreamt of jumping off the seat when the pendulum reached its highest apex and soaring through the sky like a bird.

That was the time when she truly felt free and invincible. She was pleased she was able to feel that way again, even though it was in her unconscious mind.

It was a very good dream to have.

•••

The road stretched flat across the landscape, as far as she could see in either direction. It was as if it had no beginning and no end. The sun was high in the milky sky and its rays strained to break through the thin cover of the clouds.

It was still cold, bone-chillingly so, and Antigone braced herself against the frigid gusts of wind as she stared down that chipped and worn blacktop.

She could follow the road, straight and true, or she could venture again through the tall grasses. The fields provided better cover, but the road offered her a quicker pace. It was a conundrum that she wasn't sure how to solve. Shep's code was clear on this subject, too.

Decisions, decisions, that sort of thing.

Antigone chose the road. She hadn't seen a soul out here in days; her only company was that yellow lab, who followed her from a distance, still leery and guarded. She offered the dog what little food she could. He would nervously approach, snatch the morsel she held out for him, and then run away again only to reappear a little later.

As she beat down that road, she looked over her shoulder. The dog patted its paws down pavement behind her, keeping a consistent fifty yards between them.

She had a shadow, and it was a comforting one.

The sun had finally won its struggle with the overcast and bathed her in sunshine. It was warm on her face and she no longer felt as if she were submerged in an ice bath. In fact, she was beginning to feel overheated and unzipped her coat as she strode with a long gait toward an endless horizon.

It was hours before she had seen so much as a house, but she saw one now and walked nervously past it. Who knows who would come out of those doors, she thought. *This world is full of assholes. I know that all too well.* She peered back and the dog still followed, his tongue spilling from his mouth in a pant.

By the time she could see a crop of buildings in the distance, she heard screams from the field to her left. They were the bellows of a young boy, but not the playful kind of wails. The scared kind. The frightful kind.

She turned and cupped her hand over her eyes to keep the sunlight from them and could see the boy's head poke above the tall grass. She could see the blades rustle in front of him.

Antigone sprinted across the field, her Glock drawn. The boy hollered "help" as she approached and it took until she had almost reached him to see what he feared so. Two dogs, one a male Doberman Pinscher and the other a male Rottweiler, stalked about in front of him. Both stood tall and stiff, growled and bared their teeth.

The Pinscher had a large bare spot on his withers where his hide had been chewed, presumably in a fight. The Rottweiler's coat was shiny and she could see the well defined muscles in his shoulders and upper thighs.

Antigone walked slowly to stand in front of the boy. He was maybe eight with brown hair combed forward and freckles dotted on his cheeks. He wore a threadbare coat around his shoulders, his jeans were worn almost through and his tennis shoes were frayed around the edges. He put trembling hands on her hips and dug his face into her back.

"It's okay now," she said, soothingly.

But it wasn't. Far from it. The dogs were hungry and mad that someone had trespassed on their lands. They were also menacing. The Ejection had changed domesticated animals, too. Many were abandoned by their owners, or were left on their own when the people who cared for them perished. The old instincts had taken over again and dogs hunted in packs and became more aggressive and territorial.

These two were determined to defend their turf and perhaps make a meal of them.

"Go home!" she yelled. The two dogs backed off momentarily, before resuming their stalk. She pointed, hoping the dogs remembered their training, and bellowed "I said go home!" They backed away again, but stopped and inched closer again.

She heard the boy sobbing on the back of her coat. "They're gonna eat us, aren't they?" He asked between snivels.

"No, they're not. They're probably more afraid of us than we are of them." That's what she hoped anyway. She began to slightly turn her body away from the dogs, trying to be as unthreatening to them as possible. The boy shuffled with her. She still peered at them out of the corners of her eyes. "If we show them they don't have to be afraid of us, they'll leave us alone. I promise."

The dogs still growled, but they were backing off a bit, perhaps growing weary of this dance they were engaged in. They were about to leave when the boy panicked and ran, sprinting toward the road. The Pinscher darted after him and Antigone leveled the pistol and fired a shot. The dog dropped quickly with a yelp. The Rottweiler was more interested in her and came after her, snarling as he ran. She closed her fingers to make fists and braced herself. The dog leapt on her and snapped at her face, but she was able to keep his jaws away from her flesh with her forearms jammed under his jowls. He barked loudly at her as they tussled.

She was losing her battle as the Rottweiler's teeth nipped closer at her face, his saliva dripping on her chin. Suddenly, she heard a yelp and saw the yellow lab and the Rottweiler rolling in the grass.

It was a vicious few seconds as they tangled, then backed away from each other, both striking intimidating poses. They stared each other down, each growling and snarling in a show of dominance.

The Rottweiler feigned an attack, but the lab stood his ground, barked, and then unleashed a deep gravely growl that had the Rottweiler soon bowing his head and whimpering before running off and disappearing into the tall grass.

Antigone felt the lab's tongue lick at her face. It made her laugh. "That's a good boy," she said, petting his head and scratching behind his ears as he continued to lick. "I guess I owe you my life. Again."

She stood and the lab loped at her heels as she walked toward the boy, who was sitting on the ground with his knees up to his face, crying. She rubbed his head and he looked up at her through eyes that were wet and red. His lips quivered. "I want to go home."

Antigone helped him up and the lab licked at him, too, causing him to cry hard and loud. "He won't hurt you, will you, boy?" She patted the lab on the head. "He saved our lives. He's my guardian angel."

The boy reached his hand out and the lab licked at it. He giggled.

"Do you live near here?" she asked, her voice sounding like she had sucked helium again.

"Yeah. Just over there." He pointed toward the buildings. "My mom doesn't like it when I wander off."

"I bet she doesn't. My mom hated when I went on adventures, too," she said, grabbing his hand. "Let's get you home."

As they walked into the town – it really wasn't a town as much as it was a smattering of rundown buildings built close together – a woman rushed toward her with flailing arms. She was thin – *Wasn't everyone?* – and her cheeks were wet and ruddy.

She scooped up the boy and held him in her arms, burying her face into his chest as she sobbed. "Oh, my sweet Charlie. Why do you run off like that?"

Charlie put his hands on his mother's face. "I'm sorry, Momma." He pointed a chubby finger at Antigone. "This lady saved me."

The woman turned her gaze to Antigone, who cracked a half smile. The lab sat next to her and she scratched his head nervously.

"Thank you. Thank you so much," the woman said, her voice filled with gratitude. "People don't look out for each other anymore. At least someone is."

"This guy here looked out for both of us," Antigone said, rubbing the lab's head fast and hard. He closed his eyes and he panted. "Didn't you, boy?"

He licked her hand.

The woman put the boy down and threw her arms around Antigone, squeezing her so tightly that she struggled to breathe. Her arms were still at her side while the woman embraced her. She finally wrapped her arms around her and patted her back. It had been so long since someone other than Shep or Patrick hugged her. She had forgotten how much she missed it.

The woman finally released her and smiled, "Please. Come and have something to eat."

Antigone wasn't about to turn down a meal. She just hoped it was better than the last dinner party she attended.

Charlie and his mother dwelled in a building that was once a small post office. The front counter was still intact, complete with a scale and a cash register. Machines that were used to cull and sort the mail littered the room.

They sat on stools at a table that was probably once used to stack the letters and packages. Charlie's mother poured a beefy broth into a bowl. Antigone couldn't identify the meat, which deeply concerned her.

She figured this woman was unlikely to be a cannibal and dipped her spoon into the stew and slurped. It tasted good enough. That didn't matter as much as it was real food, and her stomach thanked her for it.

The woman sat next to her son, staring at her as she ate. "What's your name?"

"Antigone. But you can call me Tig."

"And your canine companion. What's his name?"

Antigone did not know. The lab looked up at her now with a little drool rolling down from a corner of his snout. He had a large bone with a few small chunks of meat on it sitting at his paws, but he cared more for what she was eating. She reached into the bowl and grabbed a piece of meat and gave it to him. He devoured it quickly.

What would she call him? She figured it needed to be a name befitting such a hero. He had saved her after all. "I don't know. He followed me for awhile and I'm glad he did." He lay down and began chewing on his bone.

"Well, I'm glad both of you came along when you did," the woman said. "I'm Clara. I'm so glad to meet you."

Clara had dark circles around her eyes. Her brown hair was frizzy and her teeth rotting. Antigone could see, though, that she once was a very attractive woman. The Ejection had changed that.

It had a way of knocking the pretty out of people.

"Where you headed?" Clara asked as Charlie scooted off his chair and played with the lab.

"West. My brother is waiting for me in Colorado. I've come a long way."

"How'd a young girl like you get all the way out here?"

"I had a little help," Antigone said as she spooned more broth into her mouth. "But I can take care of myself."

"I see that."

Antigone finished her meal and wiped her chin with the back of her hand. She smiled at Clara and thanked her for the meal and then asked, "Have you lived here long?"

"Since I was no bigger than Charlie," Clara said, chuckling. "I love living out here. No one around. Isolated. I always felt like I was on a strange new planet. I would explore the countryside and pretend I was an astronaut on a mission. I would be gone for hours and worried my parents so. I think my boy gets that from me."

Antigone smiled. She knew the type. "Why do you live here?"

"It's safe," Clara said. "No one would think to look for people or food in a post office. No one comes around much and that's the way we like it. No offense."

"Is it just you and Charlie?"

"Yup. Always has been and always will. Isn't that right, little bugger?" Charlie didn't respond. He was too busy scratching the lab under his jaw. The dog quite enjoyed the attention. "You can stay as long as you like. I go out hunting and it would be nice to be able to leave Charlie with someone while I did so he wouldn't get the notion to wander off by himself again."

Antigone appreciated the offer. She seemed nice enough. In fact, she admired her, looking after her son by herself, hunting game and putting meat in a broth to keep him well fed and strong.

But she had a place to be. She also didn't want to bring the wrath of Bray down upon them. If he was able to escape that house, he was out there and he had made a spiteful promise to kill her.

"Thanks. But I got places to go and people to see."

"At least stay the night. It'll be getting dark soon and it's warm and safe here."

Antigone wasn't about to turn down shelter.

•••

Her eyes opened to Charlie standing over her, giggling. He turned and pointed at the lab, Shep's bent glasses high on his snout.

"He looks funny," Charlie laughed as only a little boy could. Antigone snickered, too, at the sight. The lab was incredibly accommodating to the shenanigans.

It was a wonderful way to greet a new day, but as she looked at the dog wearing Shep's broken eyewear, she quickly became saddened. At this moment, she missed Shep terribly. She missed the way he had the knack of saying just the right thing at the right time to make her feel better and safe and cared for. Disdain for Bray welled up in her again and Charlie noticed the change. "What's wrong, Tick?"

She laughed again. The boy thought she had said "tick" instead of "Tig" when she had said her name to his mother.

"I just miss a friend of mine, that's all."

"I'll be your friend," he said and hugged her. She couldn't help but cry at the gesture.

Clara had been watching and had teary eyes, too. "Do you have to leave?" She asked as Antigone stood, took the glasses off the dog and put them back in her bag.

"I'm afraid, so. It may not safe for you if I stay here."

Clara nodded. "You've seen some pretty horrible things out there, haven't you?"

"You don't know the half of it."

"I'll pack you some food and water. We don't have much to

spare, but we'll give you what we can."

Antigone knelt to look at Charlie. He stared down at the ground and pouted. "I don't want you to leave," he said in a whiney voice that only little boys can make.

"I know, Charlie. You take care of your momma and don't wander off anymore, okay?" He nodded and hugged her, his little hands grasping and pulling on her coat. "And you take good care of the doggy, too."

Antigone stood and wrapped the bag around her shoulders. Charlie tugged at her jeans. "You should take the dog so you won't be so lonely."

The lab licked at her hand and looked up into her eyes with his tail wagging. At that moment she knew what she would call him and it brought a huge smile to her face.

As she walked down the road again, she peered back and saw them wave at her, Charlie waggling his hand wildly. She waved back and blew him a kiss. She could see him giggle, and then shyly hide behind Clara's leg.

Antigone grinned as she turned and walked again. She felt lucky to have met them.

It was reassuring to her to know that one woman alone with her son in the middle of nowhere was capable of carving out a pretty good life in this fucked-up world.

It was nice to know not everyone she came upon were killers or cannibals or rapists. It was nice to know there were still decent people out there. As long as there were, maybe this world had a chance.

The lab rushed toward her, and then walked beside her like a good little shadow.

"Come on, Shepard," she said. "We have a long way to go."

Part III
Chapter Three
Detour on the Way to Halcyon

Antigone took a swig of water from the canteen, some of it spilling over her dry and cracked lips. The water felt good going down her raw throat, but food – real food – would feel so much better. She rubbed her bloated belly and felt it rumble.

"You want some, boy?" She poured out a narrow column of water and Shepard lapped it up. Some dripped off his jowls when he was finished.

She was looking at another day of marching over increasingly difficult terrain, but she couldn't stop now. She was getting closer to seeing Niko again. The promise of his face and a warm plate of food willed her up on her feet. She wobbled, but kept her balance, sliding her feet, one after another until she had built up enough momentum to raise them off the ground. Her knees ached, her hips burned, but she ignored the pain.

She was becoming quite good at that.

The wind whipped her face and she could feel the skin on her cheeks begin to crack, but she pressed on.

She wondered what Niko would say when she saw him. *He would be so proud.* She would tell the stories of her past two years and he would praise her.

He would also weep for her losses and comfort her for them.

Yes, Niko would marvel at her fortitude. She wouldn't just be his baby sister anymore.

Her legs finally gave out on her just before sunset. They shook at first, and then weakened to the point where her left leg bent and went limp under her weight. She hadn't the strength to even break her fall as she toppled to the ground, her face smashing against the cold muck. She lay like that for hours, Shepard licking at her and whining. The sun had long since set and the cold was invading down to her marrow. For a second, probably not even that long, perhaps a jiffy, she thought about giving up.

She would see Shep and Patrick there, she thought, in heaven – she still wasn't sure if she believed in such a place. But if there were, they would be there and they would rejoice at her presence.

She would never be hungry or afraid again.

But she didn't want to be that kind of character. She wanted to be brave and bold and strong. She wanted to be the hero, so she pushed herself up out of the mud, which was caked to the side of her face, and hobbled onward.

The stars were bright in the sky above her, twinkling and flickering like a billion tiny flames from a billion tiny candles. She soon found a suitable place to make a fire and she warmed her hands in front of it, chewed on some roots she had dug up and vowed to not fall again.

•••

The morning brought a second wind to her. She awoke refreshed and her joints no longer ached so much. She felt queasy and her stomach seemed to be doing somersaults, but she felt much better than the morn before.

She kicked dirt on the fire and collected some water from a nearby creek that cut shallow through a field. It was more of a ditch really; the water was muddy, but fresh, and it would sustain her for this day's march.

Shepard dutifully walked beside her, matching her pace. He was a devoted companion.

Her legs were growing weary again when her stumbling gait brought her to a spot where she could see a group of large tents off to her right. Smoke rose from a fire among them and she could see people milling about. The wise thing would be to keep walking on her course, the memory of her last encounter with people still fresh in her mind. But even that horror couldn't overwhelm the rumblings in her stomach. She needed something solid and substantial to put in her belly and she was willing to risk whatever she would find in the distance.

As she got closer, she drew the attention of a wrinkly old woman who was boiling water over the fire in a big black kettle. The woman was startled at first, but seeing the state Antigone was in, calmed and approached. "Oh, child, you look frightful," the old woman said.

"You should see me without my makeup." *That was something Shep would have appreciated.*

The woman chuckled. "At least you still have your sense of humor. Come. You need help."

She was Antigone's hero now.

•••

The old woman's name was Alma Chutz and she had lived near the small town of Eads most of her life. It was an unremarkable town with unremarkable people, but it was home and she liked it. Her husband passed "many moons ago," and her son was "gone," she said with great sadness.

Luckily, a few army reservists stationed in Eads had rescued her from a brutal attack from raiders and nursed her back to health. They cared for her, fed her and housed her in this village they had constructed. It had become a community of sorts and she felt blessed.

Now Alma was returning the favor.

Antigone didn't know what she was eating; it was some kind of combination of meat, greens and liquid mashed together in a slop, but it was hearty and filling. Shepard ate, too, devouring a mush that Alma had put in a bowl for him.

She couldn't eat much and Alma wouldn't let her. "You're bloated because your stomach has shrunk so much. Something had to take up the space. You can't eat too much too quickly. You're liable to explode."

Antigone found she had quickly become full. Shepard also had finished his meal and lay down at her feet, sighing as his eyes gently closed.

"You must be just as tired as this guy," Alma said. All Antigone could do was nod; she was far too fatigued to even mutter a single word.

Alma smiled and escorted her to a small tent that was empty except for a sleeping bag resting on top of a worn bedroll. Antigone took a pair of wobbly steps and collapsed on the makeshift bed. Shepard sprawled out at her feet.

"You sleep, child," Alma said softly. "You sleep."

•••

Antigone awoke to muffled voices coming from outside the tent. She crawled to the tent flap and listened. "Nonsense, Jackson" Alma said. "We have enough for one more."

Jackson, a bearish man in boots, camouflage pants and a flannel shirt didn't seem to agree. "Alma, we are barely feeding the people we got now."

"What kind of people are we if you don't help someone like her, especially in the condition she's in," Alma said sternly. "You are better than this. We are better than this. I don't want to hear another word about it. She stays."

Alma turned and walked slowly toward the tent. Antigone scurried back to the sleeping bag, not wanting Alma to discover she was an eavesdropper. She pretended to sleep as Alma gently nudged her. "Time to wake up, child. You need to eat something again."

The slop tasted better the second time and slid down her throat with ease. She was feeling so much stronger that she thought she could begin her journey toward Halcyon again, but Alma would hear nothing of it. "You're not nearly strong enough, child," she said through her old woman voice.

Antigone hadn't the will to argue now. Perhaps Alma was right, she thought. *Halcyon could wait a little while longer.*

Jackson entered the tent and folded his arms on his chest as he stared at Antigone. It gave her the heebie-jeebies, the way his eyes burned through her, the way his lips snarled. Alma, noticing the discomfort on Antigone's face, turned to identify the source and shooed Jackson from the tent. "Don't mind him. He's a kitten on the inside."

Antigone cracked a half smile and finished the last of her slop. "What's his deal, anyway?"

Alma chuckled. "He is wildly protective of this camp. Once a soldier, always a soldier, I guess. He trusts no strangers since the Ejection. His guard is always up. We need that, I suppose. He's kept us from harm."

Alma handed her a canteen and Antigone sloshed the water around in her mouth before swallowing. Shepard lapped at the water in a dish on the other side of the tent. "How far is it to Halcyon from here?"

Alma's face turned morose. "Oh, dear, is that where you are going? You haven't heard? Well, how could you have heard? The military base that people started calling Halcyon – such a strange name to call a place – was overrun and destroyed. I'm sorry, child. There is no Halcyon."

Antigone heard the words, but did not believe them. *It was impossible. Halcyon HAD to exist. Niko was there and Niko wouldn't have let that happen. He would have struggled and clawed and fought to keep that place safe.*

That's why he didn't come for me. He was too busy protecting the one place where people could thrive.

That's why he didn't come for me. He was too busy giving humanity a fighting chance.

That's why he didn't come for me. He was waiting for me to come to him.

"No! That can't be true! My brother is there and he wouldn't let that happen. You're wrong!"

Alma tried to calm her. She shushed her, patting her back with her frail and wrinkled hand. "I wish I was. Jackson was there and he saw it fall. I'm so sorry, child. But you have a home here now. You'll be safe and warm and fed."

Alma stood and looked down lovingly at Antigone. "You rest now."

There would be no rest for Antigone. She blustered her way out of the tent, Shepard following her like the shadow he was. Alma tried to calm her and coax her back to bed, but she brushed by on her march toward Jackson.

He towered over her – *he must be six-foot-five* – and he peered down at her through disapproving eyes. "You just won't give up, will you?"

"No. And neither would my brother."

Jackson looked over at the darkening horizon and clenched his jaw. She could tell he was biting down hard, perhaps tussling with what he should say and what he wanted to say. Finally, after what seemed to her like an eternity, he turned and looked into her eyes again. "It's gone and he's probably gone. The sooner you accept it, the sooner you can get on with your life."

Antigone cocked her head in disbelief. "Alma said you were there. Tell me what happened."

Jackson swallowed harshly, and then proceeded to tell the story of "Halcyon." It was never called that, at least by the people who mattered. It was simply known as Cheyenne Mountain Air Force Station, built under more than two-thousand feet of solid granite in the side of Cheyenne Mountain. That's all it was, and even with its metal gates and barbed wire and security forces, it could not be defended against the hoards who thought it would be their salvation.

It became a mythical place, an ideal that people clung to for hope. But it was no more real than Oz or Wonderland or Eden.

"I'm sorry to disappoint you," Jackson said. "But you're chasing a work of fiction."

"Did you know my brother, Niko Raptis?"

"Honey, I was just an army reservist called up into a shitty situation," he said. "I never saw the inside of that place. Once hell started breaking loose, we got out of there. Nothing else we could do. The only thing we would have got from sticking around was dead."

Antigone's eyes widened and her words were soaked with hope. "So, there could be people inside."

"We never saw those doors open. Not even once. After a few weeks, we lost all communication with them. My guess is what happened on the outside happened in there. My guess is they all turned on each other. Sorry, kid."

Antigone didn't believe him. Niko would never have let that happen. He was good and caring and kind. He was a hero.

"I still want to see for myself. Will you take me there?"

Jackson grabbed her shoulders and squeezed. "You just don't get it. There's nothing there to see. Alma wants you to stay here and you will stay here. She'll take care of you. You're gonna need it."

As he walked away, Antigone looked around the camp, at the tents and the people who dwelled in them. *This was no kind of life, eking out an existence, wondering if the next day would be the last.* Sure, they had trained men with guns who protected the small band of people, sixteen by her count, but things were precarious at best.

Not much had changed in the two years since the Ejection. Little progress had been made in resurrecting that old life. Antigone remembered how hard it was for her during those years after the sky burned and the world became dark.

Part III
Chapter Four
Antigone Before the Ejection

Antigone Raptis was home alone, her parents in Greece to celebrate their wedding anniversary. They had debated leaving her, a sixteen-year-old girl and a beauty at that, unsupervised.

But they trusted her. She was not the type of girl who would see this as an opportunity to go wild, throw parties and run around with boys.

She was a loner and saw this as a chance to write a few more chapters of her first attempt at a novel.

She loathed the way girls were portrayed in literature as giggly, love-struck things, weak and dainty. She wanted to write a strong female character, one who bucked the stereotypes. One who saved the boy. One who was the hero.

Antigone was stuck in a writing rut when her iPhone buzzed on the dining room table. She enjoyed watching it crawl across the surface when someone called her. It was mildly entertaining.

It was Niko. *It had to be important if Niko was calling.* He was stationed in the Cheyenne Mountain Complex in Colorado Springs, Colorado, for the past year and every time Antigone asked him what he was doing there, he would snicker and say, "That's classified."

He wasn't snickering this time. His voice was harried. "Tig, you need to get to the shelter. Now."

The way he said it scared her. "What's going on, Niko? What's happening?"

"Just go. I'll come for you if I can."

"Niko!" she yelled. "Niko!" He wasn't there. Her phone had no service now, which she found odd. She always had strong service in their home on Mt. Washington.

She always listened to her brother, especially when his voice had an inflection like that. Niko was quiet, his voice always soft and soothing. But when things were dire, when he was worried or angry or flustered, his voice changed.

It had changed now.

Antigone sprinted into the backyard, past the old swing set and toward the hatch that led down to the shelter, but stopped and gazed at the sky in awe. The light was brilliant with prismatic hues both random and stunning. The light seemed to dance, swirling across the sky like a raging river. She thought it may have been the most breathtaking thing she had ever seen.

Then it turned blood red and she felt a tingling sensation on her arms and on her neck. The sky was as bright as midday.

She walked to the edge of her property and put her hands on the back of a marble bench that overlooked the city. She loved sitting up here at night and gazing at the buildings, at the cars crawling across the many bridges and the way the lights danced off the ripples in the rivers. *It was the most beautiful city in the world.*

The entire city was clear in the glow and she could make out the three rivers converging. She could even see the water gushing out of the fountain at The Point.

She wanted to stay there and watch, but the words of Niko caused her to move once again toward the hatch. She climbed briskly down the steps and threw the breaker. She heard the hum of the generator seconds before the lights bathed the room.

It was a small shelter, but comfortable for a family of four. The main chamber housed a small couch and a chair. A desk with a florescent overhead light was built into the wall. The middle chamber was the sleeping area with concrete slabs built like bunk beds on each side and the third chamber was stocked with canned goods, jarred fruits and vegetables and two large one-hundred gallon tanks of clean drinking water.

All of it was under a roof that curved like a half moon.

The shelter was state-of-the art when it was built ten years ago. Niko thought it wise for the family to have one after some of the things he had seen on his tours of duty all over the world, and he had arranged for the leading shelter construction company in the industry to install this one. It was encased in ten-feet of concrete, was air tight – scrubbers cleaned the recycled air – and impervious to manmade or natural destruction. To Antigone, it was already becoming a coffin.

She examined her dining choices and was unimpressed. She found it in particular bad taste to have cans of baked beans in an enclosed shelter – her unusual sense of humor poking through. She was delighted to see a wide variety of offerings and figured she would christen the shelter with a bowl of SpaghettiOs.

"Niko will be here soon," she told herself. Then her thoughts wandered to her parents in Greece. She wondered if the sky was like that there, and thought the likely answer to be yes.

She, unlike many of her classmates at Central Catholic, was alert during science class and had learned about solar flares and Coronal Mass Ejections. She thought surely this was one of them. That was the only explanation.

No big deal, she thought. It zapped the satellites and the power grid, but everything would be restored shortly. She had learned that the solar storm of 1859 was more of a nuisance than anything else. Telegraph operators were shocked by the sizzling lines. People could read newspapers by the light of the sky at one o'clock in the morning and gold miners in the Rocky Mountains awoke and began to make breakfast, thinking it was morning.

Things quickly went back to normal.

Surely the same would happen now.

She had also learned, though, that there were no satellites in Earth's orbit and no power grid in 1859. There was no technology to get mucked up by the copious amounts of electromagnetic radiation.

Perhaps that is why Niko wanted her to seek shelter, not for protection from the radiation, but for protection from the people in the aftermath.

•••

The solar storm still raged and the aurora still streaked across the sky when Antigone decided to stray from the shelter. She had been down there for a week, perhaps ten days – she had lost track already – and was becoming restless. For all she knew, everything was back to normal. For all she knew, the Pirates were playing again at PNC Park and the cars on the Incline were making their inching sojourn up and down the mountain.

She was wrong.

She looked out over the dark city and was horrified by what she saw. Fires burned and smoke from them obscured the skyline. She could hear the faint echo of car alarms and a few screams carrying up to her from below.

The world was different now, irrevocably different. If she hadn't grown up, matured, before, she had in that moment. The rest of her childhood was lost. The house where she had grown up, where she had taken her first steps, lost her first tooth, kissed her first boy, was in shambles. The windows were broken out and the back door kicked in. She decided to go in to see if there was anything of that old life left to salvage.

Her white Nikes crunched over the broken glass as she walked into the kitchen. All the cupboards were open, plates were strewn about, some cracked, some shattered, and jars that once contained preserves had the tops busted off.

The living room, with its plush leather couch and chairs and thick shag carpet that felt so good on her bare feet, was largely untouched, although someone had decided to steal the family's large flat screen television, to do what with, she did not know. *It wasn't like they could plug it in and watch South Park reruns.*

The study was also untouched. She hoped no intruders had noticed the fake panel on the wall behind the painting of Jesus, his hands clasped and faint halo around his head. She found it in bad taste, too, to hide a safe full of semi-automatic weapons behind a picture of Jesus, but that was Niko's odd sense of humor poking through.

She opened the panel and dialed in the combination. She heard a click and swung the safe open. The handgun she had learned to shoot with was there and she grabbed it with a smile. Just then, something knocked her to the floor.

Dazed, she looked up and saw her neighbor, Sal Carrington, pillaging through the safe. He grabbed a couple of handguns and stuffed one into the pocket of his leather jacket.

He pointed the other at her. "I'm sorry, Antigone. I knew your family had weapons in here and I need them. My family needs them. You don't know what it is like out there."

She was beginning to get an idea. She reached out for her favorite pistol, but Carrington shook his gun at her. "Please, don't do that. I don't want to kill you."

"Mr. Carrington, this isn't like you," she said calmly. "Take what you need, but leave my gun. I need to protect myself, too."

Carrington was dispassionate. "You'll just shoot me in the back with it." He picked it up and shoved it into his other pocket. "Now take me into that shelter of yours. I know you have clean water and food in there. Come on. Get up."

Antigone slowly stood. He grabbed her V-neck shirt and she heard it rip. She gave him an unhappy glance. *I liked that shirt.* He nudged the gun into her back several times on their way outside.

The aurora cast a strange hue on everything, a constantly

changing kaleidoscope of color. It was like one of those discos she had heard about with the spinning balls reflecting light in all directions. She figured Carrington, a portly man with a face as round as the moon, a terrible looking mustache that hung on his lip like a dark caterpillar and a hairless head as smooth as a fortune teller's crystal ball, probably remembered them vividly.

She heard the creaking of the swings that glided to and fro in the breeze and she could smell the lilies that were planted at the edge of the yard as he opened the hatch and led her down the steps and into the shelter. He closed the door with a loud bang behind him. He saw the pantry across the shelter and bolted for the canned goods, grabbing as many as he could hold. He hadn't thought his plan through very well, though, Antigone quickly discovered. He had no bag with which to carry the cans and no container to fill with water.

He wasn't thinking clearly.

Panic, that sort of thing.

Carrington began to sob and whine as he realized his error. He rubbed his hands over his smooth head vigorously and he looked around agitated.

"Your family can stay here, Mr. Carrington," Antigone said. The offer was genuine, even though he stuck a gun in her back just moments before.

Carrington became calm and looked back at her in disbelief.

"You'd do that for me? For us?"

"It's lonely down here and there is room. No sense for you to be out there. It's obviously fucked you up in the head."

Carrington laughed, softly at first, then loudly, uncontrollably. It had Antigone reconsidering her decision. He charged at her and Antigone ran through possible scenarios in her head. *A swift kick to the testicles would do the job, perhaps a couple of thumbs to the eyes or a punch to the neck.* Niko had given her a self-defense lesson and she rather liked that one, too.

But she didn't need to do any of those things because Carrington threw his arms around her and hugged her like a bear, a big bear with an iron kettle belly. He wept on the shoulder of her ripped V-neck shirt.

"I .. I … I don't know what to say," he whimpered. "I'll go get them now."

Carrington climbed the steps and closed the hatch behind him. Antigone contemplated locking it to keep crazy Carrington and his batshit crazy wife and batshit crazy daughter from coming back and adding a side of psychosis to the cans and jars of food.

She had climbed the steps and was set to bar the hatch when she decided to descend them again. It had been only been a week or ten days – she couldn't tell – and the world was already going to hell.

Someone had to rise above it. Someone had to be strong and fearless.

Someone had to be the hero.

•••

Carrington was frazzled. He had a long beard now, and his mustache was full and bushy. "There's not a whole lot left."

The food stores had dwindled. Antigone tried to warn Carrington that they weren't rationing enough, that he was eating too much, but he didn't listen.

He was the eldest, therefore he knew best, that sort of thing.

Carrington's wife, Stella, tried to tell him the same, but he wouldn't listen to her, either. Now they were almost out of provisions, long before they should have been.

The worst part was Carrington should have known better. He was the science teacher at Central Catholic and always lectured the class about how unpredictable and wild Mother Nature was. *She was an angry bitch.* He didn't say that in so many words, but that was what Antigone inferred. The universe was wondrous, but just as cruel and unyielding, full of sights and pleasures to satiate any man, but also full of perils and terrors to make that same man tremble.

It was eloquent then and Antigone thought Carrington to be a wise, wise man. Now she just looked at him with a loathing sadness.

Their daughter, Amy, a dour girl about Antigone's age, plump and homely, had become catatonic months ago. Antigone couldn't remember the last time she spoke a word. No, wait, she remembered. It was when the generator lost power and Antigone set out to scrounge for more fuel to keep it purring. She said something to the effect of, "You're gonna die out there." *Always encouraging, that Amy Carrington. Always looking at the glass half full.*

Now Antigone feared Carrington himself was on the verge of a meltdown.

"Nine meals, that's all it takes," he muttered. "Nine missed meals and anarchy. Civilization can overcome many things, but not hunger. Hunger will turn even the most gentle man into a savage."

Carrington was the proof. He had a master's degree, had never struck anyone with malice in his life and was a tender and loving husband and father. Now, he had rage and desperation in his eyes.

It was time for Antigone to leave.

"Mr. Carrington, don't worry," Antigone said, trying to calm him. "I'll go look for some food."

She grabbed her favorite gun from the counter, but Carrington stopped her. "What do you need with that?"

"I need to protect myself."

"No. The guns stay here. And bring back something good, please."

With that she left. She looked down at the closed hatch somberly. She wondered what would become of them, but knew the answer all too well. She couldn't go down with them.

The fires that consumed the city had long since died, just as most of the population. At least out here she would have a fighting chance.

She walked briskly out of the city. Few people milled about the streets, more concerned with getting out of sight and getting something to put in their stomachs than with her. She figured most of the people she saw were more afraid of her than she of them. She wanted to keep it that way.

She could no longer see the city when she glanced over her left shoulder as she pushed her way through thick brush into the woods. Travel was difficult and the branches lashed and whipped at her, but she had to stay covert. On her excursion to find gasoline to power the generator she had seen some horrific acts of cruelty. She was able to avoid such a fate herself and was determined to do so again.

She emerged from the thick trees into a clearing, grass up to her knees. Insects she didn't even know existed feasted on her and she had small welts all over her arms and hands. They itched and burned, but she didn't scratch. She knew better. Niko had taught her well.

She saw a man and woman shuffle through the clearing. She tried to hide, but they spotted her.

The woman was the first to yell, "Hey, you! Hey, you!" Then the man bellowed the same.

Antigone was frozen. She could flee back into the woods and become the dessêrt of the insects, or take her chances with the skinny wanderers before her.

"Hey, you!" the woman yelled again. "We won't hurt you."

Antigone figured that was the common greeting these days: "We won't hurt you." *What else are they going to scream? Hey, you! Wanna get raped and brutally murdered? Come here then.* Most probably meant no harm. Others, however, most likely did. She had nothing to lose, though. No food. No water. Nothing they could possibly take from her. She approached them cautiously. The man lumbered in front of the woman now, his feet punching down the grass like a Yeti.

He was tall, but thin and sickly with a scruffy beard and beady eyes. His hair was long and dirty and his voice was loud. "Well, aren't you a sight for sore eyes. I'm Paul Bray, and this is my wife."

•••

They were nice to her at first as they showed her off to anyone they came across. "Please, our daughter is hungry. Please, just a little food," they would beg and surprisingly, the cries for sympathy worked. She thought it would be a good deal for her as well, but they didn't share the bounty they had received.

Antigone mentioned she was on her way to Halcyon and Bray laughed mockingly. "Why don't you stop in Oz and see the wizard on your way, Dorothy."

He was cruel and damaged. She had learned that quite quickly … and painfully.

She tried to leave once in the dark of night when they were sleeping, but Bray woke and clubbed her on the head with a thick branch he had used as a cane – more for sympathy than to steady his gait. Blood spilled from the cut and dripped from her brow. "Where the fuck do you think you're going?" He said with that voice that was as loud as it was grating. "You're our meal ticket. People can't resist a pretty face."

His wife, whom she knew as Maggie, watched and Antigone could tell she disapproved deeply, but was either too afraid or too timid to do anything to put a stop to the abuse. When Bray fell asleep again, she quietly came to Antigone and held a ripped piece of clothing over the cut. "He was a gentleman … before," Maggie said in a hushed voice. "He's just desperate. I'm sorry for what we're doing to you. I really am."

For some reason, Antigone believed it. Maybe it was because it was the first decent thing anyone had done for her since the Ejection. Maybe it was because she missed her mother and this woman was the closest thing she had to one now.

"He used to be a cop, you know," she continued. "A detective. Sometimes he wakes in the middle of the night with his arms swinging and screaming. He saw some terrible things in those days just after the Ejection. He saw friends turn on friends and spouses turn on spouses. He saw people beaten and murdered. He saw the worst in people and I think it brought out the worst in him."

Antigone felt sorry for Bray. It must have been awful trying to keep the peace in such chaos. She feared the same had happened to Niko in Colorado where she figured things were just as dire. "There are better ways to survive," Antigone said earnestly. "I can hunt, you know. My brother would take me on hunting trips. There are lots of deer around here. I'm pretty good with a gun."

The woman snickered. "The only gun we have is this old revolver and it has no bullets. I'm not sure if it would even fire if it did.

We've tried to hunt, but we don't have a damn thing to hunt with. Paul has wanted to try to steal a gun or a knife or something, but he'd have to kill someone for it and I won't let him. I'm beginning to think maybe I should. We've tried everything else. You have been the best thing to come along. I'm sorry."

Antigone balled herself up on the ground and tried to sleep. The woman still pressed the cloth on her head to stop the bleeding. "Paul saved my life, you know." She spoke as if she were trying to convince Antigone of his virtues, and maybe a little to convince herself. "I was a junkie. Meth mostly. A nasty drug. Have you ever taken it? It makes you do some pretty messed up things when you are on it. You do even more messed up things when you are trying to get more. He busted me and kept tabs on me. Kept me clean. Married me. Made me a happy woman again."

Maggie pulled the cloth away and smiled. "The bleeding has stopped. You sleep."

Antigone couldn't. Not now. She had more questions. "Why do you stay? We can both leave here together. We can get away from him. Someone will help us."

Maggie shook her head passionately. "No. I can never leave him. Paul and I have a very complicated relationship. No matter how much I screw up or he screws up, we will always stay together."

Antigone was unimpressed. "You're an idiot, if you ask me," she whispered angrily. "He doesn't deserve you."

Maggie lowered her head. "No. I don't deserve him."

"How can you say that? He's a fucking asshole."

Maggie chuckled and shook her head. "Oh, you just don't understand. The night before the Ejection, I relapsed. Went back on meth. We had a fight. He was always working and I was tired of being left alone all the time. I went out and found an old dealer of mine. When I came down from the first hit, I desperately wanted another, but I didn't have any money left. I saw this woman. She was attractive and sitting in a nice car in a shitty part of town, right outside of a dump of a hotel. She didn't belong there, anyone could tell that. She must have sat in the car for an hour before she got out."

Maggie wiped away the tears that were streaming down her cheeks. "I wanted another hit so bad. Meth is like that. It's so addictive. I dragged that poor woman into the alley next to the hotel. It was so dark I could barely see her face when I told her to give me all her money. You know what she said? She said, 'No.' Do you believe that?"

She gritted her teeth and pounded her chest with her fist. "I lost it. All the rage and hate I had balled up inside me, all the sadness I had about wasting my life and being left alone by Paul just exploded out of me, you know. I pulled out a pocket knife that Paul had given me for protection. It was one of those big ones and it was personalized. It said "Maggie, my love" on the handle. I stabbed her with it, over and over and over again, maybe eight or nine times. I remember the blood splashing up on my shirt and arms and her cold eyes as she stared at me in shock. She was still holding her key chain. It was some kind of animal, a whale. No. It was a dolphin. She had nine dollars in her purse. Nine dollars. I killed her for a five and four ones. I still have them. Well, I did until the Ejection. I used to fan them out and stare at them. Her blood was still on them from my fingers. I would sit there and pray to them for forgiveness. Strange, huh?"

Antigone sat mesmerized by the story. She felt sorry for her. She pitied her.

"I wanted to tell Paul, but I couldn't. He'd be so ashamed of me and I'd lose him. I couldn't lose him then. I especially can't lose him now. He's all I got."

To Antigone, she was no better than Bray. Maybe a little worse.

That was definitely not what a hero would do.

"When you kill someone, I mean make a conscious effort to end their life, it changes you," Maggie said, staring sadly into Antigone's eyes. "There is nothing worse you can do to your soul than that. That's why I can't let Bray kill someone for their weapons or food or anything else. He had a hard enough time when he accidently killed a poor girl when he was in uniform. I know I am going to hell. I'm afraid I'm already there."

•••

The days that followed were no better for Antigone. They had stumbled upon houses full of nothing but threats. Bray, though, deftly defused the situations with his tale of woe and more times than not, was able to coax some food and sometimes some homemade alcohol from the strangers.

Maggie slipped her some food, a stick of jerky and a handful of berries, and Antigone gobbled them down quickly. Bray was passed out after he had drunk some very strong alcohol on an empty stomach. "If Bray ever found out, he'd … he wouldn't be happy. I've never seen him this way. So angry."

Antigone awoke later that night with Bray on top of her. She wiggled, but could not free herself. His breath was hot and foul with the smell of liquor. "Wow, you are a pretty little thing."

"Get off me!"

Bray slammed his palm over Antigone's mouth and she tried to scream again, but only muffled grunts escaped. Maggie woke and watched.

Bray pushed his pelvis into hers. "Are you a virgin? I bet you are."

Antigone squirmed and was able to lift her leg enough to whip it into his crotch. *Another self-defense tip taught by my dear brother.* He rolled off of her and she quickly scooted away. Once he recovered, he came at her again, but Maggie stood in his way.

"That's enough, Paul! Leave the girl alone. What's wrong with you?"

Bray stopped, his tired and still intoxicated eyes looking into hers. "Well, well, look who decided to be the hero."

"You're better than this."

"No, I'm not," he said. "I'm a bad man, don't you know? I killed a girl once. Shot her right in the chest. All she had was a candy bar, but I thought it was a fucking gun. Didn't matter anyway. I was going to shoot whoever came out of that store. And I wasn't sorry. I was doing my job."

"I know, Paul. You told me. Don't you remember?"

"I can still see her eyes, staring back at me. I see them all the time, even when I'm sleeping." He pointed angrily at Antigone. "I see them in that girl, too."

"I know, Paul. You told me."

Bray sobbed now. Uncontrollably. He had trouble breathing, his chest heaved so violently. Maggie hugged him and tried to hush his cries. Bray buried his head into her breast, snot and tears forming a goop that dripped from his face.

"I'm sorry," he said as she squeezed him tightly. "She was just a little girl. How could I kill a little girl? I'm so sorry."

"I know, Paul," she said, shushing him again. "You told me."

Part III
Chapter Five
What a Hero Would Do

Antigone sat by the fire and counted the embers that shot off into the night. She was up to eighty-one when she decided enough was enough.

Jackson cooked a prairie dog on a stick over the fire. It wasn't the ideal meal, but it would do in a pinch if the hunting party could not bring back a deer or a wild turkey. He kept alternating his gaze between the smoking prairie dog and Antigone.

"I'm going to go to the base, you know," Antigone said. "Alma and you and all these people can't stop me."

Jackson held the prairie dog up to his face, blew on it, and then took a bite into the tough meat. He grabbed another one, skinned and skewered, and held it over the fire. "I know. No one's gonna stop you. I'm certainly not. You have to see for yourself. I feel ya."

He bit off another hunk of meat and chewed. "You know, I'll never get used to eating one of these rodents. No matter how hard I try, I can't ignore the fact that this is a giant barking squirrel. Tastes like one, too."

Antigone didn't much care about his picky palate. "First thing tomorrow morning, I'm leaving for Hal … for the base. My brother is still there."

Jackson continued his informative lecture on all things prairie dog. "I mean, there are so many of them out there now. People used to hunt them and kill them at every opportunity they got. They multiply like a virus, you know. They are kind of a nuisance. But after the sun went all crazy, there was no one left to kill them fast enough. Good thing for us, I guess, because the stupid little shits are easy to kill. Lots of protein, too."

Antigone's shoulders slumped and her lips snarled. "Didn't you hear what I said? I'm leaving tomorrow. Don't try to stop me."

"I know," Jackson said gnawing off the last shreds of meat on the bones of the prairie dog while the other cooked. "You're leaving. Blah, blah, blah. Like I said, I'm not stopping you."

Jackson offered her the other prairie dog and she begrudgingly accepted. Barking squirrel meat was better than no meat and she was famished. She took a bite and chewed. It tasted gamey, but she choked it down. Food was food. She couldn't be picky. *At least it wasn't legless man.*

"Well, I'm glad we understand each other," Antigone mumbled as she was chewing.

She heard footsteps behind her and Jackson yelled, "Alma, our guest is leaving tomorrow morning. Isn't that great?"

Antigone turned to peer at the old woman, who patted her on the head as if she was four.

"Maybe you should put those travel plans on hold, child. There's something you should see that just might make you stay."

•••

Alma had cried when Antigone told her the story, of how at first she didn't trust Billy Shepard because he had put an arrow into the brain of Maggie Bray. That woman, flawed, but repentant, didn't really deserve such a fate. The man she knew as Bray certainly did, however.

She grew to trust Shep, though. He was tortured, but kind and looked out of her and cared for her and truly loved her. And she loved him just as deeply, in a way she couldn't really describe.

She told the story of how she had to bury him in a hole on the land of a sprawling farm, of how Bray had taken his life.

An eye for an eye – literally – that sort of thing.

She told the story of Patrick, her first love, the kind of love she had only dreamt of, the kind of love her parents found and that she hoped to discover, too, someday. She told Alma of how passionate he was, adventurous and daring, of what a hero he was to her. He didn't treat her like a delicate thing that needed to be shielded. He treated her like a woman who was capable of protecting him as well. That was perhaps the thing she loved most about him, his way of making her feel like a hero, too.

But she couldn't protect him. He went off and never came back and she felt oddly responsible. She should have gone, too.

She told the story of the last time she saw him, the way he kissed her on the forehead and rubbed her cheek with the back of his soft hand as he left. And she told the story of his brutal death at the hands of Bray.

For the first time since she had met her, Alma was speechless as she left the tent that night.

Now, on this night, she was speechless again as she slowly led Antigone to a tent she had never seen anyone enter or exit before, a tent on the edge of the camp and guarded by two men with automatic rifles.

They stopped at the flap and Alma put her hands on Antigone's shoulders. "This is your decision. No one else's. Take as much time as you need."

Antigone put her hand on the flap and hesitated. Her mind took an inventory of a million things that could be inside. *My decision, no one else's? What did Alma mean by that?*

Finally, she marshaled the nerve to pass through the opening. The tent was lit by two hanging lanterns. A pole jutted out from the ground in the back and lashed to it was a man. His feet were bound and tied with a long rope to his wrists, which were trussed above his head to the post. His back was arched in what looked like a very uncomfortable pose. His clothes were dirty and smattered with blood and his head was limp, his long greasy and wet black hair hung down over his face.

Antigone slowly walked toward the man. Her legs trembled as she got closer. She knew who it was, the only person it could be, but she had to be certain. She took more hesitant steps until she was standing close enough to smell his foulness. She grabbed his stringy hair and pulled his head up. The one eye he still had was shut and blood dripped from the corner of his mouth.

It was Bray and she smiled. He was all hers.

•••

She opened and closed the pocket knife. It made a click each time she did and it began to sound rhythmic like a song. She would call it the "Bray gets his" song and it was a catchy tune.

Finally, Bray stirred. It seemed like it took forever for him to wake. She didn't want to kill him while he was unconscious. *What was the sport in that*? She wanted him to see her do it. During the time he dangled there, hog-tied like a piece of meat, she pondered the method of his end. There were so many ways, each equally tantalizing. She contemplated doing it quickly and doing it slowly. She thought about plucking one piece of him at a time, a finger here, an ear there; just rip things away from him like he had ripped things away from her, before ending his miserable existence. She even thought about unleashing Shepard on him, watching the lab, who was fiercely protective of her, rip at his flesh with his powerful jaws.

She hadn't come to a decision when he looked up at her through that one eye and gasped when he saw her sitting there.

"Well, lookie who's tied to a pole now," she said coldly and opened and closed her pocket knife again.

Bray just hung there and looked at her, emotionless.

"What? No clever comeback? No zinger? You can't even call me a bitch? Wow, how disappointing."

Bray swallowed hard. "I saved your life from those zombies. You won't kill me. You don't have it in you."

That angered Antigone, even more than she thought it would. She stood from the chair, walked over to him with long, angry strides and kneed him hard in the groin. He howled and vomited on her new boots. "Wanna bet? I'll kill you slowly, painfully, like you deserve. I want you to beg for your life first. Did Patrick beg for his before you killed him? Did you torture him and promise he'd see me again before you slit his throat?"

Bray exhaled a plume of putrid breath, "No. He was already dead when I slit his throat."

Antigone boiled with rage. She screamed loudly, spittle splashing against the dried blood on his brow. She pressed the blade of the knife to his throat, the tip drawing a droplet of blood that trickled down his neck. "How does a man like you exist? There is a hell and it spat you out."

Bray laughed. It was a giddy one, an uncontrollable one. It was one of those laughs that shake your whole body and make your eyes water. The kind of laugh that makes you piss a little. And it only made Antigone angrier.

"Wow, did you rehearse that?" Bray asked between cackles. "Spat me out from hell? No one has ever said that to me before."

Antigone dug the tip of the knife a little harder into his skin, causing a small column of blood to flow out. She thought this would make her happy, would erase all the pain. She thought one act of vengeance would make everything right again, but she was beginning to realize it would not.

Vengeance had not gotten Bray very far. Vengeance had gotten him in this sorry state, one eye, a scarred hand, and bound uncomfortably, contorted on a post in the middle of nowhere.

Antigone felt something she never thought she would when she looked at him. Pity. She felt sorry for him, sorry that he had let his rage consume him. It was his undoing.

Antigone removed the blade from his throat and closed it with a click. She grabbed his hair and pulled it, staring right into his one good eye. "I'm not going to kill you, you sonofabitch. At least not yet."

She began to walk away, but Bray's words stopped her. "I knew you wouldn't have the guts. I knew you couldn't do it. What does the little girl know about killing?"

Antigone lowered her head and closed her eyes. She clenched her fists tightly, so harshly her skin burned and her nails dug into her palms. Every single part of her wanted to turn around and gut him like a fish, skin him and skewer him like one of those prairie dogs.

Well, almost every part of her. The part of her that strived to be better, to rise above the desperation and the hatred of this world, to live with mercy in her heart won out again. She wanted to kill him, wanted her vengeance just as badly as he wanted his.

She couldn't have it, not right now, not right away. She wasn't ready. *Will I ever be ready?* She would have to swallow that hatred and learn to live with it, on this night anyway.

That's what a hero would do.

Part III
Chapter Six
Antigone and Patrick's Great Escape

Antigone Raptis didn't want to leave, but she had no choice. "Hurry," Patrick said, gripping her tender right hand as they moved through the field, the dim light reflecting off the snow cover. The squeeze of his hand on hers inflamed the pain in her raw knuckles.

Their feet crunched through the snow as they ran. Patrick never let go of his grip as they sprinted. The windmills that spun and clanked behind them got smaller each time she looked over her shoulder until she could no longer see nor hear them. Once they got far enough away from Attica, *from that wretched place*, they slowed to a walk.

"I know where we can stay," Patrick said, gasping for air. "It's about a half-day walk from here. If we keep going, we'll be there by morning."

Antigone hesitated, second-guessing her decision to flee with Patrick. Shep had sacrificed himself and that didn't sit well with her. Despite assurances from them, she feared Shep would suffer a price for staying behind.

What if he hangs from his neck? I would never forgive myself. A hero wouldn't run like a coward.

Patrick snatched her hand again and held it carefully this time. "We can go back. Whatever we do, we'll do it together."

Moments of indecision were rare for Antigone. She had always been as decisive as she was daring. She had never faced an impossible situation like this before. *What do I do? Risk the life of one man I love to save another?* She rubbed the top of Patrick's soft hand with her thumb. "Let's get moving."

Hard pellets of snow lashed at her face and a terrible wind howled. Her teeth chattered as they walked through the ankle deep snow and her feet and hands were stiff and numb. It was beginning to get brighter, which just enabled her to see just how frigid and desolate everything was around them. Her hands were red, swollen and cracked even though she had stuffed them as far as she could into her pockets.

Patrick fared much better. He zipped along through the drifts, every now and then slowing his pace so she could catch up. "We're almost there."

Finally, they came upon a farm surrounded by red pines. They grew tall and straight and were blanketed by a white canopy. Those trees would have looked beautiful to her under normal circumstances, but she was too chilled, tired and worried to enjoy them.

A slight man with a harried face, but a warm smile, shot out of the house to meet them. Patrick hugged the man, patting him firmly on the back. "This is Cyril. He was an old friend of my father, and hated my mother. So that makes him our friend."

"Hurry inside," Cyril said. "You need to warm up."

The heat from the fire was welcome on her face and hands. She moved her fingers and was pleased to be able to feel them again. The ripe red skin on her knuckles oozed as she watched Patrick and Cyril sit at the dining room table to speak. Antigone couldn't quite hear what they were saying, but gathered from Cyril's facial contortions that Patrick was filling him in on the state of Attica and why they had left.

Patrick waved her over and Cyril grinned at Antigone. "I've known Pat since he was no taller than a grasshopper. He always had his nose in a book. He always was off on his own, alone with his thoughts. I'm glad he found someone to fight for – and someone who will fight for him, I hear."

"No one messes with Antigone Raptis," Patrick said.

Cyril chortled. "Get something to eat and rest. There are places to sleep in the cellar. You'll be safe down there while I'm hunting."

•••

The cellar was dark and cold, but clean. Two bedrolls lay on the floor and Antigone flopped on one. Her leg muscles seized and she tried to relax them by curling her toes. Patrick lay on the other bedroll, staring across the shadows.

"I know you're worried about him," Patrick said. "I don't know him that well, but I get the feeling he can take care of himself. I think my mom is losing her hold on Ward and the others."

Antigone lay on her back and picked at the loose skin on her knuckles. "What if you're wrong? What if she kills him?"

"She won't be able to. She's smart. She knows if she tries to kill him without the support of the people, she'll lose her power. And she's all about power now. It's weird how people can change. She used to be kind. When I was little and my brothers picked on me, she always told me not to take it personally, that was just what big brothers did and that they loved me even though they didn't show it. She sang to me, old songs. When my dad and brothers died, something happened to her. She changed. She started talking weird and I didn't even know her anymore. I only went along with her craziness because she is my mother and I love her."

Antigone crawled over to Patrick. He flinched when her cold hand touched his chest, and then wrapped his arm around her waist. "That's just so fucked-up."

There were lots of fucked-up things in Attica.

Antigone was to be promised to a man of fifty. He was nice enough, tall and handsome, a lawyer in that other life. He looked younger than his age, which was odd for these times. The Ejection had rapidly aged most. The thought of lying down for him sickened her. She had no idea why her longing for Patrick was such a crime. *We'd make a great pair and our kids would be gorgeous.* Patrick, though, had been promised to the man's young daughter and the lawyer was important to Rhian's grasp on power.

Politics, that sort of thing.

When she asked Patrick about it, she could hear his frustrated exhale. "My mom turned into a monster. After the Ejection, everyone kind of went crazy. My mom went nuts. She thought she was building a super community or something messed up like that. She thought towns like Attica were going to be the model for the world going forward and she wanted to be the example everyone followed. She was delusional, but I can't blame her for that. Everyone is delusional now in some way."

Antigone leaned over and kissed Patrick deeply on the lips. She felt his chest heave and his heart flutter.

Patrick pulled away nervously. "Um, here? Right … now?"

She giggled. "Why not? No one can hear us."

Antigone always worried about what her first time would be like. She wanted it to be special, like in the movies. She wanted candlelight and roses and the sweet touch of a caring man. While she was strong and independent, she still wanted to be the girl who was swept off her feet.

"Tell me, Patrick, you've never been with a girl before?" She kissed him hard again.

"Oh, and how many boys have you been with?" he chided her. "I bet you made all the boys swoon."

"Maybe one or two," she said before she realized that could have been misinterpreted. "Boys who swooned, not how many I've been with."

He smiled and kissed her again. "I know what you meant." His lips pecked at the curve of her neck and she felt his tongue dance on her skin.

"We can stop," he said, smiling.

She didn't want to stop. She wanted this more than she could imagine. "Shut up," she said, kissing him again.

•••

When they awoke some time later, her cares and worries came back, more furious and determined as ever.

"I hope Shep is all right," Antigone whispered with desperation.

Patrick rubbed her bare back. She could feel him tracing his fingers down her vertebrae. "I know. I'm going back."

Antigone lifted her head and tossed her hair out of her eyes with a quick whip of her head. "No. I should go."

Patrick protested. "You can't go. My mother would have no qualms about hanging you. Me, well, she wouldn't do that to her only living son. Even she's not that insane. She'd have to hang Shep and me both, or none of us. It seems like a no-brainer. Probably should have done that to begin with."

He pushed himself up off the bedroll and began hastily dressing himself. "I better go now before it's too late. They know we're gone by now and that Shep helped us get away. I'm sure he'll be in front of that stupid tribunal soon."

Antigone stood, prompting Patrick to stop what he was doing and stare. She quite liked that she had the ability to drop his jaw. "Hey, eyes on your own paper," she said as she dressed, slipping layer after layer over her now freezing body.

She rooted through her bag and pulled out the tube of Twilight Nude lipstick. She put it in Patrick's open hand and closed his fingers around it. "Take this with you. Something to remind you that I'll be right here when you guys get back."

She grabbed the back of his head and scratched his scalp. "And tell Shep you saved his ass for me."

Patrick smiled, nodded and bowed. "Yes, my lady." He rubbed her cheek with the back of his soft hand and kissed her lightly on the forehead. He slung his bag over his shoulder and got halfway up the cellar steps before he looked back at her. "I love you, Antigone Raptis," he said as he opened the cellar door, light bathing him like an Adonis, she thought.

"Don't get killed," she yelled.

•••

Cyril poked at his stew with a spoon and Mia cried into hers. Antigone was at a loss to say anything at first, searching for any kind of consoling words.

"I'm sure Skye's fine," Antigone said. Cyril and Mia smiled politely, and then went back to their jabs and sobs. "She knows this area well. Maybe she lost track of time?"

It had been dark for hours and she could hear the wind howling against the windows. Outside was no place for a fourteen-year-old girl during the day, let alone on a frigid night.

"I'll go out and look for her," Antigone volunteered, prompting Cyril to shake his head rapidly.

"I don't need two lost girls on my conscience," Cyril barked, then flashed a false smile again. "I appreciate the offer. I really do, but it's not safe out there."

Antigone hated it when people treated her like a child. She hated it even more when they treated her like a female one. She was perfectly capable of handling herself. She always had been. She knew how to protect herself, how to use a firearm, and she had pulled Shep's ass out of the fire more times than she could count. There was another girl out there, alone, perhaps hurt or trapped, that needed help and she wanted to be the one to render it.

That's what a hero would do.

Skye was prone to wandering off on her own, Cyril had said. A free spirit was she. But she had always returned home before nightfall. She was daring and adventurous – Antigone knew the type – but she was not stupid or careless.

Antigone volunteered to search for her again and Cyril protested, more vehemently this time. "I'm going to go look for her now. Patrick will be back with what's his name, Shep, soon. Then you can all go out looking for her with me."

Antigone thought maybe she was with Patrick. Maybe he had seen her and brought her along with him on his way to Attica. *That must be where she is.* She told her theory to Cyril and it was met with a somber, "Maybe."

Just then there was a rap on the door. Cyril's head shot up.

All Antigone heard was muffled voices at first, then a loud, deep one that was not Cyril's. "I'm just looking for some food," the voice boomed. "Maybe you can help out a poor, hungry soul?"

Antigone's mouth gaped and her heart pounded. It was Bray. She raced down to the cellar and bolted the door, listening to the heavy steps on the ceiling above her.

Stomp! Stomp! Stomp!

Why was he here?

Stomp! Stomp! Stomp!

Cyril, kill him! Kill him now!

Stomp! Stomp! Stomp!

Part III
Chapter Seven
Heroes Don't Cry

Antigone Raptis left the man she loathed, the man she wanted wiped off the face of the Earth, hanging there on that post as she emerged from the tent into the darkness of the camp. There was no one there to greet her; nothing but the sound of the wind rustling the tall grass.

She listened to that din of nature. It helped calm her in situations like these, those rare situations when she hadn't known what to do. Several times she began to march back into the tent and end his miserable life, but each time she stopped.

She recalled her brother telling her about a great method of making what seems like an impossible choice. It always resonated with her. Take a coin. Heads is one course of action, tails is another. Flip it and when the piece of silver is spinning in the air, rushing up before gravity pulls it back down, think hard about what side you wish it to land.

That is your answer.

Heads? Tails? It is really moot. Your true desire would be ascertained well before the coin clanks off the table or the floor or the ground.

She wished she had a coin.

Lacking one, she decided to walk back to her tent and stare into the darkness to decide. She thought, "What would Shep do?" and figured he would have driven that knife into his heart hours ago. He would have been done with it quickly. Then she thought, "What would Pat do?" and she concluded he would have let him live.

But they weren't here. She was. Bray was. The only question that mattered now was "what would Antigone Raptis do?"

What would a hero do?

•••

Antigone was surprised she had gotten any sleep at all, but she had. The sun hitting the tent cast a soothing glow within it and warmed it like a greenhouse. It felt safe, like a womb. She never wanted to leave it.

Loud voices from outside prompted her to exit the tent anyway. Alma and Jackson were arguing – it seemed they always did – and Alma was winning as Jackson closed his lips tightly and clenched his jaw in a sign of concession. She had learned that was his way of waving the white flag.

Did Alma ever lose an argument?

They saw her and flashed stilted smiles. "Bray is still alive," Alma said. "Is that your final decision?"

"I …" Antigone said and paused, not even sure what she would say next. "I don't know."

"If she didn't do it last night, she'll never kill the bastard. We have to let him go," Jackson said as Alma lifted her hand to hush him.

"Let him go? You're going to let him go?" Antigone bellowed, puzzled.

Jackson threw his arms out in frustration. "We can't keep him tied up like a hog in there forever. We can't keep him hostage. What else are we going to do with him? His life is yours, not ours."

Antigone tried to hold back her tears, but couldn't. It was the stress of it all and she was finding it more and more difficult lately to control her emotions.

"I don't know what to do," Antigone cried. "What am I supposed to do, Alma?"

Alma smiled sweetly. Antigone hadn't known her long, be she had figured out rather quickly that she was gentle and kind and caring and had a way of comforting everyone around her with a simple look. It was her superpower, Antigone guessed, a trait she had always possessed and one that made Jackson and his men rally around her like they did, even when they disagreed with her vehemently.

Alma took Antigone in her arms and squeezed her, like her mother used to when she was child, when she had jumped off that swing at its apex and crashed to the ground, skinning her knees.

"It's all right, child," Alma said, squeezing her even more tightly. "Let it all out."

Antigone hated to cry. Girls cry. Heroes don't. But she bawled now, wetting Alma's sweater as she did. She sobbed for Shep. She sobbed for Patrick. She even sobbed for Bray because she knew somewhere under that pain and hatred that so consumed him was a man who was sorry for his sins, sorry for the path he had taken to destruction. She knew he was once a hero, a flawed one, but still a hero. He had put aside his hatred to save her in that horror house, after all. He had put the legless man out of his misery. He was capable of kindness.

Antigone felt a relief once she was done. It felt like all the pain she was swallowing had finally been vomited.

Alma rubbed the back of her head and whispered, "You are in a very delicate condition. You need to rest."

But there would never be rest for Antigone Raptis, at least not yet.

•••

Jackson told the story of Paul Bray's capture. It really wasn't a very compelling one. After hearing the haunting stories of Bray's savage ways, Alma had ordered a couple of men to search the countryside for him. He was undoubtedly out there, if he had survived the evil of that house. He wouldn't be satisfied with only his revenge on Shep. He would be out for more blood.

Alma was correct.

Bray put up little fight against the reservists with the rifles. He was just a few klicks away, lumbering toward the tent camp, bloody and cold, when they snatched him.

Now he belonged to Antigone Raptis, who slipped into sleep with the weight of a life on her head. A life she didn't know if she would take or spare.

•••

Antigone woke from her nap to Shepard licking her forehead. The tent still glowed in the shining sun. She gathered her things. She had decided that it was time to leave, time to leave Bray and all that hate and death behind her, time to go to Halcyon – if it existed – and time to see if she could find Niko.

He is there. He has to be there.

She emerged from the tent to see Alma and Jackson standing guard.

"You can't leave, child," Alma said with that disarming voice. It wasn't working this time.

Antigone was incredulous. "Am I a prisoner here?"

"Of course not," Jackson said. "Go ahead. Leave. No one is stopping you."

Alma waved her hand at Jackson, "Hush, you."

She walked to Antigone and grabbed her hands. Alma's fingers felt rough as they rubbed her soft skin. "No, you are not a prisoner, but you can't leave. Not in the condition you're in. And you still have a decision to make."

"I feel fine now. Jackson, how far is it to Halcyon?"

Before Jackson could answer, Alma pressed her hand against Antigone's bloated belly. "I don't think you understand the condition I am referring to, child."

Antigone was confused.

"You're pregnant, at least four months so," Alma said. "You're going to be a mother. You can't go gallivanting out there alone while carrying a baby. You have more than yourself and your dog to look after now."

Antigone lurched backward and held her stomach in her hands. For the first time the churning and rumbling she interpreted as hunger, she now felt as movement and kicks from a fetus. It was equal parts excitement and terror. *What do I know about raising a kid? I'm a kid myself.*

Babies having babies, that sort of thing.

Oh my God, I'm bringing a new life into this world. What chance does my baby have? That was especially true if Alma was correct and Halcyon no longer existed. *Oh my God, what am I going to do?*

"I know it's quite the shock," Alma said, escorting her back into the tent. "But you have to look out for her now."

"Her? How do you know it's a girl?"

Alma smiled and patted Antigone's stomach. "I just know these things. I've delivered more babies than I can count, probably more babies than people who once filled this county. When you do it as long as I have, you just have an inkling. She's going to be a pretty girl."

Antigone closed her eyes and sighed. How could she have not known she was pregnant? The signs were so clear now. The bloated stomach, the nausea in the morning, the emotional outbursts that were not like her. Her sudden craving for dandelions. What kind of mother would that make her?

"Does this make your decision about Mr. Bray easier?" Alma asked.

"Why would it make it easier?"

"If you let him go, he'll come after you and that little girl you're carrying. He won't stop. You know that."

Antigone did, all too well. "So, you're saying I should kill him?" Antigone rubbed her belly. "What kind of example would that set for her?"

"It's you choice, child. But sometimes we have to do things we don't want to do, things we thought we would never do, to protect ourselves and others." A tear rolled down Alma's wrinkled cheek. It seemed to Antigone she spoke from experience.

"What did you do?" Antigone asked.

Alma brushed the tear away from her face. "I killed a man. Things are not like they used to be, child. Things never will be again. The rules have changed. We do what we need to do to survive. God will forgive us for that. We all have to make sacrifices and sometimes those sacrifices are made from within."

"Who'd you kill?"

"My son. He was a lot like that Mr. Bray. He needed to be put down or he would have meant the end to us all. He was tied to that very post in that tent. My hand trembled something terrible before I stuck the knife in his heart. I'll always remember those eyes looking back at me, big and wide like saucers. He didn't think I could do it, but I did. I told him I was sorry. But I wasn't. I will never apologize for doing what I did. It saved lives. And Jackson saved me. He gave me the same choice I'm giving you, to save yourself and your baby."

"Your son. He was one of the raiders?"

Alma nodded, wiping away another tear that had escaped from her tired eyes. "I tried to stop them from killing a poor man for his food. I failed. The other men beat me. My son, who had changed so much after the Ejection I didn't even recognize him anymore, watched as they kicked at me something fierce. I would have surely been killed had it not been for Jackson and his men. Everything happens for a reason, child. Jackson came along at just the right time for a reason. There is no such thing as a random event. Everything you have been through led you to here and to this moment."

Antigone had a greater appreciation for Alma now. What she must have gone through, she thought. What horrors she must have seen. Everyone has his or her own demons locked inside and the loving old woman was no different. *Who's to say what is right and what is wrong? Who's to say what is justified and what is not?* Alma did what she thought was right when she jabbed that blade into her son's chest.

Antigone wasn't sure she had that kind of gumption.

"I don't know if I can do it," she lamented.

Alma laughed. It was a curious laugh, an odd one that caught Antigone by surprise. "If I could kill my son, you can surely kill that man in there. You'll be amazed at what you can do in dire times like these."

Antigone Raptis knew that all too well.

Part III
Chapter Eight
What Antigone Did to Save Shep's Sorry Ass

Antigone Raptis closed the door behind her and let a tear slide down her cheek. "I don't have to ask how he's doing, do I?" Mia said, glumly.

Antigone shook her head. She held back more tears, but felt her lips quiver with worry. Shep was already near death, his hand ravaged by that bullet, and she feared the worst. She was amazed at how quickly the infection had set in, but that was the way things were now. Any wound, no matter how insignificant, could kill and kill fast. Big wounds like that one were the worst. Disease was just as opportunistic as the gangs and the wretches in this new world, and snuffed people out just as efficiently, too.

He wouldn't last long with a temperature like that.

It was time for her to be a hero again.

She dug through Shep's bag, looking for anything that could help him, but she found nothing of use.

She rummaged through the pockets of his coat, hoping he had a bottle of antibiotics or something to bring down his fever – he was always prepared. She felt a cylinder. It was smooth and she prayed that it was a bottle of medicine.

It wasn't.

She held the tube of Twilight Nude lipstick in her hand, stared at it as the light glistened off its sleek surface, and wondered just how in the hell Shep came to possess it.

There was only one conclusion she could draw: Shep had lied.

And if Shep had lied to her, that most likely meant Pat was dead.

Her heart fluttered and she felt like vomiting, but choked it down.

Skye peeked over her shoulder in an attempt to glimpse what she held.

"Whatya got?" Skye asked as her neck strained.

"Nothing that will help him," Antigone answered, her voice cracking. "Mia, do you know where I can find antibiotics and fast?"

Mia shook her head and uttered a panicked "no."

Skye interjected. "I do. But it's dangerous."

Of course it was. Nothing in this life was easy. "Where, Skye? He doesn't have much time."

"There's another farm about a mile from here. Terrible people live there. But I know they have antibiotics because Parker needed some for his pecker."

Antigone was shocked by that statement, but was too distracted by more pressing issues to ask for details. "Where is it?"

"Just across the field to the East."

She grabbed a bag and stuffed it with food and clean water. Food and water was currency in the economy of survival and she figured it would surely buy her a prescription of antibiotics.

The snow was thick and broke like glass as her feet pounded through the glaze. Her leg muscles burned as she trudged through the shin-deep pack. She crossed a line of trees and saw the decrepit house in the distance.

That shithole has to be it.

She approached the house slowly and crept onto the porch. The door swung open and an old man with a shotgun stood in the arch. "Great. Another pretty girl." He turned and walked away, leaving the door wide open. *Was that an invitation?* She took it as such.

The house reeked and dried blood was caked on the hardwood floor a few feet away from her. She felt her heart beat faster at the sight. She assumed by the way the old man walked up the stairs, groaning with each strained step, that blood on his floors was nothing new. That made her heart beat faster still. "Come on. He's up here."

Antigone hurried to the base of the steps and looked up at the old man, whose ascent was slow, but steady. "I'm sorry. I'm not here for someone. I was told you have antibiotics. I can pay for them."

The old man stopped his climb, looked down at her and shook his head. "You'll pay for them sure enough. Come on."

Antigone raced up the steps and followed closely behind him. *To catch his fall if he stumbles if nothing else; wouldn't want him to break a hip.* The upstairs smelled just as pungent as the first floor. They walked past a room and she peered into it. A man lay there, moaning, with a blood-soaked cloth on his crotch. In the next room, another man sat on the edge of a bed, his head buried deep in his hands.

"We have another live one, Sammy," the old man announced, prompting Sam's head to shoot up quickly. "I don't know what you boys do to get all this pussy. You should bottle that, too."

Antigone sheepishly entered the room, which was lit only by the flames from a pair of candles that burned on a dresser. Sam stood and smiled. "What do we have here?"

Antigone cleared her throat. "I was told you had antibiotics. My friend needs some desperately."

Sam chuckled. "Everyone needs drugs desperately. That never changes." He knelt by an old floor safe and quickly dialed in the combination. The door swung open and he pillaged through an assortment of bottles. "I have amoxicillin, penicillin, cephalexin and ciprofloxacin. Did you know you used to be able to buy these at a pet store? Crazy, huh? They are fish antibiotics. Crazy. Just crazy."

As he continued to comb though his stores of drugs, Sam gave a synopsis of his life. He was a chemistry wiz and a pharmacist in that other time, and he also dabbled in the art of making illegal concoctions – crystal methamphetamine in particular. No one much cared for meth any longer. The demand for recreation drugs had plummeted after the Ejection. The drug in highest demand was a simple antibiotic. "Bacteria are indiscriminant. They don't care if you're good or bad, rich or poor, black or white, Christian or a Jew. They'll attack you all the same and one little bug can bring down the toughest SOB."

Antigone did not care for his autobiography. "That's great and all, but I'm in a fucking hurry. What's the best kind for an infected wound?"

Sam turned his head to peer at her. He smirked and sighed. "Well, Bactrim would be best, but it looks like I don't have any of that. Probably the cephalexin."

Antigone held out her hand and wiggled her fingers. "Great. I'll take a couple of bottles of that then. Come on!"

Sam chuckled and his eyes moved from her feet up to her head. "I'm not a free clinic. You have to pay me first."

"Fine." Antigone dropped the bag. "There's lots of food and water in there. You can have it all. Just give me the medicine. Hurry!"

Sam snickered again. His eyes narrowed and he appeared annoyed. "Jesus. Where's the fire? I don't need food and water. I have that."

"Then what do you want?"

Sam stood and prowled slowly to her. He pushed his body against hers. "You. You would be perfect payment."

Antigone pushed him away. Sam stumbled as he backpedaled, falling into a sit on the corner of the bed. He giggled the whole time.

"No fucking way," Antigone bellowed. "You're disgusting. I don't have time for this."

"Suit yourself," Sam said, crossing his arms on his chest. "I hope your friend dies quickly and doesn't suffer too much. I'm sure his fever is out of control by now and his brain is cooking in his skull like a hard-boiled egg. I have all night. I can wait until you come to your senses and realize this is the only way you are going to be able to save your friend's life."

How bad could it be? It was just sex and, by the look of him, it would be over quickly.

Antigone unzipped her coat and let it fall to the floor. Sam smiled. "See. I knew you were reasonable."

She unbuttoned and unzipped her pants and let them fall around her ankles. She pulled her sweater over her head and then her sports bra. Her breasts spilled out and were met with a sigh of delight from Sam the Pervert.

"Wow. You are spectacular."

She wanted him to shut up. She grabbed the waistband of her panties and pulled them down, letting them slip and fall to her ankles. She stepped out of the pile of clothes and walked slowly toward Sam, who was already beginning to disrobe.

"I'll be gentle. I'm not some beast," he promised, flipping Antigone to her back.

She lay there and endured it, feeling nothing that she felt when she was with Pat. She dulled her perception as much as she could and thought of other things, pleasant things, like butterflies and swing sets and the laughter only children can make. And of Halcyon. She imagined how perfect and peaceful it would be there.

Those were pleasant thoughts to have, even at an unpleasant time like this.

She hoped each of his moaning thrusts would be the last. As she figured, it was over quickly and Sam rolled off her with a loud groan. His sweaty chest heaved up and down. "See, that wasn't so bad," he said through a heavy breath.

Oh, it was, you prick. It was.

Sam peeled himself off the bed, still naked, and knelt down in front of the floor safe. Antigone cringed at the sight of his dangling testicles. "You certainly earned these," he said, tossing a couple of bottles on the bed. He closed the safe and it locked with a click, then he hopped back over to her. She looked away from the disgusting sight of his jiggling junk as he moved.

She felt his hot, smelly breath on her face. "I really hope your friend recovers. I'll give you some privacy to get dressed. I am a gentleman, after all."

He grabbed his clothes from the bed, bowed to her with a silly grin and closed the door behind him. She shut her eyes and lay back, trying to wash the experience out of her head. She felt dirty and cheap, and tried to wipe his sweaty stench off of her with her hands.

She figured she would one day forgive herself, that the ends justified the means. She realized she would do anything – and had – for Shep, and she knew he, too, would do anything for her, even if it meant keeping her from a horrible truth.

Antigone opened her eyes and saw another man hanging over her. It was the man who bled from the crotch. Sweat was beaded on his forehead and his eyes were red and bloodshot. He snarled. "Aren't you the whore?"

He pulled his pants down and Antigone screamed at the sight. His mangled and flaccid penis hung there, blood and puss oozing from it. She tried to push him off of her, but he slammed her down and punched her in the face. She could already feel her cheek swell. She tried to scream, but he covered her mouth with his clammy hands and pressed down hard. "Now you are going to fuck me."

Antigone squirmed, her knee coming up to jab him in the crotch. He rolled off of her and onto the floor, groaning and crying and clutching at his wound. She hastily slipped on her panties then her pants and pulled her sports bra over her head before he recovered, pushed himself up and slashed at her with a pocket knife. It was a reckless swipe and it caught her on the arm just below the shoulder. Blood seeped immediately out of the gash and it burned when her sweat rolled into the opening.

He slashed at her again, but missed, and Antigone brought her fist down on his elbow, dislocating it. The knife fell to the floor just before he did.

She grabbed the knife, peering down as he cradled his arm. "You better run because I'm gonna kill you," he bellowed.

Antigone squeezed the handle of the knife so tightly her knuckles turned a bright white. She shoved him to his back and kicked him in the ribs. He moaned. She kicked him again and he moaned louder. And again, and he began to whimper and cough. She knelt, pressed the blade of the knife against his neck, and he looked up at her, his eyes wide and wet, more from the kicks to the ribs and the fever than from remorse or fear.

Her hand shook, the blade scraping at the skin on his neck, making it red and raw. She bit her lip and blood oozed out of it and she screamed, loud and long until her voice was hoarse. It drew the attention of Sam, who burst into the room to see the scene before him.

"Don't kill my brother," Sam whispered in shock. "He's messed up, but he's still my kin."

Antigone stood, folded the knife with a click and slipped it into her pocket. She calmly finished dressing.

Sam stood there motionless. His brother writhed on the floor bleating and blubbering from the pain.

"I won't kill him, even though the bastard deserves it," she said sharply. "I guess I don't have it in me."

Killing him wasn't what a hero would do, she thought.

Then again, perhaps it was.

Part III
Chapter Nine
Inside the Looking Glass

Antigone lay on the sleeping bag, pulled up her shirt and gently rubbed her bare stomach. She didn't know why she began to sing softly, but she did.

"How many miles to Halcyon? Three score miles and ten. Can I get there by candle-light? Yes, and back again. If your heels are nimble and light, you may get there by candle-light."

She thought about Patrick. *He would have made such a great father. He was caring and decent and kind – nothing like his loony mother.* And she thought about Shep and wondered what his take would have been on this. That made her smile. He would have been so mad at first, probably would have scolded her for being so careless, but would have adored her child and would have held the baby girl in his tender arms, protecting her from harm.

Antigone wiped some sweat that had beaded on her forehead and slipped into sleep, dreaming of the first tooth lost and the first steps taken, of swings, tea parties and mud pies, of dances and first kisses.

It was a good dream to have.

•••

Antigone heard a whimper, forced her eyes open and looked at Shepard. Her heart sunk at the horror of the sight. Shepard lay dead, his right eye punctured. Blood flowed out of the wound like a waterfall of crimson. Shep's glasses lay next to the dog's snout.

Bray hulked over him, blood dripping from her pocket knife, which he held firmly in his right hand. He turned his one-eyed gaze down at Antigone and smiled lustfully. “You should have killed me when you had the chance.”

Antigone wiggled off the bedroll and pushed herself backward on her rump toward the back of the tent. Her eyes were wide and full of terror, she supposed. That only fueled Bray more.

“I’ll try to make it quick and painless,” Bray said, his voice booming as loudly as ever. “You are such a lush thing.”

Bray’s feet pounded on the ground as he lumbered over to her. He grabbed her hair tight in his hand and yanked her to her feet. He chuckled as he noticed her belly. “A two-for-one deal,” he said cruelly.

“Please. My baby has done nothing to you,” Antigone pleaded, her voice earnest and desperate. “I can’t believe even you could be so evil.”

Bray smiled as he gently rubbed the edge of the blade on her face and down to her neck, her hair still wound around his hand in a tight hold. “Before I kill you, tell me something. What do you miss?”

The question caught Antigone by surprise.

“What?” She blurted, squinting out of the corners of her eyes at him.

“What do you miss?” He yelled. She could feel the blade scraping at her throat.

She missed her innocence. She missed feeling human. She missed Shep and Patrick, her brother and her parents. She missed hot Earl Grey tea, digging her toes in the sand on a beach and feeling the salty breeze in her face. She missed all the things she once loved in that old life, and the few good things she had discovered in this new one. If she were to die, she wouldn’t go quietly.

“I miss gouging your fucking eye out,” she bellowed.

Bray simply repeated the question, calmly this time. “What do you miss?”

When he didn’t get an immediate answer, he thrust the knife into her stomach with short, rapid jabs. Over and over again. Nine times. Each time the blade punctured her, it burned. She fell to the ground and peered up at the ceiling of the tent. It morphed, changing colors as if seen through a kaleidoscope. Ribbons of light swirled like an aurora, then turned blood red. She watched the ruddy liquid fall on her like rain.

Bray stood over her. He looked like Shep, but wasn’t. He sounded like Patrick, but didn’t. “You know what you have to do.”

•••

Antigone’s eyes shot open and she gasped. She coughed violently, a little bit of yellowish phlegm coming up and spat it onto the ground. Her heart pounded and the back of her neck was drenched in sweat. The tent glowed green again, casting that comforting light upon her.

She needed all the comfort she could get.

Her eyes quickly scanned for Shepard, who was sleeping at her feet. The dog lifted his head and looked at her, sensing her panic. He trotted over and licked at her face. Antigone closed her eyes and took a deep breath, finally realizing it was just a nightmare, a vivid dream. Nothing more.

Alma walked in and stood by the flap. "Have you made your choice, child?"

Antigone took another deep breath and let it out through puckered lips. It was as if she were releasing all of her demons in one exhale. It felt wondrous. "Yes. I have made my choice."

•••

Bray hung on the pole in the same awkward pose as the day before. He groaned and grunted every time he tried to move. Jackson stood behind her, his arms crossed on his chest.

Antigone turned to Jackson. "Cut him down."

Jackson obeyed. Bray collapsed to the ground in a heavy heap. He tried to work his arms and legs, but failed miserably. "Sit him on the chair," Antigone commanded and Jackson complied. Bray could barely balance himself upon it. He swayed like a red pine in a brisk wind and his head bobbed from side to side.

"You can go now," Antigone said. Jackson hesitated, but left the tent.

Antigone looked at Bray with compassion. He looked like that beaten down man again, the one who wandered onto the wrong property and tangled with the wrong man. He looked like that frail man who set all of this in motion.

Such a waste, a needless waste. The world was tough enough without men like Bray, bent on a warped sense of vengeance, she thought.

She walked slowly to him, a shadow of his former self, a man at her mercy, a man broken and busted like this new world and a man without a shred of hope or dignity. It saddened her.

Such a waste, a needless waste.

She lifted his head up gently with a light touch of her index finger on his chin. He peered up at her through his one eye. "Look what you have become," she said.

He tried to speak, but couldn't, either too weak to utter a word or too dumbfounded to.

Antigone kissed him on the forehead, and then whispered in his ear. "I'm going to free you."

Bray strained to look up at her and sneered. "I knew you couldn't do it. I will come after you. I have followed you for hundreds of miles, stalked you, waiting to kill you and I will do it. Mark my words. I will do it."

Antigone got on her knees in front of him, his shoulders slumped, his head waggling and his body swaying. She placed her left hand on his cheek and steadied his face so she could look into his eye. "No, Bray. No, you won't."

The blade slipped into his chest easily. She was surprised at just how smooth it was going through his flesh and into his heart. She could feel his blood pour out onto the handle and over her right hand, dripping onto the dirt and dead grass below them.

He coughed and bright red blood spat out, spraying crimson dots onto her neck and shirt.

Her whole body convulsed and she couldn't help but sob as his life slowly drained away. She felt like vomiting and heaved, but nothing came up. He looked down at the blood oozing from his chest, the knife still in it, and then back at her and smirked.

Bray's voice was weak. "Good for you. Maybe there is hope for you yet."

Antigone pulled the knife out, stared at it, and then cast her gaze back to Bray. He was dead now, his head hanging limp and his eye glazed.

She closed her eyes and took a deep breath. She had killed a man, made a conscious decision to take a life, and in that moment it changed her, but not like she had thought. It had become easy in this life to kill. It had become easy after the Ejection to chalk up murder as a necessary part of survival.

And now, she understood why. She felt no remorse for what she had just done. She felt no pangs of guilt, no crisis of conscience. No regret. She did it more for the life that grew inside her than for her own lust for vengeance. She did it to free Bray from the prison of his own hate as much as to free herself.

It felt good.

She had no problem with that feeling.

Antigone Raptis emerged from the tent and Jackson peered in, then back at her. "I didn't think you had it in you."

She was full of surprises lately as she put her hands on her belly, leaving a bloody handprint on her shirt, and felt her girl move and kick, knowing she had done the best thing she could for her.

She was about to do another.

"I'm going to Halcyon and you and Alma and all of your men can kiss my ass," Antigone said in a raspy voice.

Jackson smiled. "I'll be right with you. Let me get my gear."

Antigone could use the companionship, but not his protection. She wasn't some giggly, lovestruck thing, weak and dainty. She could take care of herself, after all, and she had proven it, more to herself than anyone else.

Antigone gathered her things in the tent. She would miss the warmth of it.

All good things, that sort of thing.

Alma shuffled in, smiling and crying all at once. "I'm going to miss you, child."

"I'll be back some day," Antigone said.

Alma nodded. "I look forward to that."

Antigone walked out into the warm sun that beat down on her face and felt the breeze kick up her hair. She tied it back with a rubber band as Jackson approached with a large backpack strapped around his muscular shoulder.

"It's about a hundred or so miles to the base. On foot, that'll take us a few days," Jackson said.

She coughed up more phlegm, but swallowed it. "Then we better get going."

•••

Antigone's strides were long and rapid, Shepard keeping pace at her side. She walked with the same purpose she had for the past two days. She was more focused and single-minded than she ever had been in her short life. Jackson followed behind her, trying to maintain the speed she had set. "I know how badly you want to get there, but you have to slow down. This is no good for you or the baby. You don't look well."

Antigone stopped to let Jackson catch up before she yelled at him. "Don't tell me what is good for me or my baby. She is the most precious thing in my life right now."

Jackson held his hands up in a show of contrition. "Hold your fire. I'm just looking out for you."

"Let's move." She walked faster now in defiance of Jackson, even though the ground in front of her swayed from side to side as if she were walking on the deck of a ship in rough seas. She didn't care, though. She wanted to show him that her previous pace was slow in comparison.

Her forehead felt warm to the touch and her hands were clammy as she wiped the sweat from her brow. She could see a hint of mountains on the horizon, the peaks covered by a blanket of white. They almost looked like the frosting on the top of a cupcake. She missed cupcakes. She wanted her daughter to know the wonders of such things and she was determined that she would.

She had never seen mountains like that before and marveled at their beauty against the backdrop of the setting sun. It was as if she were walking into a painting.

"We should make camp soon, unless you just want to keep walking in the dark," Jackson said with sarcasm.

They found a nice, secure spot. Antigone built the fire quickly, impressing Jackson.

He caught them something fresh to eat – a couple of prairie dogs. "Those stupid shits," he joked. They sizzled over the fire as he peered at her, the light from the flames dancing off his granite-like jaw. "You were dead set against killing that Bray bastard. Why'd you do it?"

Wasn't it obvious? "I freed him."

Jackson was puzzled. "Freed him? What kind of bullshit is that? You killed him because you wanted him to pay for what he had done to you. Own it."

Jackson handed her a skewered prairie dog and she took a bite. She came to the conclusion she would never grow fond of the taste, just like she would never grow fond of the flavor of killing, no matter how right the reason.

"All he knew was hate. He only lived to destroy. No one loved him. He had no one to love. He was already dead. I showed him a tremendous amount of mercy. It was the best way he could have gone."

The meat did not sit well in her stomach and she vomited it back up. Jackson looked at her, worried. "Are you feeling ill?"

Antigone bristled at the question. "No, it's just that I can't stand the taste of fucking prairie dog."

Jackson tore a bit of meat off the stick with his fingers and tossed it toward Shepard. Jackson then took a bite and swallowed it down hard. "I feel ya. Disgusting little shits, aren't they? Your dog seems to like it, though." He pointed his prairie dog on a stick at Antigone's small, round stomach. "How do you know it's a girl?"

She smiled. "I have an inkling."

•••

Antigone had a dream again, this of her daughter, her face covered in icing, a cupcake smashed in her tiny right hand. She giggled as only a little girl can.

It was a good dream to have.

When she awoke, Jackson was stomping out the fire and Shepard was sniffing about the ground. "Let's go. We can make it by nightfall."

One more day. One more day to Halcyon.

She strode even more quickly than the days before, but her joints ached and her head pounded. Her eyes had trouble focusing and the whole world seemed to shake as if she were in a snow globe in the hands of a zealous kid. Jackson didn't even think of trying to slow her pace. She figured he had learned quickly and knew better than to challenge her.

The mountains rose high to their left. They looked like the biggest things in the universe as she looked up at them. She could barely see the peaks.

By dusk they had reached the winding road that led up to the entrance to the base. Antigone stomped up that hill, expecting to be greeted by Niko, but there was no one there. She walked down the paved road, right down the middle of double-yellow lines toward the half-circle tunnel that jutted out from the face of the mountain. She stood at the entrance of the portal. Bones littered the inside, big ones and small ones. Antigone thought the small ones must have belonged to children and that sickened her stomach. She vomited a putrid yellow liquid.

Nothing so much as stirred from inside the portal now.

She stared into the arch for what seemed like an eternity, but was in reality only a few minutes. Jackson stood beside her. She could sense his unease.

"I'm sorry, Antigone," he said softly. "I told you there would be no one here. There's nothing left but these bones."

Antigone didn't lose faith. She sat on the hard blacktop road, tucked her legs under her and rocked to and fro, staring into the abyss. Shepard sat next to her and whined a little as he, too, stared straight ahead. She tried to will the blast door, which sat at the end of the corridor, to open, but it didn't budge.

"Come on. It's getting dark," Jackson pleaded. "There are coyotes and other wild animals all over this place. That's probably what plucked those bones clean. We need to find a better place to make camp for the night."

Antigone did not move. Neither did Shepard, who sat dutifully at her side. "Do you know what it took me to get here, what I lost? I'm not fucking leaving until that door opens or until I'm satisfied it never will."

Jackson's shoulders slumped and he sat down right next to her. "Well, I guess we're staying then."

Antigone nodded and began to rock again, her pregnant belly rested on her lap. She felt dampness on her pants and reached down to dab it. Her fingers were stained with blood. She was relieved that she could still feel her baby move and kick. The movement was fierce now, as if she, too, were stubborn and determined.

Like mother, like daughter, that sort of thing.

The moon filled the sky and cast an eerie glow into the mouth of the portal. Her eyes became heavy and her head bobbed with fatigue. Jackson pleaded once more for them to leave and make a more suitable shelter for the night, the cries of the coyotes loud and threatening now, but Antigone still would not yield.

Just a minute longer.

She strained to keep her eyes open and her head still.

It'll open any minute now. You'll see. Any minute now, it will open.

The entrance to the arch shook violently, and then turned 90 degrees on its side. The portal looked like the letter 'D' now and she wondered what kept all those bones from falling.

"Antigone! Antigone!" she heard Jackson yell. She did not move to address his cries. She only stared ahead, wanting. Shepard barked and licked at her cheek. It tickled and it made her smile.

She thought she could smell the lilies that grew tall in her backyard and the cherry pie her mother had baked cooling on the window sill.

"Antigone! Antigone!" Jackson yelled again, but she did not move.

She felt warm and soothed and safe. She felt at peace.

A bright light bathed her and she saw several figures of men and women, only the blackness of their forms in front of the casted light, walk from the portal and slowly toward her. She saw a hand reach out for her and touch her face.

She heard a man's voice whisper, "Tig," and a cold hand lift her head. "Tig, you are safe now. Nothing will ever hurt you again."

•••

She awoke to a finger jabbing at her forehead. Her eyes strained to open in the brightly lit room. An IV was stuck in her left arm and liquid dripped through it from a hanging bag. A crisp white sheet was pulled up to her chest and she felt a shiver run through her.

Once her eyes could finally focus, she saw Niko standing in front of her, smiling wide and proud. He didn't look as she remembered, his face was worn down by time, and thick black stubble covered his face. She had never seen him with as much as a whisker before. *I guess things have changed.*

Antigone fearfully grabbed at her stomach and felt the bulge and its warmth. She pressed her hands down on her belly and held her breath. *Move! Kick! Do something!* She felt her baby give quite the wallop and she could breathe again. *Thank God my precious girl is all right.*

"When you were a little girl, you always had scraped knees and tangled hair," Niko said. "I guess you still have that fight in you."

Antigone closed her eyes and smiled, perhaps the biggest one yet. She imagined those wrinkles around the corners of her lips that boys went crazy for were thick and deep now. She felt his hand caress her face when she spoke. "I knew you would still be here."

"And I'm going to be an uncle, apparently."

She thanked God again that her baby was safe. "Is this Halcyon?"

He chuckled. "Not quite."

"Where is it?"

"You'll see."

"What happened here?"

"People stormed this place. Thousands and thousands of them. The choice was made to not open the blast doors. They banged and banged on it and then turned on each other. All we could do was watch through the security cameras as they tore each other apart."

Human nature, that sort of thing.

"Many people spent many nights mourning for them," Niko said, somberly. "But sometimes you have to do certain things to survive."

Antigone knew that all too well.

Niko continued: "Sometimes you have to sacrifice a little bit of yourself."

She could tell he was not proud of what they had done. She didn't judge him. It was not her place.

•••

It took a week for her to recover enough to move. Niko took her down to the real Halcyon, hundreds of feet below the surface, deep under the mountain. The elevator moved in fits and starts at first, then smoothly descended for what seemed to her like an eternity.

When it stopped and the door finally opened, Antigone was left with nothing but wonder.

People walked about, bathed in the artificial light that simulated the sun. Trees and plants grew and an underground spring spilled into a lake from a waterfall.

"This," Niko said, his smile wide, "is Halcyon."

It was like a world unto itself. Trees – evergreens and oaks and maples – grew straight and tall. Birds – robins and bluebirds and blackbirds and sparrows – sang and chirped. Animals, all kinds of them, roamed the plains and the woodlands. Spiders crawled and bees buzzed and butterflies batted their wings, fresh from their cocoons.

A monarch landed on Antigone's hand, its wings orange and black. She could hardly believe her eyes. *Yes. I must be dreaming.*

It was a good dream to have.

Niko smiled as he watched Antigone stare at the butterfly in delight. "This place has its own ecosystem. Thousands of species and thousands of people live down here. They have for years. It's the single greatest feat of engineering in human history."

Niko held Antigone. "I don't know how long we will stay here, however long it takes, I guess."

She never wanted to leave this place. It was heaven.

•••

She cried in her arms and Antigone shushed her, rocking her to and fro. Boys and girls kicked their legs on a nearby swing set and others laughed as only children could. Shepard playfully barked, chasing the running children, nipping at their feet.

There was no breeze, not inside here, but the artificial sun felt warm on her skin. The baby girl stopped crying now, cooed and smiled, shoving her bent fingers and fist into her mouth.

She has Patrick's eyes. Yes, those are Patrick's eyes.

Antigone kissed her soft forehead and rocked her, humming a verse from a nursery rhyme she had learned as a child.

"Hush little baby don't say a word. Momma's gonna buy you a mocking bird. If that mocking bird don't sing. Momma's gonna buy you a diamond ring. If that diamond ring turns brass, momma's gonna buy you a looking glass."

It was catchy and she quite liked singing it.

Her name was Skye Anna Raptis and she would never be hungry or afraid. Her mother would protect her from now until the end of time.

That's what a hero would do.

ABOUT THE AUTHOR

MIKE KILROY is an award-winning journalist and has been hooked on writing since he was a young boy growing up in a small Ohio town. The critically acclaimed *Nine Meals* is his first foray into fiction.

52852821R00112

Made in the USA
Lexington, KY
12 June 2016